All books by this author

Relics of Ar'Zac
Rise of the Sparrows
Wardens of Archos
Blood of the Dragon
Shadow in Ar'Sanciond (#0.5)
The Relics of Ar'Zac Box Set

Darkened Light
Darkened Light
Brightened Shadows

Blood Wisp
Blood Wisp
Blood Song
Blood Vow

Chaos of Esta Anderson
A Dream of Death and Magic
A Dream of Stars and Curses
A Dream of Storms and Mourning

Anthologies
Once Upon a Name
Twice Upon a Name
Third Name's a Charm

Find out more about Sarina's books at
sarinalanger.com

Content Warning

It's time, folks! As promised from Book 1, this series turns spicy *now*! Please note, however, that the graphic sex scenes are still the exception rather than the rule – Esta has too much to worry about to jump on her partner every other page. When they are there, though, they don't hold back. Where possible, I made them easy to skip for those of you who'd rather do that. I hope you find they were worth the wait!

Besides the smut many of us have been waiting for, this book also contains:

The results of trauma manifesting in panic attacks, depression, death, light descriptions of blood (in non-violent settings), and mentions of a past war.

If these things are not for you, it's unlikely that you would enjoy this book/series.

I would quite like to dedicate this book to caffeine, actually. Esta and I have been through a lot together now, and the plot for this book has been through some shit, too. Caffeine made it all possible and much more bearable when I scrapped the first draft and started over.

Thank you, caffeine.
I love you.

CHAPTER ONE

I swear there's an actual bloody void inside me. That, and my crossed legs are starting to hurt. There's a stick under my bum that's been digging in for around three minutes now. Just a bit longer and I'll be numb to it, I can feel it. The forest breeze is calming, the few rays of sunshine are nice, I'm sensitive to all other parts of nature I'm normally barely aware of—yadda yadda—but *inside* me? Where I'm supposed to look and find some kind of elusive resonance? Fucking nothing.

'Do you feel anything?' Kate asks, just in front of me.

I bite my lip to stop all my frustrations from pouring out.

'*No*,' I say, a little too harshly. Kate is trying to help me find my magic again. It's not her fault I'm utterly untalented.

It seems that time I pushed Chiara down the stairs with magic was a one-off... an impossible anomaly of a one-off, at that. One I can't seem to replicate. Kate wants me to find the source of my magic inside me, but I'm not patient enough for this. I'm not convinced there's anything *to* find.

'Let's try again in a moment,' Kate says. 'Take a break for now.'

I sigh but do as she says. I get up to walk around a little. Kate says it's important to stretch my legs between attempts, to shake out my limbs. I really don't think it makes a difference, though, at least not to me finding the unfindable. I'm grateful that she wants to help me do this, but we've been trying for the last two days, and I've got nothing to show for it. I know what I did, and so does Chiara; she was pissed about it, too, like I should have told her that I have magic before she kidnapped me. Well, joke's on her, because it was news to me, too, and I can't do it again. If only she knew how badly I'm failing at this. I'm sure she'd be delighted.

Mischief says hating on her at every opportunity isn't a healthy coping mechanism, but I don't care. I think I'm entitled to a little salt… and I'd much rather hate on her hateful ass than on my own ungifted one.

'How are you feeling today?' Kate asks as I walk around trying to shake the discomfort out of my legs. 'Do you still have nightmares?'

'My lucid dreams are fine.' No nightmares there since the Dreamcatcher left me alone. 'My regular dreams, though…'

I don't want to go there. My lucid dreams have always been a sanctuary, and I need their safety and my dream guide cat's sass more than ever now, because when I don't step into my lucid dreams, when I opt for a night of regular sleep, Chiara is there in nightmares that would give the Dreamcatcher a run for his money.

'I can give you a tea to help you sleep, if you like,' Kate offers.

I shake my head. 'I need to work through this on my own,

don't I? That's the usual advice?'

Kate gives me a sympathetic smile. 'It's alright to accept help when you've experienced trauma.'

I slowly nod. *Trauma.* That's what Chiara left me with. But she's gone now and won't hurt me anymore—there's not even a smidgen of a doubt in my mind that she took Leverett's threat seriously: If she ever comes near me again, he will kill her.

'I'm alright, really,' I say. 'Helps that I'm not around a bunch of vampires in my everyday life.' Except for Leverett, and I know he'd never hurt me. 'I just wish I could control *this*, you know?' I vaguely wave my hand at her like that's where my magic lives. 'It's the only thing I did that worked against her.'

I knew when I decided to make a run for it that I could never beat Chiara in a fight. Being a vampire, she's faster and stronger than me in every way; I knew she would never just let me escape. I tried kicking and screaming and helplessly swiping my hands at her. It probably amused her. But then Mischief did something in my unconscious that let me use magic—real magic I've had all along. I panicked, my magic burst out of me and shoved Chiara down her basement stairs, and I ran.

Pretty sure it's the only real defence against the Veiled I had. And now, it seems, that one defence is gone. It's not like I'm looking for a fight, and as far as I know, most Veiled aren't eager to find me just to hurt me, either. Chiara did, though. One angry Veiled I don't see coming is all it'll take to kill me—

Unless I can convince my magic to come back. Unless I can learn to call it when I need it so I don't survive out of sheer luck next time.

'It's only been a few days,' Kate says. 'It's normal for Veiled witches to need some time to recover when they've used large amounts of magic. Your body and mind weren't used to it, and you reacted on instinct. Don't forget, that was only a little under two weeks ago. Give it time, Esta. You're a good pupil. I have every faith that you'll be able to use magic again.'

Her words coax a weak smile out of me. 'Well, I'll certainly try. Magic can't just disappear, can it?'

Kate puts on her beautiful patient teacher smile. 'No, at least not on its own. The fact that you used magic without anyone teaching you proves that it's a skill you were born with. We have discussed the difference between human witches and Veiled witches. Do you remember it?'

I nod. 'Human witches use magick, with a k, and it's stuff anyone can learn. Veiled witches use magic, without the k, and it's the flashy kind we see on TV. Throwing fireballs around and such.'

Or shoving a concentrated ball of air at angry vampires.

Kate nods. 'That's right. Veiled witches don't simply appear, Esta. No one is born human and suddenly becomes Veiled without the interference of another Veiled, which is never subtle and never without risks. You used magic; therefore, it was always in you and always will be.'

Kate always knows just what to say. My magic hasn't vanished—I just need to find it again. Last time, Mischief did something to unleash it, but she's made it clear to me that she mustn't do it again. Rules were broken, she said. I won't ask her to break more; if Kate is right, like she always is, I won't have to. The magic is *there*.

I just need to figure out where.

Newly fired up, I sit down and cross my legs. 'Let's try again.'

I half expect Kate to lecture me about not pushing myself, that I should be taking it easy after Chiara, but instead, she sits before me.

'Same thing as before,' Kate says. 'Close your eyes, and look inward.'

I place my palms flat on the moss to ground myself, then do as she says. It's difficult to "look inward" when I'm not sure what to look *for*. When I used magic against Chiara, I wasn't trying, I was panicking. My magic shot out of my hand without me needing to find it first. Mischief is the one who did all the hard work, but I can't rely on her to do it again. Not unless I want to get her in trouble, and not unless I want to be able to do this myself whenever I want.

I really do try. I still my mind as much as I can, silently beg the magic to hear me and answer. I recall the feeling of it bursting out of me, how terrified I was in that moment in case that's the trigger.

But just as before, there's nothing except silence.

I shake my head. 'What am I supposed to feel for?'

Kate has explained it before, but I'm getting frustrated. Patience was never my strong suit. I know it's only been a few short days, but shouldn't I have made some kind of progress by now? At the very least, shouldn't I have felt *some* sign that the magic is still inside me and… and sparkling, or glowing, or whatever it does?

'Your magic will feel like a concentrated sphere of energy inside you, usually near your centre. If you have an affinity for a specific element, you might sense something related to it, like heat for fire or a refreshing coolness for water. From your description, it sounds like you used air or possibly pure energy. The latter would be rare but not unheard of. Try to find a breeze inside you, or a ball of energy.'

I slowly shake my head again. 'Nope. Sorry, I think all I feel is caffeine.' I sigh, place my arms behind me, and lean onto my elbows. 'Why can't I do this?'

I suppose I should be grateful that I used magic when I needed it, and I am, but that can't be all I had in me. Kate said herself that's not how it works.

'You're too hard on yourself,' she says. 'You weren't taught how to cast magic from birth. I know you're doing everything you can.' She pauses; I sense a *but* coming. 'I admit, however, that I expected you to have felt something, if only a small trace. Don't let that you haven't discourage you. I will help you. I'm confident that we can find the source of your magic again.'

I nod, but it's hard not to be disappointed. We've never discussed it, but I imagine she's taught her share of witches, albeit the human variety. She's a great teacher; I'm the problem.

Kate slightly cocks her head at me. 'One more try? We'll go home after that.'

'Alright.' I really want to hug my dog for comfort. Lady and Kate's dogs, Keano and Bruin, stayed home today, because we thought they might have distracted me last time. It was a fair assumption—I am easily distracted by dogs.

I close my eyes again and focus on nothing in particular. The moss under my hands and ankles. The birdsong around me. Maybe even that is too much distraction, but I don't know how to ignore it.

'I have an idea,' Kate says. 'Since there's a chance you used air magic to defend yourself, focus on the breeze. See if that helps.'

That I can do. The wind isn't strong today, especially shielded by trees as we are, but I'll never not be able to find the breeze. I take a deep breath in and focus.

I feel the wind on my bare arms. On my feet through my sandals. Feel it gently tousle my hair, brush fine strands out of my face. The breeze caresses my neck, flows down my back. It feels wonderful, but nothing is changing inside me. I don't suddenly feel a breeze in my core, only gratitude in my heart for the wind's presence. If nothing else, it softens my continued failure a little.

'Careful, now,' Kate whispers. 'Open your eyes and look.'

I open one eye and peek towards my feet, to where Kate nods.

The grass near my legs is moving. Like a small breeze is sighing through it.

Both my eyes fly wide open. '*Oh!* Am *I* doing that? Is that me?'

Just like that, the grass settles again, and my heart drops with it.

But Kate says, 'Yes, I believe you did it. Well done, Esta.'

My heart swells with pride. 'I didn't feel any different,

though. Does that mean I don't need to feel the magic inside me first?'

Kate gives me a stern look. 'No. Although…' Her expression softens into contemplation. 'It has given me an idea. I believe my approach may have been incorrect. I wonder… There's something I would like to try, but I will need a few days to look into it. Don't get your hopes up, Esta. It's an idea, nothing more, but I think I might know why my method didn't work for you; or rather, I have my suspicions.'

I nod, still happy I managed to do anything at all—*if* it was me and not just the wind around me. Kate's hunches are usually correct. I'm more than happy to give her all the time she needs.

'Sure, let me know when you know.'

'Make sure you rest for a few days, Esta. You've been pushing yourself, and you're still recovering from your ordeal with Chiara. You're also going back to work soon, correct?'

I frown. 'Don't remind me.'

I'm fortunate to work term-time at a university, meaning I get nearly three months off over the summer. And yet, it never feels long enough. Funny how that works. But I'm being unfair; it's not a bad job, and I get along swimmingly with my manager. Not everyone is so lucky. It may not be the photography career I always wanted, but the Dreamcatcher and the Mara made sure I don't pursue that. So, my gallery job isn't perfect, but it pays the bills and no overpowered supernatural beings destroy my sanity over it, so I can't complain too much. I do have a little over a month left of my summer break, so it's not like I'm going back next Monday.

'Promise me, Esta,' Kate says with the practiced look of a lifelong teacher reminding me to do my homework. 'You won't do yourself any favours if you burn out.'

'I know. I'll take it easy, I promise.'

And as we walk back home together, I try not to get too excited about whatever plan Kate has thought of.

CHAPTER TWO

Lady, my rottweiler daughter, barely left my side the first two days after Leverett and Kate saved me from Chiara except to eat, and even then she didn't take her eyes off me. The moment I get home today, she jumps at me like she was scared I wouldn't come home. I hate that I worried her.

I'm so happy I get to hug her again.

'It's alright, baby, I'm home.' I take her face into my hands and kiss her nose. She licks mine in response.

Bonnie walks through the living room door to greet me. 'How did it go?'

'Eh.' I sigh. 'Could be worse, I guess, but could be better.'

I follow her into the living room with my dog walking between my feet. I sit on the sofa; Lady jumps up and plants her bum firmly on my lap.

Bonnie sits next to me, but I don't miss the keys in her hand. 'Still no sign of that magic you used, huh?' she asks.

'None. Well, maybe a little.' My sister's eyes widen. 'Don't get too excited, it could just have been the wind.'

She huffs and playfully punches my arm. 'I bet you're just

not giving yourself enough credit. How long does it normally take to learn magic? For a non-Veiled witch, I mean?'

I throw her a look, but I don't mean it. We've been over this before; she knows non-Veiled witches can't do this magic at all. That I could is something between impossible and a miracle… maybe there are some questions for my parents in there, too. I don't visit as often as other kids do, and we're not as close as my mum thinks we are, but I believe Kate. She said before that, if there were Veiled magic in my family, I wouldn't have found out by accident.

'Doesn't matter,' I finally say, 'because the magick non-Veiled witches do is different. I don't know how I did it.'

I began to see the Veiled when I stepped into the void lake in my lucid dreams. A lot of shit has happened since then, much of it unpleasant. That I can use real magic is one of the only genuinely wonderful results; figures that I can't do it now.

'I'd love to stay and talk more encouragement at you, but I need to go,' Bonnie says. 'My apprenticeship has actually placed me in the field today. I need to leave if I don't want to be late.' She gives me an awkward but pleading look. 'I really don't want to make a bad impression.'

I wave her away before she's done talking. 'Go. Impress your future employers and save the ocean.'

'Will you be al—'

'*Yes*. Does this look like our dog will let me be sad for long?'

Lady whines and shoves her heavy head at mine. Her wagging tail hits Bonnie in the knee.

'Gods, fine!' She laughs. 'But we'll talk properly tonight, alright?'

11

I nod. 'I might know what Kate's planning by then, too. She seems to have an idea.'

Bonnie looks crestfallen. 'Damn, now I want to hear all about it.'

I gently nudge Lady. 'Go, chase her to the car. She'll lose all her future work prospects if you don't.'

Lady, being the goodest puppy, ignores my command. Instead, she falls against me and snuggles her head against my shoulder.

'*Fine.*' Bonnie sighs. 'But we will catch up tonight! Walk the dog, it'll help.'

Lady's head shoots up at that.

'I just might, since you've put ideas in her head now,' I say. 'What time will you be back? I'll order pizza.'

'Wait with that until I'm back,' she says. 'I've a feeling they'll make me wade into something. I might smell when I get home, which should be around eight. I don't know for sure, though. I might be later.'

I really appreciate that we're all avoiding the topic of Leverett like the plague. Do I want to talk about my feelings? Yes. Absolutely. Does it hurt too much? Also yes. I haven't been back in his bookshop since he said he needs time to think about us, but that doesn't mean I haven't been thinking about him. If he decides loving a human is too painful, I'll respect it. But if he doesn't… If he says he wants to be with me… Ugh. It was only ever going to be a matter of time before my brain brought it up. I can just imagine Mischief pawing at me to talk to him already. Which I won't.

'I'll see you tonight,' I say to Bonnie. She waves me and

Lady goodbye, and I hug my dog, who lets out a very happy huff. 'How about that walk?'

She's on her paws and waddling to the door faster than my eyes can follow. If there's one thing that'll get her to move, it's the promise of light outdoor exercise.

So, I attach her leash, she sets the pace, and I silently beg the breeze to give me some sign—any sign—that what happened with Kate wasn't a fluke.

'Do you have time to talk?'

Lady and I returned from our walk five minutes ago. I've sat on the sofa since, staring at Leverett's text message, because my knees don't feel strong enough to support me.

The last time we talked, he told me he has feelings for me but isn't sure if he can put himself through loving a human. I left his shop with mixed emotions. I understand—or as much as I can in my non-vampire position, anyway—what he was battling with, but we'd also kissed that same evening. Since then, I've learned that I can be his friend, because that's better than not being in his life at all. I don't fall in love easily, but when I do, I fall hard. I felt safe with him so quickly. I felt seen and accepted. Now the emotional connection is there, I can't stop thinking about him.

Still, I understand his concerns. I haven't texted him since I last saw him just over a week ago.

Until now.

Or I *would* text him, *if* I could get out of my head long enough to formulate a response.

I hope against all reason that he's decided he can love me

after all, that I'll go over there or he comes over and we'll be a couple by the end of today. Really, though, I know it's more likely that he'll tell me he can't do it, and I have no right to argue. It can't be easy, loving someone you'll not only outlive by several centuries but who'll also age while you stay young… or young-ish, anyway. Leverett doesn't drink blood, so he ages, too. He doesn't look like a twenty-year-old, but he's not an old man, either. When we first met, I thought of him as being middle-aged, though in reality he's several hundred years old—419, in fact. He's four hundred years older than me by almost exactly a decade. I don't care about any of that. I care that he makes me feel safe.

Bonnie will be gone for at least five hours yet, so if Leverett came over, we'd be alone. That's if things go well. If they don't, I guess it doesn't matter how much longer Bonnie will be out. I've already done two disappointed walks from his bookshop—once when the boggart twisted his opinion into definitely not wanting to be with me, and again when he told me he needed time. I'd rather not make it a third walk of shame, or I guess sadness would be more fitting. But if it does go well…

An invisible paw swipes at my face—Mischief's new way outside my dreamscape of telling me to stop thinking and start doing.

I quickly type, 'Sure! Shall I come over?' and then I grab my shoes, because I'm fully expecting him to say yes.

But he doesn't.

Roughly one minute later, as I'm fiddling with my sandal straps and wondering whether my knee-length yellow dress is too provocative or not sexy enough, Leverett's shadow appears behind our door's stained-glass window. I open the door just as his hand is on his way up to knock. For a second, all I can do is stare at him. This can't be bad news, right? He wouldn't have rushed over if it were bad news. No one hurries to deliver bad news.

I awkwardly shuffle back out of my one sandal while I wave him into the living room. Leverett doesn't take his eyes off me as he follows me. His eyes darken when he sees me, like he's… Like… Damn it, I'm still not sure what it means, but it looks like lust and it's doing things to me.

'You wanted to ta—' I start.

'I'm sorry,' he says at the same time.

I fall silent. My heart falls with my voice. He's *sorry*. It's fine. I can still be his friend. I want him in my life, one way or another.

Leverett clears his throat. 'I'm sorry I ever needed time to think. The moment you left my shop, I hated myself for letting you walk away when all I wanted was to bend you over my counter.'

My throat goes dry. I mean, I would have preferred that, too.

'But since I'd already asked for time to think, I decided to take that time to consider the pros and cons of loving a human, to—' He sighs. 'And I've thought of you every second since you walked away. I care about you, Esta. A lot. I didn't want either of us to be deluded about what we're getting into. I can spend your life with you, but I will lose you one day. I will have to bury you, and those years will fly by for me. And

15

it will hurt when you go. But those years will pass just as fast either way, and one day I will lose you either way. It will hurt infinitely worse when that day comes and I regret not having been yours this whole time.'

He stands closer, so close I could easily kiss him if only I tilted my head up just so. But I don't dare move. Not yet.

Leverett takes my hands into his; I realise how much mine are shaking.

'Esta. Do you still want me? Because I will not waste another damn second if you'll have me.'

I kiss him.

He wraps his arms around me. His tongue claims mine like he's starving and I'm all he needs. I hold on to him with just as much desperation, but he's so much stronger than I am that he effortlessly guides me backwards until I walk into the table. His growing erection presses against my centre. A breathless moan escapes me. He wants me. He's mine. After all this—

Supported by the table, I close my legs around him, then let him carry me up the stairs. If he were anyone else, I'd have exactly zero trust in his ability to not drop me, but vampires are strong, and I've never felt safer... even when he kicks my door shut behind him and hastily lowers me onto my bed. His erection pressing against my leg makes it impossible to think.

'Your car isn't here,' he whispers against my lips. 'We're alone?'

I nod against him, desperate to feel his lips on mine again. 'For at least five hours.'

A dark smile slowly spreads on his face. 'Good.'

He gently spreads my legs and slides two fingers into my

underwear. Into *me*.

I gasp. My eyes flutter shut, my mind suddenly blank. The way he strokes me, I can't—

'*Lev*. Inside me. *Please*.'

I've never been so desperate, and I don't care that I sound it, too. I feel like I've wanted him for *months*. Except for this past week, where I've made an effort not to think about him, I've thought of little else. Even my dreams have been torturing me. Actually having him here, in my bedroom and between my legs, is too much. I don't want to fall apart within one minute of him stroking my clit, but I don't know how to hold on.

Lev chuckles at my torment. I almost cum from the sound alone.

'Oh no, my beautiful Esta. Not yet. First I want to see you come undone at my hands.' He leans over me, kisses me, licks my lips, his fingers moving in slow, rhythmic waves, and whispers, 'Cum for me, Esta.'

My back arches at his command, and a strained gasp escapes me.

His fingers slow down, but he doesn't stop. His eyes darken further, and in this moment, at least, I don't doubt what it means.

Once he's sure that I've ridden out my orgasm, he kisses me again, then slides my dress over my head. He throws my underwear into some corner, I don't care where. I watch his face as he undoes my bra and throws that off the bed, too, mesmerised by the simple fact that we're here and this is happening. He kisses me again, first my lips, then my neck, then my breasts. I rake my fingers through his hair.

'You're even more beautiful when you cum for me than I imagined,' he says.

A smirk crosses my lips. 'You've imagined us, have you?'

He chuckles again. 'Oh, yes. Many times.'

I can only guess what a vampire's imagination is capable of, so I'm just relieved I didn't let it down.

I let my hands roam over his neck, his chest. Tug at his shirt and run my hand under the fabric. Let my other hand move down his stomach and stroke his erection through his trousers.

I'm much too pleased with myself when his eyes flutter shut and he moans.

'Esta— I'm not done with you.'

I rub a little harder and love that his head falls back a little, like my touch is bringing out something primal in him.

'Hmm?' I tease. 'You want me to stop?'

'No. I want your mouth around my cock, but there'll be time for that later.'

The raw want in his voice nearly undoes me all over again, but he said *later*. Whatever he wants right now, I will give it.

This time when I tug at his shirt, he vanishes into fog. One second later, he reappears before me, his clothes on the floor under him.

I've *never* seen anyone undress that fast.

'Wha— I—'

He pulls me forwards on the bed and places his tip at my entrance, my shaking legs around him. My whole body is trembling.

'Are you *sure* you're ready for this?' But his voice is trembling almost as hard as I am. 'You won't get rid of me if I take you, Esta. I will be yours—body, mind, and soul. I need you to be mine, too.'

I remember he said something like that a few weeks ago, at the party—about whether I'm really ready to have an utterly devoted vampire partner. I was ready then, and I'm ready now.

I wiggle forwards a tiny bit so he can feel how wet I am. 'I'm yours.'

He grips my legs and thrusts into me. I moan. My back arches as I feel him against my inner walls. It's too much, I can't— I thought I'd be able to hang on more easily after my first orgasm, but *gods*, I was wrong. All of this is overwhelming in the best possible way.

'Did I hurt you?' he whispers.

'No,' I pant out. 'Harder.'

He *growls*, and begins to thrust in and out, harder and harder every time he enters me. I'm barely clinging to sanity as is, but then he begins to slow, the bastard, and— Just as I'm about to complain, he slides one finger against my clit. He brings his finger to his mouth and licks it.

Leverett smirks again. 'Just a taste for now, since you were so desperate to have me inside you.'

Before I can think of something to say—it's hard, because all logic has left my head—he returns his fingers to my middle and begins to stroke me in time with his thrusts. My need builds fast. I grip the sheets under me and keep pace with him as he steadily fucks me closer to the edge.

And then, I fall apart under him. I feel him finish inside me at the same time. He growls again as we ride out our joined climax together.

Leverett kisses me once, twice. Again and again. Slowly. Indulgently. I begin to move back a little and pull him onto the bed next to me until Leverett cradles me in his arms.

'I'm sorry it took me so long to come to my senses,' he whispers against my lips. He strokes my back with one hand while caressing my face with the other. His nose gently moves against mine. I can't get enough of him. All this touch, and it's still not enough. We've only just cuddled up together, and I already miss him inside me.

I shake my head. 'You're here now. I'm glad you're sure.'

He kisses me deeper, his tongue stroking mine, and I want to fall into him. 'I am. And I'm utterly obsessed with you, Esta Anderson.'

I almost laugh. Does he have any idea how much *I've* obsessed over *him*? Oh, the stories Mischief could tell. Oh, the things my poor dream guide has seen.

'No more obsessed than I am with you.'

He chuckles. The sound reverberates through my chest and right into my heart. 'We'll see about that.'

We stay like that—intertwined with each other and marvelling at the other's hands on naked skin—until I dose off in Leverett's arms.

CHAPTER
THREE

I open my eyes to the purple leaves of the tree in my dreamscape. I must have fallen asleep in Leverett's arms—Mischief is going to be insufferable. At least my dreams won't torture me with naked Leveretts now... or they still might, but the real one will be waiting for me when I wake up, so...

I suppose if anything, my dreams will be a lot more detailed from now on.

'Hehe. Good evening. Having fun, are you?'

I squint up at the tree. Mischief loafs between two branches in a way that can't possibly be comfortable. Cats can get comfy in the strangest positions, but she's not really a cat. She only takes the shape of one because I really wanted a cat when we first met. I know she can shift into other shapes, too; it's never bothered me. But now that I know she's Veiled... What kind of Veiled, exactly? Would she still be comfy sitting like this in her natural form, whatever that is? I don't remember what she looked like when we first met, before she changed into a cat. Perhaps she's always taken this form with me. I mean, she does know my thoughts; it's part of her job as dream guide.

She probably adopted this form so I'd immediately feel safe with her.

A shiver runs down my back. That… doesn't sit quite well with me, actually, but what else was she supposed to do? Dream guides gonna dream guide. Whatever that means. I can't judge her when I barely know the real her or the first thing about her background.

'Don't overthink it, Esta,' she purrs, then licks her paw. 'In fact, I'd appreciate it if you never thought about it again.'

I sit up and lean against the tree trunk. This purple-leafed tree is probably the oldest thing here except for Mischief, or at least they are the only two things that haven't really changed. There are plenty of places in my dreamscape that represent my childhood or my memories, but even they have shifted and reformed over time as my perception and knowledge has changed. I don't remember this tree ever looking any different, though. It's always been here—black trunk, purple leaves, grounding comfort. Maybe all dreamscapes have a… *feature* like my tree, some kind of mental focal point that keeps everything centred and stable. This is where I become lucid every time. It's like an unshakable safe space where nothing bad can happen.

I smirk at her. 'Got something to hide, do you?'

She stretches and jumps from the branch straight onto my legs. No claws dig in as she lands and inevitably slides off the sides—it's all soft paws with her by choice, unless she wants to get my attention and decides that only claws will do.

'Don't we all.' She sighs. 'It's complicated. I already wasn't supposed to help you with Chiara the way I did. Don't ask for more.'

That's not exactly the same thing as us talking about her true form, but if she can't talk about it, I won't push her.

I hug her to me. 'Thank you again for that.'

When I was trapped in Chiara's basement and convinced I was going to die, hugging her again was one of the things I wished I could do, so I'll make up for it now.

Mischief affectionately headbutts my arm. 'I would *much* rather talk about you and Leverett.'

'Nope!' I laugh. 'Not doing that.' It's bad enough that Bonnie will ask for all the details. I don't mind showing off a little, but he's all mine now, *all mine*, and those details are too private. I want to keep them that way. Mischief likely already knows more than I'd normally be comfortable sharing through our connection. No need for me to spell any of it out.

She puts a fluffy paw on my arm. 'I'm just happy for you.'

I hug her again. 'Thank you. *I* would much rather talk about what Kate said. Any idea what plan she might have? Or if I actually used magic?'

Mischief huffs. 'I'm in *your* head, not hers. I don't know what she's thinking. And… Forgive me, Esta. I can't comment on the magic thing. Besides, there's nothing to talk about. I sealed it away again, remember?'

That would explain why I've been struggling so much, but there's something in her voice when she said that last bit that makes me wonder.

'*Did* you seal it again?'

She paws at my face, like a light slap. Her claws lightly scrape against my face. 'Of course I did. Please, Esta. I can't

23

talk about it.'

I sigh, but I'm not angry. Clearly, dream guide politics are complicated. I wish we could discuss it, but her claws on my face got the message across.

'Alright. Do you think I'm really part Veiled, though?' I'm just wondering out loud like I've always done with her, so that should be safe. This is business as usual for us; it would be stranger if I didn't ask.

Mischief licks her paw and cleans her head with it like she regrets that she ever let me pet her. 'How would I know if you don't?'

I sigh again. 'Yeah, fair point. It's just not adding up. I'd know if there was a Veiled in my family, right? Kate said the Veiled are far too proud of their bloodlines to not raise me their way.'

Heh, or maybe they saw how weak my feeble little magic really is and deemed me unworthy of their heritage. Maybe I'd be more shame than joy to the family. I suppose that's possible.

Mischief gets comfy on my legs and rests her head on my knee. 'It does sound like it. There must be some other possibility you haven't considered.'

I make a mental note of that. It very much sounds like she's trying to nudge me in the right direction; so, she does know something, but she can't tell me outright.

Mischief gets up again and nestles herself against my chest instead. She tugs in her front paws and closes her eyes. My dream guide kitty is about to fall asleep on me.

I smile. 'You alright there?'

Mischief has copied many typical cat mannerisms over the years, but she's never cuddled me like this before.

'Let me have this, Esta. Just for a moment. Please?'

I still. This isn't like her. I stroke her head down to her back. She purrs, but there's something sad about it.

'Mischief?'

'Let me have this and I'll never bug you about Leverett again.'

I nod and close my arms around her. I don't know why she needs this, but clearly, she does. Maybe it's because, when Chiara kept me trapped in her basement, Mischief hoped to see me again, too.

I yawn. 'Alright. You're safe with me.'

I don't know why I said that. It felt appropriate somehow, like she needed to hear it.

Hopefully, Kate's hunch is right, whatever it is. Maybe there's something in Saif's impressive home library—he did say I could come back to use it—but I wouldn't even know where to start. So, all my hope rests on Kate, at least for now.

All I can do is wait.

Bonnie did not, in fact, make it home by eight. She messaged me around eight-thirty saying they were running late and not to wait up, so Leverett and I, erm, made the most of it. When I eventually heard her keys in the door, it was nearly midnight, and I was about ready to pass out in Leverett's arms again.

The next morning, Leverett wakes me with a kiss to let me know he can hear her sneaking through the house.

'I'll go say hello,' I say as I reluctantly slide out of bed.

Leverett nods. 'I'll give you a moment.'

I smile, throw on a dress—though his shirt is tempting if only to see Bonnie's reaction—and make my way downstairs. I smell coffee; we're both tea people, but Bonnie insists coffee has a stronger caffeine hit and will drink it instead when she's particularly exhausted. Last night must have been a lot.

Heh, I guess I'm not the only one who had it rough last night.

'Good morning!' I say as I sway into the kitchen with a huge grin. I meant to play it cool, but I can't stop thinking about the naked vampire in my bed. I compose myself before Bonnie turns around. I'm dying to tell her, but I think this'll be funnier... *if* my face doesn't give it away first. 'How did it go yesterday?'

Bonnie turns around from making a tea for Lady and gives me that look that begs for pizza and a movie night.

'I love my internship,' she says, 'but it's kicking my butt. I'll definitely try to find a job closer to home. Last night's field trip was awesome, but I'm not making that trip every day.' She falls into my arms. 'I can't wait for it to be over. Uni is stressful, too, but at least it doesn't take me so long to get there.' She gives our rottweiler daughter a regretful look, then looks back to me. 'I'm sorry, but can you walk her again today? I desperately need more sleep.'

'Don't you need to be at the internship today?'

She raises her coffee at me with a tired smile. 'As a thank-you for all my hard work yesterday, I've been given today off, so I'm gonna sleep.' She takes a sip and freezes. 'I'm going to regret this coffee, aren't I.'

'No problem, I'll take Lady. And you love it really.'

She gives her coffee another unsure look, then downs half the cup in one go. 'The internship? Yes. Absolutely. It's everything I want. The drive? That can fuck off.'

I laugh; this seems like a good moment to let out some of my excitement before I burst.

Bonnie frowns at me. 'It wasn't *that* funny. How was *your* evening?' She looks me up and down like she can see traces of Leverett's hands on me. 'You weren't bored, I h—'

A floorboard right above us creaks. Bonnie glances at it, then at me, tapping her fingernails on her cup.

'Who is— *Esta.*'

I giggle after all, and I'm very aware that I'm blushing again. I don't care, I can't hold it in anymore.

'Yes?' I ask innocently.

Bonnie playfully punches my arm. 'You might have led with that!'

'Where's the fun in that?'

Leverett enters the room and Bonnie shakes her head at him. 'I'm out for two seconds, mister, and this is what you do to my sister? What have you got to say for yourself?' She throws her best glower at him, but I see the light in her empty threat. Leverett chuckles and gives me a smile so warm I want to melt into him.

'I assure you I only want to make her happy.'

I lean into him and return his smile. 'You do.' And I will spend every minute of my life making him happy, too.

He kisses me.

Bonnie gags. 'Gawd, alright, you're too cute. You two

lovebirds get out of here. Go walk Lady together.' She gives Leverett a heavy look. 'She's your daughter now, too. Welcome to the family.'

Lady barks in approval and cosies up to his legs.

Bonnie passes me on her way upstairs, whispers, 'Tell me *everything*,' and then Leverett and I are off for our first walk together.

It's barely eight-thirty a.m., but it's already approaching unbearable temperatures. Over the last few weeks, the grass in the park has turned to hay. Lady couldn't care less and is running circles around us.

Next to me, Leverett chuckles again, the sound that will be the end of me. 'Do you think your sister approves of me?'

I snort. 'She'll be pestering me for details later.' I look at him. 'Don't worry, I won't actually tell her everything. She's just happy for me.'

'Then I hope you have no complaints.'

I giggle again. Hopefully, I won't continue to act like a teenager now we're together or I might start to annoy myself before the week is over.

'None,' I say with a smile.

Leverett puts an arm around my waist, pulls me to him, and kisses me. In front of everyone in the park. They all know about us now.

All four of them.

I'm so wrapped up in the handsome vampire at my side I don't notice that my dog leads us straight into another couple. Fortunately, Leverett slows us down before I walk into them.

It's the fairy couple—the first Veiled I saw after I stepped into the void lake, whose names I learned and immediately forgot at Anton's party.

'Esta!' one of them says. 'It's so good to see you.' She glances at Leverett. 'Both of you.'

Great. Of course *they* remember *my* name. Not a huge surprise, I guess, since apparently the Veiled community is all abuzz about my epic standoff with the Dreamcatcher and the Mara, but it still bugs me that I don't remember theirs. I do remember they want to adopt a dog, though.

'Oh, hey!' I hope I don't sound as awkward as I feel. 'Any news on adopting a puppy?' I whisper the last bit in case their kids are around, but I don't see them, so it's probably unnecessary. For all I know, though, fairy children can turn invisible whenever, so I'd rather be careful.

'No, not yet,' the first fairy's wife says. 'We were actually wondering if you could recommend somewhere.'

I blink. 'Me? Erm... There's a rescue centre nearby, but we had our dog from another one before we realised this one is closer. I can give you their names, but I don't really know anywhere else. Sorry.'

'Oh, no, we're sorry,' the first fairy says. 'We thought you might work with dogs, the way you care for yours and took an interest in our plans. We should have asked.'

I wave them off. 'No, it's fine. I just really love my dog.' It's not the worst assumption strangers have made about me recently. 'I actually work at the university gallery in town, so, erm... No dog adoption advice from there.'

'That sounds lovely,' the second fairy with the Irish accent says. 'Poppy here paints. She even makes money from it. She's so talented.'

Poppy. Her name is Poppy. Now if only I could remember Poppy's wife's name… I'd actually make a point to remember this time.

'Sorcha is too kind,' Poppy says. *Sorcha. Sorchasorchasorcha.* 'I make a little money from my painting, but it's hardly a fortune. Do you paint, too?'

It takes me a second to realise she means me.

I quickly shake my head. 'I studied photography, but…' They know a little about what happened with the Dreamcatcher—all Veiled seem to—but do they know *why* it happened?

Sorcha's eyes brighten. 'How wonderful!' They share a glance. 'Say, would you consider taking our family portrait? Some individual ones, too. We'll pay you, of course!' She smiles. 'We haven't been able to find a Veiled photographer, and we'd love to have professional photos of *us*. You know?'

My heart does a flip, sinks, and does another flip only to sink deeper than before. The first thing people do when I tell them I studied photography is ask me to photograph them. I hate this response, though that's because they don't usually offer to pay me. They just see it as an easy way to get some good photos while paying me in "experience," something to add to my portfolio. Poppy and Sorcha would actually pay me. This is everything I wanted not that long ago: to take photos of the Veiled as they are, with their wings out bright and proud.

But even as I half consider it, I hear Mischief's bones snap all over again.

I've never regretted anything like I regret shaking my head in that moment. 'I don't actually do photography that much anymore. Sorry. A-and I already took loads of photos in this park and never saw any wings, so… Sorry.'

I hope they don't think badly of me for saying no; they must think I just don't want to photograph *them* for whatever reason. Leverett tightens his arm around me and pulls me in a little. I draw strength from it as I try not to dwell on how I just declined the one chance I was desperate to have.

'You wouldn't have seen them, not like that,' Poppy says. She continues in a whisper, 'It's part of the magic we place on ourselves to blend in. Otherwise, there'd be photos of us everywhere.' Ah. Well, that explains that. 'But if you don't want to pursue it further, that's alright. I hear many people lose the passion for their chosen subject during their degree.'

I nod, like that's absolutely me even though I'm the opposite.

'We've taken up enough of your time,' Sorcha says. 'I'm sure we'll run into each other again.'

I nod again and force myself to smile. 'Yeah. See you later.'

I hope the Dreamcatcher and the Mara are watching. I hope they know how much it hurt to turn down this offer, and that I did it anyway.

Leverett kisses my head and leads me away, towards the forest. He doesn't say anything, and I don't try to make small talk just to sound like I'm fine when really, I feel like I've just buried a piece of me.

CHAPTER
FOUR

An hour later, I stand outside Kate's front door with my heart in my throat. I had a text from her not long after we got home asking me to come over, and since Leverett has a few things to take care of in his shop, I made sure Lady was happy and then went over.

I knock and try not to overthink it. Has she found a spell that can coax out my magic? Has she found someone who has taught people like me before? Although, I don't really know what *people like me* even means in this context. There probably aren't many who discovered their secret, hidden magic under the same circumstances I did.

But this is me overthinking it, so I remind myself that I don't know why she called me over and try to forget about it.

My heart nearly rips out of my chest when Kate opens the door. I'm totally expecting too much from this.

'Ah, Esta!' Kate says as she waves me into her home, her dogs taking turns to jump up my legs for a head pat. 'I didn't think you'd be here quite so soon. Come in.'

'Am I too early?' I did as good as fly over. 'I can come back later if it's better.'

Kate smiles at me. 'No, not at all. Please, take a seat in the living room.'

I freeze when I realise someone is already there.

The stranger is *tall*. And *white*, actual chalk-white—his skin, his eyes, his long hair. He's so incredibly pale he looks like he should be translucent but defies logic by still appearing solid. His slightly stooped posture looks uncomfortable, like Kate's living room is too small for him; I instinctively want to ask him if he'd rather talk outside. Mum would call him lanky; despite his slight frame, there's an unexpected strength to him, though at the same time he looks like the smallest breeze might carry him away. His smile is kind, though, just a little... I don't know. Like he hasn't smiled in a while and is trying to remember how it works.

He's sitting down, but his limbs look too big to sit comfortably, and I wonder if he only chose the sofa because his head would go through the ceiling otherwise. He stares at me as I enter and freeze in the doorway, but not in a creepy way, more like he's literally just looking *at* me, or like he's acknowledging me as someone new in the room.

'Hello, Esta Anderson.' His voice is light, melodic. It reminds me of a spring breeze, or clear blue skies. Gods, I think I feel a breeze inside me, even, like what Kate told me to find within myself. If just his presence gets my magic to respond, we're off to a good start.

'Hello,' I say. 'Just Esta, please.'

Kate walks in after me. 'Esta, this is Zeru. I asked them here because of a suspicion I had.' She smiles at Zeru. 'Does this mean my hunch was right?'

Zeru continues to stare at me in their oddly non-staring way. 'It seems so. How curious.'

I look between Zeru and Kate and have no idea what they're talking about. 'What hunch? How do you already know if Kate was right? We haven't done anything yet.'

'A simple test,' Zeru says. 'When you arrived and I greeted you, you responded.'

I've never passed a test so easily. 'I mean… Well… Yeah? It would have been rude not to?'

One of Kate's dogs, Keano, shoves his head at my hand, and I scratch his ear while I try to figure out what's going on. How is a simple greeting a test? How can that possibly confirm anything?

'I did not speak the words aloud,' Zeru says. 'I spoke into your mind, as I do with all my sylph brethren.'

I shiver, but I'm not sure why. For a moment, I just stand there. I even stop petting Keano. I look to Kate so she can make sense of this for me.

She gives me her patient teacher smile. 'Zeru isn't saying you're a sylph yourself, but rather that your magic is sylph in origin.'

'A very distant origin,' Zeru clarifies. 'I would like to ask you a few questions to determine how to proceed.'

I nod again. My legs shaking, I slide to the floor next to Keano. The sofa looks so very far away, and Keano is thrilled. Bruin waddles up beside me and begs to be cuddled, so I hug both dogs to myself. Kate sits in her armchair, while Zeru continues to absolutely and effortlessly dominate the room with their brightness and height and pure existence.

'Sure,' I say. 'I don't know that I have any answers, though. I'm so confused.'

'Understandable,' Zeru says. 'I believe I may be able to help, but before I decide, there are a few things I must know.'

It occurs to me how still they are, yet it doesn't feel unnatural. Not with them. More like they have no need to rush.

'Can I ask a few things, too?' I ask. 'When you're done, I mean?'

Zeru mimics my nod, a stiffer version of my own.

'Kate told me you possess a kind of magic she can't teach,' Zeru says. 'She also told me you acquired your power through unusual means. Please tell me about the first time you realised you could use magic.'

'Erm… That's complicated, maybe?' My gut and Kate both say I can trust Zeru. I don't want to hide anything from them, but Mischief asked me not to talk about it. How much can I say without getting her involved? 'I first used magic two weeks ago, but I've known magic exists for over a month now.'

Bloody hell, it feels much longer ago than that. Funny how time flies when your dreams are invaded and you get kidnapped by a vampire.

Zeru nods again, the movement a little smoother this time, like they're getting used to it. 'We are aware of the incident that allowed you to see the Veiled, as you call us. Kate mentioned you first used magic yourself in self-defence. Tell me about that.'

Of course Zeru knows about that. I seem to be every

Veiled's favourite topic of gossip lately. Why wouldn't that stretch to actual forces of nature?

'A vampire kidnapped me,' I say. 'I saw an opening and ran for it. She came after me, I panicked, and just... kinda... did it?'

Zeru hasn't blinked once since I met them. I can't decide if the atmosphere in this room is the calm before one hell of a storm, or if it's more like we're at the safe centre of a hurricane.

'I don't understand,' Zeru says. 'You shouldn't have been able to access dormant magic without help. Are you certain it was only you and the vampire?'

I bite my lip. Inside myself, I think I feel Mischief's ears ping back. I promised I wouldn't talk about it, but if I don't, Zeru has wasted their time, and we won't get anywhere. But I *promised*.

'I can't talk about it. I'm sorry. I swore I wouldn't.'

'That is commendable.' Zeru gently waves their hand, and the room feels... softer. Like they've just thrown a blanket over us. 'No one will hear us, and I will keep your secret if it is safe to do so. You have my word.'

I *want* to trust them, but I don't even know them. I do trust Kate, though. Still, I—

I sigh.

'I know you're conflicted,' Kate says. 'Zeru means you no harm, however. I can vouch for them.'

'What did you do just now?' I ask, partially to buy time and partially to judge if it really is safe. 'Something changed in the air, I felt it.'

'Very good,' Zeru says. 'I placed a shield over the house to keep our conversation confidential. Whoever you're worried about listening in won't hear us.'

Still, I hesitate. The breaking of promises doesn't come easily to me.

'I can't teach you if you're not honest with me,' Zeru says. 'I need to fully understand the steps that led to your unique situation if I am to help you.'

Kate smiles at me. 'I believe I know who you're worried for, and I can assure you nothing gets through Zeru's shield. They have shaped the air to hide us, and no one understands air better than a sylph.'

I want to shake my head again—I already lost my one chance to pursue my dream photography career today; why not lose out on a second awesome thing while I'm at it?—but I feel a light touch to my cheek, and I feel a purr inside me. Mischief's way of letting me know it's alright.

I swallow. 'Technically, it was just me and Chiara—that's the vampire. But my dream guide was there, too. You know, in my mind. She knew there was magic hiding somewhere in me, and she did something to free it. If she hadn't, I'd be dead.' I glance from Zeru to Kate and back again. 'She knows she wasn't supposed to meddle like that, but I really would be dead if she hadn't helped me. She saved my life.' I deflate against Bruin, who licks my face in response. 'She isn't in trouble, is she?'

Mischief told me that she's broken some rules to help me, but I didn't realise how bad it sounds until I summarised it out loud. What if the magic was hidden inside me for a reason?

Wouldn't the void lake have unlocked it otherwise? Freeing magic that's supposed to be secret and locked up tight is probably a huge problem. And I just explained it all, like an idiot.

'Please, don't worry.' Zeru's voice is gentle, and I feel myself relax into it. 'I promised that no word would leave this room, and I spoke true. But that a dream guide would go to such lengths... Remarkable. How odd.'

'Mischief didn't know anything about my magic. She just didn't want me to die and saw a potential solution. She did what any friend would do. I'd do the same in her, uh, paws.'

Slowly, Zeru shakes their head, and I get the feeling that I couldn't be more wrong. 'You don't understand the role of dream guides, and I am not here to discuss it with you. Right now, you have a more pressing question to ponder.'

'Will she be alright?' I'm too worried I messed up and doomed Mischief in the process to think about my magic.

'That's not for us to say,' Kate says. 'Neither of us hold any power over dream guide laws. I can, however, vouch for Zeru. If Mischief's superiors weren't already aware of what happened before this conversation, they won't have heard about it now. Sylphs have an understanding of magic few others possess. I swear to you that you can trust Zeru.'

I nod and hold on to Bruin and Keano, one arm around each dog. 'Alright.'

'As I said earlier, your magic is sylph in origin, though it would have been dormant for several lives. That your dream guide not only sensed it but also managed to unleash it is... intriguing.'

Sounds like they really meant to say *troubling* or *fascinating* and met in the middle.

'What do you mean, several lives?' I look at Kate. 'Like, my ancestors? Previous generations?'

'Not quite,' she says. 'The truth may be harder to understand, though.'

'It's certainly more surprising,' Zeru says. 'To keep it simple, your mortal souls are the sum of your combined lives. All of you carry fragments, if you will, of past experiences, but they are just that: vague memories you cannot grasp. They still exist within you because their lives had a deep impact on you, or because the information can be of use to you in this life. That is all you need to know.'

Frankly, even that is confusing. 'Hang on,' I say. 'So, I was a sylph in a past life?'

I don't know how to begin to wrap my head around that.

'It would seem so,' Zeru says. 'Your magic's signature is unmistakable. Coming across the reincarnated soul of a sylph is extremely rare, but it's not impossible.'

So many questions about that statement alone, though I doubt Zeru is here to explain sylph reproduction and the rules of rebirth to me. Probably for the best if we don't do this right now; I wouldn't know where to begin.

'That you can access your dormant sylph magic now,' Zeru continues, 'as a human, has no precedent. I'm unsure what it means, what effects it might have.'

'I just want to be able to defend myself,' I say. 'That's all I ever wanted.' Or ever since I stepped into the void lake, anyway.

39

'Where do we go from here?' Kate asks. Despite sitting in her armchair and being a fair bit smaller than Zeru, her presence feels larger. Must be because it's her home; she simply looks more at ease here.

'Esta and I have two options,' Zeru says, their white eyes on me. 'You can attempt to learn how to use the remnants of your magic, or we sylphs can seal it again. Forever this time.'

I frown. 'But Mischief already sealed it. She told me.'

'Your dream guide lied to you.'

I feel like they punched me in the face. 'Why would she do that?'

'I can't say. Perhaps she didn't know how, or she saw the need to protect herself?'

'Esta and Mischief are close,' Kate jumps in. 'Closer than dream guides and their charges usually are, I won't deny it. I believe Mischief may have lied to give Esta a gift without further implicating herself.'

Zeru is silent for a moment. 'Then that is more unusual still, but it is not for me to judge. I am here to present you with the choice I have just given you. In truth, I need time to consider the best course of action. Kate has told me that you struggle to use your magic. It is my belief that you would also struggle to call on it, let alone master it. Therefore, attempting to teach you should pose little risk. However, I cannot ignore that this is a power you were not supposed to have. The smallest breeze can rattle many leaves. Removing your magic altogether would be the safest option.'

'No. I had that option once and I didn't take it then, either.'

'With the Dreamcatcher and the Mara,' Zeru says. 'That was

a slightly different choice.'

I look to Kate for help again, but she simply watches me.

I sigh and sink against Bruin. 'If it's unlikely I'll be able to do much anyway, what's the harm in me keeping my magic? Can't I at least try?'

Zeru inclines their head. 'I would like you to consider these questions carefully. I will do the same. When next we meet, we will know how to proceed.'

I want to protest, to say there's nothing for me to think about, but I keep quiet. I don't want to give them the impression that I'm impulsive or can't be trusted to apply reason. While it's an easy choice for me, it's clearly a difficult choice for Zeru. I will trust them to consider every angle while I will do the same. Hopefully, we'll reach the same conclusion…

Because if I decide to keep my magic and they decide to remove it, I'm not convinced I'd have any say in the matter this time.

CHAPTER
FIVE

I need this movie night as much as Bonnie does. She's exhausted from her internship, and I have about a thousand questions I need to talk through with her... Okay, I have two, but they're big ones. I hate that part of me already knows the answers, because I don't like either of them. There's got to be a loophole, or maybe I only think I know the answer because I'm scared? Everything that's happened with the Dreamcatcher, the boggart, and Chiara has me second-guessing everything. I've done my best to not think about any of that today, which being with Leverett made easy. Now that I'm mixing our cocktails, though, and Bonnie just ordered pizza, it's harder not to dwell on it.

But that's what this movie night is for. It'll magically make everything better with the power of sister-relaxation time.

'*So*!' Bonnie grins at me as I place our drinks on the table. She wiggles her eyebrows at me. 'You and Leverett, eh? I would *never* have guessed.'

I playfully punch her shoulder. 'Stop it, you're as bad as Mischief.'

Bonnie giggles. 'How did she react? I know she's been teasing you.'

I snort. 'More like torturing.' My smile falls, because that's another thing I hate: I've been close with Mischief for as long as I can remember, but are we allowed to get along this well? Zeru made it sound like it's odd, and Mischief said something along those lines, too. What if just us discussing Mischief's and my friendship counts against her somehow? But how could friendship ever go against anyone? And I've talked to Bonnie about her for years; no one's ever complained. I know this particular problem is different, that I can't talk about what Mischief did with my magic, but I'm scared to mention her at all now and I hate it. My head hurts and I haven't started drinking yet.

Bonnie hands me my cocktail. 'You look like you need this.' She takes a sip of her own while she waits for me to do the same. 'Now, talk. What's troubling you?'

I sigh. Where do I even start?

'Leverett has been wonderful, so don't go thinking it's anything he's done.'

Bonnie narrows her eyes at me over the brim of her glass like she dares him to try, but she nods for me to continue.

'A Veiled family asked me to take photos for them, wings out and all, but I can't do it because I swore to the Dreamcatcher that I wouldn't. My magic, turns out, is sylph in origin, diluted by several reincarnations or something like that, and I should never have known I have it. Kate knows someone who could teach me, but they said—' I sigh again; none of this feels fair. 'They said they can remove my magic,

43

which is probably the best option if we're being honest. Even if I were to keep it, I wouldn't be able to do anything useful with it anyway, so what's the point? And I think Mischief is in trouble because she helped me. I don't know what to do about any of it.'

Bonnie drinks half her cocktail in one swig. 'Damn, sister. That's a lot.'

Lady, who's sitting on the floor by my feet, whines up at me.

I nod and look pleadingly at both of them to fix it. 'I know.'

Bonnie puts her glass to her lips, then frowns at it when she remembers it's empty already. 'Are you *sure* that photography offer is definitely a problem?'

'The Dreamcatcher and the Mara were happy to destroy my mind over it, remember? I'm pretty sure that means it's a problem.'

'Hmm…' Bonnie thinks for a moment. 'Wasn't the problem that you were going to just… take photos? And that they were worried you'd out the entire Veiled community that way? Like, against their will?'

'That was a big part of it, yes.' There's also the issue that someone else sent the Mara and the Dreamcatcher after me in the first place and I still don't know who it is. Whoever it is, I clearly pissed off the wrong Veiled. The brownie-boggart problem was just me being naïve, but who knows what'll happen next? What if I can't talk it out with the next Veiled who comes after me? Because I definitely can't fight them.

'So, this is different, isn't it?' Bonnie asks. 'You have permission this time, and you're not making the photos public.

They wouldn't have asked you to take photos of them "wings and all" if they weren't happy for the photos to show their, erm, Veiledness.'

I slowly sip my drink and nod to show I've heard her. It makes sense when Bonnie puts it that way. But what if whoever sent the Dreamcatcher after me doesn't see it this way? It's not like I can ask. I got away with a warning once; I doubt I'd be let off the hook again. Next time, I might not even get the chance to argue my case.

I shake my head. 'It's too risky. What if it goes wrong?'

Bonnie shrugs. 'It's your call, but I wouldn't give up on this just yet. This has been your dream for how long? So your first approach didn't go well. You know better now, and you're not the one who started it this time. You were *invited*. Doesn't that count for something?'

My turn to shrug, because I really don't know. 'I want to agree, but…' I remember all the nightmares the Dreamcatcher showed me. The blood and death that might result from my ambition. It's not worth that; I have other dreams. Isn't moving on despite the pain supposed to be the mature approach? I'm over thirty. Time to act like an adult.

I huff and finish my drink. Yes, I have other dreams—other dreams like learning magic.

'I'll think about it, I guess.' Bonnie is right, I shouldn't give up just because it didn't work the first time, but I'm scared. The Dreamcatcher put my mind through hell, and Chiara physically tortured me. I want to be strong and all that, but I also know I can't go through something like that again. It's been too much in too little time. I've never even broken a bone before. I've known stress, but not like this. I've been hurt, but never like that. Life doesn't prepare you for challenges, trials, whatever like these ones. Like having your dreams turned against you, or being some vampire's blood toy.

Bonnie takes our glasses and goes to make another cocktail.

'Hold on, what was that about you being a sylph?' she calls from the kitchen.

I get up and join her. 'I'm not one now, obviously, but Kate's friend thinks I was. Like, a *really* long time ago. In another life.'

Bonnie's eyes go wide. 'Whoa. That's so cool!'

Despite myself, I smile. 'Well, it doesn't actually mean anything, does it? It's probably true for everyone, and it's not like it's given me a step up or anything. I can't do much with my magic. I shouldn't even have known it's there. That's part of the problem, I think. It was mine in another life, but it's not meant to be mine now. That I used it once anyway violated the natural order, or something like that.'

Bonnie tops up the gin with cranberry juice and frowns at me. 'That's a shame. But if you can't do much anyway, what's the big deal?'

I shrug again and gratefully accept the drink. 'I dunno. As I said, it upsets the natural balance. I'm a regular mortal who somehow got at her long-since-dormant Veiled magic, so that's a problem. I mean, I can see why. If everyone somehow figured this out, lots of humans could run around with powers they're not supposed to have. And who knows? Maybe I'll somehow break the space-time continuum just by practicing. I definitely don't want to do that.'

I can see why that Veiled who has it in for me might take offence at that, and I wouldn't disagree.

Bonnie makes a face. 'That seems extremely unlikely, though, doesn't it? I mean, you used enough magic to shove Chiara down the stairs. If that didn't break reality, I doubt you barely rustling some grass will.'

I snort a laugh. That sounds sensible to me, but what do I know of reincarnation and Veiled magic and the natural order?

'I just know I don't want to lose it again,' I say. 'Zeru—Kate's friend—said they'd remove only my magic, so it's not like I wouldn't remember the Veiled exist. Really, the worst thing that would happen is some major disappointment for me. Two weeks ago, I wasn't trying to learn magic, either—not Veiled magic, anyway. So, nothing would really change, right?'

Bonnie nods. 'Right.'

The doorbell rings. Bonnie does a fast shuffle to collect the pizzas, and I sit back down on the sofa. The smell of cheese and pepperoni fills the room as she sets the boxes on the table and sits next to me.

'Except it did kinda save your life with Chiara,' Bonnie continues. 'Isn't that worth a thought?'

I pull my pizza box onto my lap, open it, and inhale. My stomach rumbles; my mouth waters.

'That's my first choice, too,' I say. 'But I don't think I can argue if Zeru comes back and doesn't agree. Me having magic I'm not meant to have is probably a greater threat than the photographs I'll never take. I'll be gutted if they say no, but I'll understand it.'

Bonnie turns the TV on and finds the movie. 'Well then, I'm glad I could help clear things up.'

I laugh. 'It did help, actually. Thank you.'

Because, while I would hate to lose my magic now that I've felt it, I really would understand if I couldn't keep it. But I do think self-defence is a valid point, too. Bonnie is right, it did save my life. Zeru seems to know a lot more about me—about everything—than I'd have guessed from a stranger. Hopefully, they can also see that I'm not a violent person, that I really only want to learn so I can protect myself.

This time, at least, being okay with whatever Zeru decides is easy. I'd keep my memories and knowledge of the Veiled; I wouldn't even really lose a part of myself, since the remnants of this magic don't truly belong to me. They belonged to another me, in another time. I'm lucky to have used so much of it; I can be grateful for that much without demanding more.

And so, as we settle in with our pizzas, cocktails, and a movie, I'm at peace with whatever happens next with my magic, which leaves me very open to missing photography instead.

CHAPTER SIX

I become lucid under my purple-leafed tree as usual tonight. I don't see Mischief in the branches or on the other side of the trunk, so I take a moment to stretch. I feel hopeful after my chat with Bonnie. I've willed the grass a vibrant yellow and the sky a bright blue and lavender nebula to match how I feel. It looks like daylight, but I kept the big full moon. There's something soothing about it, something energising, and that's exactly how I want to feel. Besides, it's been ages since I adjusted the appearance of my dreamscape. Last time I made the grass yellow, Mischief said it looked like a cat's litter tray, but the colour was more muted then. It's so much brighter today, like little blades of optimism while the sky sings of reassurance and relaxation.

'Alright,' I say, knowing Mischief will hear me just fine. 'You can come out now.'

Talking to her after everything that happened with Chiara hasn't been tense, exactly, but I definitely watched what I said so I wouldn't cause more problems for her. Maybe Mischief needs a moment, too, or maybe she's off investigating something without me. It's not like she can't do either. I'm excited to discuss my magic with her, though. I can't wait to hypothesise about its sylphid origin, to daydream about using awesome wind magic like some superhero. I'll never be able to do that while I'm awake, but maybe here, in my dreamscape, I can have some fun with the knowledge. It'll be just like old times, a wonderful reminder that we're alright and can get back to regular lucid dream fun now.

I feel like I've aged at least one year for every day since I stepped into the void lake. Everything before that feels like it happened to another me, and in a sense, it has. That's the thing with life-altering events—you're never quite the same after. I'm ready for at least this one thing to go back to normal.

'Mischief?'

I sigh in relief when she materialises a little ahead of me. Last time I had to call her, the Dreamcatcher had—

I shake my head. Mischief is right there. I can see that she's fine now, and technically speaking, she was fine then, too. Although… she's not a figment of my imagination, like I believed at the time. Did it hurt after all when the Dreamcatcher snapped her bones? She didn't seem traumatised, but surely… I shake my head again. Maybe I'll ask her. It's behind us, though; I'm sure she'd rather move on, too.

I get to my feet and walk over to her. 'Wanna play superhero with me?'

I expect her to make some comment about me being childish or wash her paw in boredom, but she just sits there. I stop and frown. Mischief cocks her head a little, so at least I know she's a real cat—or *my* real dream guide cat, anyway.

She's not just some cutout.

'Play… superhero? If you wish.'

My heart misses a beat. I grow cold.

'You're not Mischief.'

My eyes burn, though I'm not sure where the tears come from. I just know this isn't right.

The cat straightens. 'I will be your dream guide from now on. You can call me—'

'Where is Mischief?'

My dreamscape spins in response to me feeling faint. Is it something I said? Did I condemn her somehow? Is it because I talked to Zeru? They and Kate said our conversation would be private, but what if they lied, or if someone else has even more power than the sylph and listened in on us? What if we weren't alone in Kate's house without her knowing?

'The dream guide you call Mischief has been asked to return. I have been assigned as their replacement.'

My head swirls. I've known Mischief since I was little, and she's never mentioned a home to me, assuming that's what this imposter means. Where else would she return to? And I've always seen her as female, and she's never said anything. It doesn't feel quite right; wouldn't she have told me? I did suspect that Mischief wasn't her real name since I gave it to her, so at least that bit isn't surprising.

I shake my head at the newcomer. 'What does that mean? Returned where?'

'That information is classified,' the new cat says. 'Don't worry about *Mischief's* well-being. I can help you in every way they did.'

51

I doubt that. It seems unlikely anyone else would have freed my magic to save my life, for one, but I also can't imagine anyone else would have summoned all those naked dream-Leveretts just to tease me.

I shake my head and flick my hand at the imposter. 'Don't do that. Take her shape, I mean. You're not her.'

'Which form would you prefer? We believed you would appreciate the—'

'I don't want any form!'

Presumably, taking a shape I'll trust is just what dream guides do. I did find it comforting with Mischief. This stranger asking me which form they should take so I'll feel more at ease has the opposite effect.

I don't care that I probably sound like a whiny kid who's been told she can't have cake five minutes before dinner. How can they just take my friend away? How am I supposed to just be okay with this?

'That form isn't *yours*. It's too weird.' I throw a glare at them I'm sure they don't deserve. 'And I don't want another dream guide. I already have one, thank you.'

'Very well.' The dream guide does a flip and lands as a dog. A rottweiler, like Lady. 'Is this better? I sense you like this dog breed.'

'I— I guess, but also no.' I pout. It's probably not this guide's fault that Mischief isn't here, but that doesn't change that Mischief is just... *gone*. Did anyone ask if she wanted to say goodbye first, or did she choose to leave without a word? Did she leave without arguing because it's what's expected of her? Maybe I've been lying to myself. Maybe I really was just a job to her.

I remember last night, when she asked me to let her cuddle to me, to not make a big fuss over it, to just let her have it. She seemed sad then. Did she know this would happen?

'It would be best if you let it go, Esta,' the stranger says.

'But *why*?' I ask. There's more I want to say, but I suspect this dream guide isn't allowed to say anything helpful. 'Just tell me one thing. Is Mischief in trouble because of me? What will happen to her? Yes, I *know* that's two things.'

Mischief would have called me out on it, but Mischief gets to do that. This dream guide hasn't earned the right to sass me.

'Our superiors have watched them closely for a while,' the dream guide says. 'They were aware Mischief was growing closer to you than a dream guide should to their charge, but they chose to observe the situation due to your unique circumstances. They believed it best to have someone guide you whom you trust.'

I sink to the ground and sit. Run my hand through the grass and consider changing it back to the shade of yellow Mischief made fun of.

'But is she alright? What will happen to her now?'

She's broken a few rules, but I don't know if it's bad enough to warrant punishment or what kind.

'After some time to reflect on their choices, they will be trained anew until they are deemed fit to be reassigned.' My heart jumps, but the dream guide shakes their head at me. 'They won't be reassigned to you, Esta. If you have no more questions, please simply go about your dream as you usually would. Pretend I'm not here. I will guide you as needed.'

I huff. No more questions? I have *all the questions*. But Mischief wasn't allowed to elaborate on anything work-related, and I'm guessing this dream guide isn't, either. And it's impossible to go about my usual dream business without Mischief being a part of it, but I don't say that. I worry it would only make her situation worse.

'I have been given leave to answer your questions within reason.'

I slowly nod to myself. It seems it's normal for dream guides to know their dreamers' minds and wasn't a Mischief thing, though that's not really surprising. Maybe I can use this opportunity to get at least some answers.

'Is that all you're meant to do, then?' I ask. 'Read my mind and guide me down the "right" path from the shadows?'

The guide, still in rottweiler form, barks in agreement. 'It is what we are trained for. We are passive guides to our dreamers. We are not allowed to be biased.'

'But Mischief has always played with me,' I say, and immediately wish I'd think before arguing.

Fortunately, the dog nods. 'They were first sent to you when you were a child. We have some leave to bond with our youngest charges, but it is recommended we begin to distance ourselves when it is not detrimental to the child's mental health. You must consider that cases like yours are rare—most dreamers aren't aware they have dream guides and write us off as being part of their dreams.'

I frown. 'I can't be the only person in the world who can lucid dream and has a dream guide.'

'That is correct. When we are assigned to guide a lucid dreamer, we stay in the background. We guide you by shaping your dreams in minor ways, not by interfering directly as Mischief has done.'

'And just who decides what the right path is?' I ask. 'Why would you think you know enough about me to lead me down one way over another?'

That's bugged me more than the fact that dream guides take a shape we trust. I've explored my dreamscape as much as I physically can that I know of, but I've always decided where to go. Mischief has never suggested something I hadn't thought of first. She never tried to influence my choices when I didn't express a preference myself.

'We do not,' the dog says. 'When you go about your day, no one approaches you to give you directions. When you're lost and want to know the way, someone might tell you where to look, though you still have to take the necessary steps yourself. This is what we do.'

'Fine,' I sigh. 'I suppose that's fair. But—' I bite my lip. Mischief did more than guide my dreams—I felt her comfort me while I was wide awake, and I heard her voice once or twice. But I can't ask about that. If they aren't aware Mischief did those things, I won't be the one to tell them.

But the dog cocks its head. 'This was another transgression. Mischief overstepped the line between dream guide and spirit guide. This will be investigated, too.'

I could kick myself. This is too risky. How am I supposed to watch what I *think* all the time?

'Does everyone have a dream guide?' I ask.

'No,' the dog says. 'Most people have one dream guide for a short period of time. Mischief was asked to stay with you because of your situation.'

I don't know what that means, and I doubt the dog will tell me.

'Then I don't want one, either. I'll be fine on my own.'

The dog cocks its head. 'You're dismissing me?'

'Yes,' I say. 'I don't want a new dream guide. Mischief isn't replaceable.'

Maybe, in time, I might have got some more information out of this dream guide, but it seems unlikely, and I can't stand the idea of not feeling safe in my own dreamscape. My dreams have always been the easiest expression of my subconscious. How can I be sure this guide isn't here to spy on me or to dig up more dirt on Mischief? I'm not having it.

My skin crawls. How can I be sure that, even if they agree to leave me alone, someone won't stay and watch me? The thought makes me shiver, but the dream guide said themself that they're usually meant to watch from the shadows. I'd like to think I'd know if something's changed in my dreamscape, but I assume that dream guides are good at this. Dreams are their natural habitat, while I'm merely a natural lucid dreamer. Bonnie is a good swimmer, but Sunny is a mermaid—just like Sunny knows the sea far better than Bonnie ever will, I imagine dream guides know much more about my dreamscape. Doesn't seem fair.

The dog nods. 'I will withdraw. If you ever change your mind, we will answer.'

I scowl. 'So, what, you'll just keep an eye on me?'

'Watching dreamers is what my superiors do,' the dog says. 'It's nothing personal, and we don't judge. You might say dreams are my superiors' demesne.'

I nearly ask where the fuck they were when the Dreamcatcher invaded then, but I hold my tongue. I'm just feeling spiteful. As the dog explained, dream guides don't interfere, they just vaguely gesture in the right direction. Besides, the Dreamcatcher and the Mara work with dreams, too. Whoever these superiors are, they probably knew about it and allowed it.

Can't say that endears me to them.

I sigh again, because I know that I'm probably being unfair. The Dreamcatcher and the Mara mentioned that their orders came from way higher up, so maybe there was nothing Mischief's boss could have done to prevent it. Maybe the dream guide boss is powerless against whoever was after me, too.

I freeze, and a chill runs down my back.

Or maybe Mischief's boss *is* the one who sent the Dreamcatcher after me.

No reaction from the dog. Interesting.

I sigh yet again. This is too much at once; I can't reason through it all so fast. It wouldn't be the first time I got carried away and got it completely wrong. It also doesn't help that I'm angry with Mischief's boss right now.

'Alright,' I say to the dog. 'I'll, erm, reach out if I need anything.'

I blink; the dream guide is gone.

And my dreamscape is too empty without Mischief.

CHAPTER SEVEN

I want to snuggle into Leverett for emotional support when I wake up, but he didn't stay overnight. I want to confront Mischief's boss, but I've no idea where to start. I want to learn magic to distract myself, but it hasn't been that long since Zeru said they needed time to think about it.

I do the only thing I can think of that might fix it.

I get up, make one tea for myself and one for Lady, and then I go outside. Seems like ages since I just sat down on the low wall halfway up our garden. Bonnie isn't up yet, so it's just me and Lady.

And then, I text Kate to ask if she has time to talk. I'll go to Leverett after this, but I need reassurance that everything is going to be fine from someone who knows about these things, and as far as I'm concerned, Kate knows everything. Maybe Leverett sells books on dream guide hierarchy? I kinda already checked, though. Besides, this is probably a little too niche even for his bookshop.

Lady is happily sniffing around the garden and settles in the shade under the apple tree after a few minutes while I wait for Kate.

I take the moment to feel the breeze on my arms, the sun on my face, the grass I really need to cut against my ankles. Dream guides, like nature, have always been here, though I admit that's an assumption. I can't expect them to change how they operate because of me. By their definition, Mischief did break the rules. They are just trying to do for me what they do for every other dreamer. That doesn't mean it sits right with me. Mischief isn't just my dream guide, she's my friend. I know that's part of the problem, but I can't just not do anything. I don't know what I *can* do, though.

I hear a door open and look behind me. Kate walks towards me with her own cup of tea, her dogs bounding up and down the garden.

'Good morning, Esta.'

I pivot on the low wall so I can face her properly. 'Hey.'

'Is something wrong?' she asks. 'You sound upset.'

I nod, but this isn't the time to get Mischief into even more trouble. If I'm going to look into this, I'll have to be sneaky, and asking Kate in broad daylight how much she knows about the people who run Dream Guides, Ltd. isn't that. I don't think it'll be suspicious if I looked more into dreams in a general sense, though. I'm just not sure how yet.

'It's a long story,' I say. 'Have you heard anything from Zeru?'

And there's her patient teacher smile. I instantly feel a little better.

'It might feel like a long time since you spoke to them, but sylphs are much longer lived than we are. I'm afraid they might think it over for weeks, and it would be to them like a second would be to you.'

I deflate a little. 'Oh.'

'Does this mean you've thought about it?'

'Yes. I spoke it through with Bonnie, too. Could you pass on my decision? I'd do it myself, but I don't know how to reach them.'

I don't even know where sylphs live. Kate taught me that they are air elementals, and Zeru certainly looked out of place in her small living room. They probably live on the breeze or something equally ethereal, but I can't work with that. Unless I'd just kinda speak into the air? I'm too self-conscious for that. Talking at my shed while hoping the boggart was hiding behind the door was weird enough.

'I don't mind,' Kate says, 'but prepare yourself for a wait.'

I make a face and hide it in my teacup. Always with the patience.

'That's fine. Tell them I'd like to learn if they want to teach me or know someone who would. I at least want to see what I can do, and I'm aware it likely won't be much at all. If there's anything I can learn that will help me defend myself, I want to at least try.'

I wonder if flimsy air magic can defeat the dream guide manager, but probably not.

Kate's smile grows a little. She looks proud of me, and it makes my heart swell.

'I will pass it on, Esta. I wish there were more I could teach you, but I'm afraid sylph magic is not my speciality.'

'Maybe not, but you still knew who to contact. I don't know what I'd do without you.'

That last part slipped out, but I mean it. I don't know where I'd be without Kate's support and patience, and I hope I never have to find out.

'You would get by, I'm sure,' she says. 'You have come so far on your own already. You're a smart woman, Esta. You don't need me to make your decisions for you.'

I blush a little. I wasn't expecting this kind of praise. 'I... don't know that's true, but thank you. And I do rely on your advice.'

In this way I feel closer to Kate than I do to my own mum. Kate has always seemed so wise to me, and who else would I ask about Veiled stuff? She's like my witchy mother, though there's no chance I'll tell her that. But I know who I can go to with any kind of Veiled problems and when I need advice, be it magick or magic.

'Then I must do well in my role as your teacher,' she says. 'I will let you know when I have a response from Zeru. Again, please don't be disappointed if you don't hear today or even tomorrow.'

'I promise. Would it be, I dunno, easier or faster if I did it myself?'

Kate hesitates for a moment. 'It would, though as you have no doubt guessed, contacting Zeru is not as simple as messaging them as you messaged me. If they choose to teach you, I'm sure they will share the best way to stay in touch. Until then, it's not for me to share.'

I nod. 'Understood.'

We finish our tea in companionable silence, and when Kate goes back into her house, I have this strange sense that I've done everything I can without really having done anything. I'm about to go back inside, too, when my phone rings.

'Hello?' Part of me hopes against hope it's Zeru, but of course it's not.

'Hi, Esta. Sorry to disturb you for the second time on your break.'

It's Eloise, my manager. She sounds happy, but she's never called me without reason, least of all on my summer break.

'Oh, uh, fine. What's up?'

'Do you have time today? It's such a lovely day outside, I thought I'd buy you a slice of cake.'

I frown to myself. *Right.* That's not odd at all.

I hate that some small part of my brain wonders if this isn't Eloise at all but some trap to lure me away from home. Maybe I should ask Kate if there are any Veiled therapists I can talk to about what happened with Chiara and the Dreamcatcher. I sure as hell can't tell a human therapist what happened or they'd likely lock me up.

'Sure,' I say. 'When were you thinking?'

'Now?' She laughs. 'Don't worry if not. We can catch up another day.'

I dread to think what's so urgent it can't wait until I'm back at work in just over one month. The last time she called me, she told me there'll be redundancies. Maybe she wants to catch me up on the gossip? She assured me that my role is too small to be considered and she's our only manager, so I doubt one of us has lost our job.

'No, that's fine,' I say. 'I'll leave now, so I'll be in town in roughly an hour?'

'Perfect. I'll meet you outside the gallery.'

I hang up and usher Lady back into the house. If it weren't for my worry that something's wrong at work, I wouldn't care what this is about. Any distraction is welcome, and I can stop by Leverett's shop on the way home. I quickly message him to ask if I can come over this afternoon, and then I start walking.

Eloise seems happy and relaxed when I meet her outside the gallery. We hug, she suggests a café inside our shopping centre, and we walk over together. I expected her to suggest a café nearer the gallery—I know she likes two that are closer, and the café we're going to is more of a roped-off area in the middle of the busy shopping centre near the escalators. It's not exactly cosy, though as long as they do good tea and cake, I don't really care.

That, and Eloise insists she's buying. It seems we're celebrating something.

We sit, go over the menu quickly, and then she says with a smile:

'I've been made redundant.'

I blink once. 'I'm sorry, what?'

Nearly every other table is occupied and there are loads of people going around the shops, but all that noise seems so far away. Eloise's smile has a vicious quality to it, like she'll make the higher-ups pay somehow or like they've actually done her a favour so joke's on them.

Really, though, I think she's just angry. I am, too. Eloise is my manager—our *only* manager. And she's a friend—or a work friend, anyway. Working in our gallery has its ups and downs, but she's been one of the few real positives since I started. This may sound dramatic, but I can't imagine the place without her and I don't want to.

'Oh, Esta.' She says it like I'm the one who's received bad news. 'I knew this was coming. I'm not surprised they're getting rid of me.'

Well, *I* am surprised. The gallery needs a manager; she'd have said if the whole place was closing.

'I'm so sorry,' I say. 'What will you do?'

'I'm moving back to South Africa,' she says. Now her smile makes sense. 'I can be there for my grandson's second birthday. I'll help look after him, and it'll be lovely to be home again.'

Someone comes to take our orders; Eloise asks for two large teas and two of every cake.

I work up a smile for her. 'I'll miss you. If you're ever in the area, let me know. My treat next time.'

She cackles. 'Oh, I don't know that I'll come back any time soon. No offence.'

I huff a laugh. 'None taken. Do you know who'll replace you?'

'Well, I'm not supposed to talk about this…' Her laughter fills the café. 'Like I care now. Do you remember Marvin?' She laughs again when my face clearly says that I do. 'It'll be him. I heard he's not getting a pay rise with it, so they're saving quite a bit. He would probably be made redundant, too, if he hadn't agreed to it.'

'Are you serious? Marvin? That's bullshit!' I say, louder than I maybe should have.

A woman on the table next to us scowls at me like I've offended her whole family.

'Oh, I know,' Eloise says. 'I've always hated him. He used to be my manager back when I started, Esta, he's been here forever. He's always been a bully.' She picks up her cake like it's a cookie and looks at me over the chocolate sponge. 'What are you going to do?'

I shake my head. 'I don't know. The gallery won't be the same without you, but I'm so happy that you get to live with your family.' I take a bite of my own piece of chocolate cake. 'I imagine your husband is happy with this, too?'

She never talked too much about him. I know she's married, and I think she said once he likes football. That's it.

Eloise waves me off. 'He's annoyed to lose his friends here, but I told him I'm going with or without him.' She cackles again; I'll miss that sound. The gallery will be so empty without her laugh ringing out from her office even with her door shut. 'But enough about me! How is your photography coming along? You had something you wanted to work on over the summer, didn't you? Looks like I won't be able to showcase your new photos in the gallery after all, but maybe you can arrange something with Marvin.'

We both laugh at that—Marvin would rather die than do a nice thing for me, I'm sure. My face falls quickly, though. The last time I talked to her about my project, I had every intention of photographing the Veiled, which ended up with the Dreamcatcher on my tail.

'It's, erm… It didn't work out. It wasn't as easy as I thought once I actually started taking pictures.'

'Ah, and you were so excited, too.' She finishes her cake and tops up her tea. My own cake tastes dry and flavourless now she's brought up my dead ambition. 'Got anything else lined up?'

I bury the truth in a generous sip of caffeine. I want to tell her it's complicated, but that wouldn't explain anything. And besides, Bonnie is probably right: The problem before, or part of it, was a lack of consent. I have Poppy's and Sorcha's, so it shouldn't be an issue this time. I try to remember what we were taught at uni. Maybe if I make them sign a contract? No, a model release form! We were told to always use those when photographing other people. I probably still have a template somewhere on my laptop. Maybe, if I tweak it a little to include something about how all Veiled Pride photos are only for use within family and other Veiled—

'Your smile says yes,' Eloise says as she unwraps a muffin.

I didn't realise I was smiling, but now she's said it, my smile grows wider. How didn't I think of a model release form before? Failing that, how hard can it be to draw up a simple contract? If I can get it in writing that they give me their full permission and that they reached out to me of their own free will, that all photos are just for their own use unless clearly stated otherwise... Gods. I think this might actually work. I won't make any money right away, but if Poppy and Sorcha recommend me... And maybe I can take pictures for Anton and Saif, too. They have so many contacts. Anton strikes me as someone who would revel in a photoshoot, though Saif might not be as into it. Still, if they're happy with the results, I'm sure Anton would show off his new photos to his friends or at least display them in his house.

I've missed photography so much, and I think I've finally cracked the code. I can do this—I can *really* do this. I have contacts, too, and given the management situation at my gallery, I might just outright ask Anton for his help in spreading the word. Frankly, I don't want to work one day for Marvin. It was always my plan to work in the gallery while I built my photography career and leave eventually, I just didn't expect things to happen like this. And it's not like I'm handing in my resignation today, though I can totally draft it and have it ready for—

I make myself finish my tea and take a deep breath, though my hands are shaking a little. If the nightmare with the Dreamcatcher has taught me anything it's that I get carried away when I'm excited, and this is the most excited I've felt in… Gods. A long time. It's nice to feel like this again.

'I've got nothing official lined up,' I say, 'but I do have a lead. Do you mind if I make a call?'

Eloise shrugs and stabs her fork into soft cheesecake. 'Go for it.'

I find a quiet spot against a wall and call Sorcha and Poppy. This isn't me getting carried away, this is me planning ahead. There's no reason to delay; the sooner I can take these first pictures, the sooner I'll know if this might work. When I go back to work next month, I'll have an action plan. It'll make Marvin that little bit easier to tolerate until I can shove my resignation in his face.

'Hello?'

I think it's Poppy who picks up; I'm not that familiar with

their voices.

'I've had a think about being your photographer,' I say. My heart is in my throat when I add, 'I'd love to do it. When are you free?'

CHAPTER
EIGHT

I'm still buzzing when I enter Leverett's bookshop. I always figured I'd be gutted if Eloise left before I do, but instead, I'm optimistic. I hate the idea of Marvin being my new manager, but all being well, I can make something of my photography. I have a plan, not just vague dreams. And with Poppy and Sorcha on my side and maybe Anton, too, I *know* I can do this.

Leverett looks up from the book he's reading behind the counter and smiles at me.

'You look happy!' He comes over to kiss me, and I wrap my arms around him.

'I'm hopeful.' I laugh. 'And I'm excited. Could you call Anton for me? There's something I want to ask him.'

Leverett chuckles. 'I can, though will you tell *me* what has you so giddy, too?'

'The short version is, my manager has been made redundant and my new manager is a dick, so I've accepted my neighbours' photography offer.'

Leverett locks the door and turns the sign over to Closed.

'I understand why the latter half would make you happy,

but I'm a little confused about the first.'

I nod to his front door. 'Is it alright to just close shop for a bit?'

He smiles and waves me after him. 'I've told you before, I don't really need the money. The shop is just a front to blend in. Besides, I'm the only one working here. If I suddenly took sick, I would need to close, too.'

I follow him and don't argue. It's his business, he can do what he wants with it. Although, if I had enough money to not need to work in retail, I definitely wouldn't.

'Make yourself comfortable,' Leverett says as we enter his flat above the shop. 'Can I get you a tea?'

'Please and thank you,' I say. I quickly message Bonnie to let her know I'll be out a little longer—I messaged her when I first walked into town, but I don't want her to worry when I might not be home for several hours yet.

'When will you get back?' she replies.

I smell cinnamon from the kitchenette—Leverett's own blend of heavenly tea.

'Not sure,' I write back. 'I'm at Leverett's.'

'Ooooh. So not at all tonight ;)'

I giggle and throw my phone in my bag.

Leverett puts two cups of tea on the small table and sits next to me. My heart misses a beat; previously, we've always sat in different seats, but now… We're a couple now. I blush, suddenly feeling sheepish. That man's my boyfriend. He's mine. I break out into a bright smile.

He chuckles again. 'How is your new manager being a dick related to you accepting the photography offer, and why is it making you this happy?'

I sit a little closer. 'Because if this job goes well and they recommend me… Maybe I can still build a photography career. I've thought about it, I think it'll be fine if I make them sign a release form.' I beam at him. 'I think I can do this.'

Leverett puts an arm around my shoulder, pulls me to him, and kisses me. 'Tell me if I can help.'

'Do you know anything about light boxes or shutter speeds?'

He kisses me again. 'I don't understand what you just said.'

I laugh. 'Then I think I'll just call you for backup if the Dreamcatcher comes to collect.'

I don't think he will, though, or at least I really hope not. I assume he would make himself known if I was in any danger of breaking our agreement, but I've never felt his influence on my mind while I was awake. He was only a threat to me while I was sleeping, so the real test will be tonight. Hopefully, if he has noticed my plans and disagrees, he can warn me before he destroys my mind so I can change my plans. Although… it would break my heart, and I don't care if that sounds dramatic. These brief few hours since I thought of the loophole have reminded me how much I truly love photography, of the excitement and energy I used to have for it. I don't want to lose that again. Frankly, I'd rather give up my magic than lose this feeling.

Leverett's face turns serious. 'Discuss all the relevant details with that couple first. Having a contract is a good idea, but words have power, too. Let it be said aloud that they understand, that they give you full consent. Verbal contracts can be even more powerful than written ones, especially amongst the Veiled.'

I gulp. I hadn't considered that.

'Thank you,' I say. 'I will.'

Leverett touches his nose to mine. 'So, when is the big day?'

'Not until next week Saturday.' When I called Poppy and Sorcha, I was prepared to jog home, grab my equipment, and set up in their living room, but life had other ideas. 'They already have plans tomorrow and will be at work every day next week, so next Saturday is the first day we're all free.'

'Then you have time to prepare,' Leverett says. 'That's not a bad thing.'

I let out a nervous laugh. 'More like I have time to be anxious about it.'

He gives me a seductive smile. 'Well, if you need a release for all that energy, you can always stop by.'

I blush furiously. I'm not nervous because of what we might do, but because *Leverett is my boyfriend now*. That'll take some getting used to, but in the best way. I might stop calling him my boyfriend, though, and opt for *partner* instead. We're not fourteen, even if I do sometimes behave like it around him.

'*Well*,' I counter, and put my legs over his. 'I'm already here, and I'm not moving any time soon.'

'Good.' Leverett kisses me, longer this time, and I melt against him. 'Is that why you want me to contact Anton? Because you want to offer to photograph him and Saif?'

I nod. 'Only if they want to. But Anton has so many paintings in his home already, I thought he might be interested.'

'Oh, I'm sure he'd love to.' Leverett strokes my arm. 'Should I be offended that you haven't asked *me*?'

I tilt my head back. 'You want me to photograph you?'

'Would I not be a good… experiment, for your theory? You have my consent. I know everything that happened with the Dreamcatcher. I can even sign your release form. Doesn't that make me a good first test?'

'I, erm—' I imagine him sprawled out, naked, while I take intimate close-ups of him. 'I suppose I could do that.'

He laughs. 'It doesn't have to be anything lewd, Esta. I'm merely volunteering as your guinea pig. Although, if you wanted to take some photos of us together, I wouldn't mind that, either.'

He whispers that last part, an edge to his voice.

I've never had photos like that, neither have I ever wanted any. Then again, I've never really had someone I'd like intimate photos with. I blush at the idea of printing them in a darkroom, of watching the images appear as I wash the prints and hang them up, one by one, while I look at us naked and wrapped up in each other as my face stays perfectly professional, considering if the contrast came out right. And then Bonnie happens upon the images and is scarred forever.

'Alright,' I say, 'but I'll need some time to research the best way to do this.' I'll probably set up a timer, because the thought of having to operate a shutter remote while Leverett thrusts into me is too weird and impractical.

Leverett nods. 'No pressure. We don't need to do this at all.'

And with anyone else, I'd have objected, but I trust Leverett completely. I know he'd never do anything to hurt me, let alone use any intimate images of us to blackmail me.

'No, I'd like to. I'm just not sure right now what the best way is to do this.' He leans in to kiss me again, but I bite my lip. Since we're already asking for things… 'There's, erm… There's something I've wondered.'

He smiles. 'And what's that?'

'Feel free to say no! But, uh… I've wondered what…' I swallow and decide to just get it out. 'I want you to bite me.'

His eyes turn black, and his breathing comes heavier. A low growl sounds from his chest.

'Esta…' He shakes his head and touches his forehead to mine. 'You don't know what you're asking.'

I immediately wave it off to dismiss the idea. 'Oh, no, you definitely don't have to, I was just wondering how—'

'You misunderstand,' he says, his voice husky. 'I very much want to. But I will need time to prepare myself or you'll be in danger.'

I swallow. 'Take as long as you need.'

When Chiara bit me, it *hurt*. I felt brutalised and violated, but I remember Leverett saying that a vampire's bite is like any touch—it can be painful, or it can be wonderful and gentle and loving. I hate that my first experience was so awful and degrading when it should always have been Leverett's. And maybe, if Leverett bites me and it feels good, it'll heal some of the emotional scarring Chiara left on my soul.

But even more than that, it's a kind of intimacy I can only have with him, and I want it.

Leverett slowly nods, but his eyes are still dark, and I can

74

clearly see his trousers straining against his erection.

'I didn't realise just the suggestion would affect you so much,' I whisper.

'I don't take your offer lightly,' he says. 'I don't drink blood anymore, as you know, so without sufficient mental preparation, I'm afraid I'll lose control. I can't bear the thought of— And your blood will taste so sweet, Esta, not only because it's been so long but because of our feelings for each other. It might be hard to stop.' He strokes my face and cradles me with his other arm around my back. 'I would be lying if I said I hadn't thought about it. A vampire's blood lust is a dangerous thing when the purpose is simply to survive, but when the purpose is to taste a lover… I never dreamed I might one day meet a human I love as I love you, who wants this as much as I want it.'

I turn to liquid in his arms. If he hadn't said all those things about how dangerous it is, I might have begged him to do it now.

I summon the strength to pull myself up so I can kiss him. Leverett responds and brings me closer, his growl a rumble in his chest. I stroke his lips with my tongue, but he grunts and pulls away.

'Careful. After what you asked for, there's a good chance you would cut yourself on my fangs.'

I gulp and nod, but he pulls away a little more.

'Do I scare you like this?'

I shake my head. 'No. You're my vampire and I love you and want all of you.'

Leverett crushes his lips to mine so hard and fast I might

75

bruise. I wrap my arms around him and let him flip me onto my back. I'm desperate for his tongue against mine, for his lips on my neck, but neither are a good idea right now. The best I can do is distract him.

I feel my hand down his chest, over his stomach, towards his hips. He moans when I stroke his length through the fabric of his trousers.

Emboldened by the sound and the power I have over this wonderful man, I say, 'You didn't say *I* can't taste *you*.'

He moans again. 'Esta. There's no chance I'll let you go unsatisfied.'

I chuckle, trying to mimic him and probably failing miserably. I kiss him and whisper against his lips, 'Just a taste, then?'

He doesn't object. Instead, he slides his hand under my dress and goes straight for my clit. I gasp, and he tightens his grip on me. His other hand moves down my neck. For a second, I wonder if he'll squeeze just a little, but he'd probably break me.

I disentangle myself from his arms and slip out of my dress. Kick my underwear away from us and throw my bra after it. His eyes don't leave me for one second; I'm not even sure if he blinks.

'On your back,' I say.

Leverett obeys.

I straddle him, kiss him, and begin to slide his shirt off. He takes it off the rest of the way. I kiss his neck, his collarbone, his chest, and work my way all the way down until I meet fabric. I undo his belt, careful to stroke his erection with every move I make. The sounds he makes threaten to undo me.

Slowly, I remove his underwear, hoping the lack of speed tortures him. I kneel on the ground beside him, because it's easier than sitting on his legs and trying to make this look graceful.

I kiss his legs first, work my way up this time from his knees to his balls. Leverett buckles slightly when I run my tongue up his shaft.

'Esta—'

I lick the precum off his tip, and he *whimpers*. This is too much. It's torturing me, too. But I do it again, fold myself over him so I can close my lips around the head—

And Leverett grips my hair. Gently pulls me back.

'Bend over.'

I don't argue and just do as he says. We're both too desperate to keep this up for long.

I get on all fours and wait. Leverett cups my sex in his hand and rubs once, twice. I let out a feral moan, and he chuckles. Damn it, all the power is back with him.

But then he gets on his knees behind me, puts an arm around my middle, and thrusts into me. I sigh in eternal bliss and push back into him.

Leverett immediately falls into a fast rhythm. I do my best to match him, but it only takes seconds before he's too fast for me. His hands grip my hips; I've a feeling they'll be bruised tomorrow. I don't care. I want every step I'll take to remind me of him inside me.

The pressure builds inside me so fast I barely get his name out before my orgasm tears through me. Leverett moans as he cums with me. He doesn't stop immediately but keeps gently fucking me like he can't bear the thought of pulling out. *This* rhythm I can match.

Eventually, he stops, sits against the sofa, and pulls me into his arms nestled against his chest and between his legs. I kiss him, again and again, because I can't get enough of this man.

When we finally get up, it's to move to his bedroom together.

CHAPTER
NINE

'Tell me how your magick studies are progressing,' Kate says, and my face falls. 'How are your experiments with tarot going? What about your independent research?'

I awkwardly shuffle alongside her as we enter the forest and leave everyone else in the park behind us. It's a nice morning for a walk. Our dogs trot together a little ahead of us.

'Erm… About that…'

Kate gives me a sympathetic smile. 'I don't mind that you took a break, Esta. Don't worry, I'm not angry with you. However, if you want Zeru to consider teaching you, it can't hurt to show them how dedicated a student you can be.'

I nod. 'Yes, of course. It's just that with Chiara and the boggart, I…' I shake my head at myself. It sounds like a weak excuse even though I know having your house catch fire and being traumatised aren't small things.

But Kate says, 'You have nothing to apologise for. You might remember that I myself insisted you take as long as you need to recover. In light of Zeru potentially teaching you, however, I think it would be good to continue. Shall we pick up where we left off?'

I sigh in relief. Kate is too good to me. 'You told me how to create sigils to protect myself, but I haven't done much with that…' Which is to say I haven't done anything. I figured some small drawing wouldn't protect me from an angry vampire or any angry Veiled, really, so I didn't prioritise it. Kate is right, though: I want Zeru to see that teaching me wouldn't be a waste of their time.

Kate continues. 'We also covered some different ways to scry, and we talked about different spirits, including sylphs.'

'Yes, that's—' I remember thinking at the time how my grandad used to call me his little sylph when I was younger. Did he know, or is it just a coincidence? I suppose since my sylph magic is a leftover from another life, he couldn't have known, but it makes me smile nonetheless. 'That's right. I… kinda spaced out, I think.'

'Let's start there, then. It would be rather fitting if we discussed sylphs today, don't you think? It will give you a better idea of what to expect from Zeru. It might also give you some insights into your own magic, though I can't promise it.'

'Thank you,' I say. 'I would love that.'

Lady gets distracted by a stick and picks it up, her tail wagging like it's the best stick she's ever found. She waddles back to me and drops it at my feet, hope in her eyes. I throw it; she nearly throws herself over Keano and Bruin to get it back. I'm amazed it doesn't tempt Kate's dogs at all. They're so well behaved.

'What do you remember?' Kate asks.

'That sylphs are air elementals,' I say. 'And, uh… They don't normally show themselves to humans.'

I try to wrack my brain for anything else she might have mentioned, but I really wasn't paying much attention at the time. I was very distracted by my dog and feeling guilty over my feelings for Leverett… or rather I was embarrassed because I'd been making an idiot of myself in front of him. That, at least, is no longer an issue, though my dog is still rather distracting. She returns with the stick, and I throw it again.

'I taught you how to draw the pentagram starting with Air. Do you remember how to do it?'

I draw a blank and hope she doesn't notice. Starting at the left-most point of the star because my hand automatically wanders there, I work my way around to the right until I've completed the shape, then draw a circle around it.

'Very good!' Kate says. 'Do you remember why I told you to draw the circle?'

'Because…' Gods, what else did we discuss in our last lesson? I'm sure I asked her to teach me some self-defence magick, and I remember drawing it like that when I cleaned my house. 'Because it activates it as a cleansing sigil!'

Kate smiles at me. 'I taught it to you in that context, yes, but more generally it's to protect. But we're getting off track. You must have some questions about sylphs yourself. Why don't you ask me what you want to know?'

I nervously glance around. 'Can't they hear us? They live on the breeze, right?'

I'm worried Kate is about to teach me something that would be better coming from Zeru. I don't want to annoy all of sylphkind before I've had one lesson with them.

'Yes, and no,' she says. 'Sylphs can exist on and move on the breeze, but that doesn't mean they are there all the time; although, it's true that some could be here right now and we wouldn't know.' Her smile turns mysterious. 'Are you worried I'm telling you forbidden knowledge?'

'Well… Kind of.'

Lady has given up on playing fetch and is once again happily walking beside Kate's dogs. I wish she'd bring me the stick, though. It would help me buy time when I'm unsure how to answer.

'I'm only teaching you information you might find yourself in the correct books. All of Zeru's secrets are safe with me, or they would be if I knew any. It is part of our arrangement with the Mara and Dreamcatcher that I teach you magick; the elements and their affinities and correspondences are a natural beginning. We will cover the other elementals in due course, too.' She slightly cocks her head at me, not dissimilar to how a dog does it. 'Although, I'm sure they will appreciate that you don't wish to overstep any boundaries. I'm certain our consideration won't go unnoticed.'

I beam at her. 'In that case, don't hold back. As for questions…' There was something Zeru mentioned, come to think of it. 'Zeru said sylphs are keepers of knowledge. What does that mean?'

Kate pauses a moment. 'In simple terms, sylphs guard all the knowledge in the universe. I said they have an understanding of magic few others possess? It is part of their nature, though it does not make them equally skilled with every element. They know the laws behind all things, and they protect that knowledge gently but firmly. Which is why there is no one better suited to teaching you how to use your dormant sylph magic than a sylph.'

'Wait, you said "few others." Who else has access to so much knowledge?' I can't even wrap my head around the idea of all knowledge ever. It's hard to imagine anyone understanding all that or even just being vaguely familiar with half of it.

'There are a few deities whose chief demesne is knowledge,' Kate says, 'magical or otherwise. No other elementals have easy access to it, though.'

'But others *could* gain access to it?' I'm not sure how to feel about that. If the Veiled who's after me could just walk in there and know what I'm going to do and when, it would give her an incredible advantage against me. But I suspect if that were the case, I wouldn't have made it this far, so that's probably not what's happening.

Kate shakes her head. 'Even most deities can't just wander in. As I said, sylphs protect that knowledge firmly. You might imagine it like a large library only a handful of members may peruse freely. Those few members aside, some students, or initiates, might be granted supervised access to limited shelves only. Nobody else is allowed entry. And before you ask: No, I haven't seen it myself.'

'So it's an actual library?' I picture the small library that's part of my gallery but struggle to imagine Zeru in there. Saif's library seems like a better fit, and even that seems tiny compared to what Kate described.

Her mysterious smile returns. 'Yes, and no.'

I nod like that answer is even remotely satisfying. 'Can we talk about deities at some point?' I ask. 'I have a lot of questions.'

Kate laughs. 'I imagine you do. And at some point, yes. For now, let's start small and focus on one elemental at a time, shall we?'

I smile to myself. 'You said sylphs have much longer lives than we do. How long are we talking?'

'Potentially infinite.'

I gape at her. 'They're immortal?' I guess that makes sense. They're elementals, after all. Part of nature. The elements have always existed, haven't they?

'No, not at all,' Kate says. 'They can die, though I won't explain how. If Zeru wishes to share this detail with you, it's their decision.'

Lady falls back until she walks next to me. She gives me The Look, and I oblige: A head massage it is. She closes her eyes in enjoyment.

'It's a little overwhelming,' I say. 'To think that someone like that might teach me anything… Would I need to go to this library?'

I mean, I would love to, but there's this feeling like I don't belong there, certainly not without a clear written invitation. I'd much rather return to Saif's comfy home library, where I don't feel watched at all times and can read what I want.

Kate smiles. 'No, I don't think so. As you might have guessed, it's not an easy place to get to. Zeru would come to you, though I don't know where exactly they might teach you.

They prefer to be outside, where they can feel the wind.'

'I do too. They might stand out, though.'

Given how tall they are and how pale, they don't exactly blend in. I imagine sunlight would bounce off their skin and hair like a beacon.

'Of course, this is only if they decide to teach you at all,' Kate reminds me. 'Sylphs are not known to change their minds on a whim. If they say no, you will have to accept it.'

'That's fine,' I say. 'I've come to the same conclusion.'

A couple walking their dog approach, and Kate and I fall silent as their Yorkshire terrier greets our dogs and we exchange courteous nods with the strangers.

'Being taught by a sylph is a great honour,' Kate says when we're alone again. 'I trust you will pay more attention to them than you normally do to me.'

I blush. 'Y-yes, sorry.'

Kate whistles, and her dogs turn around and wait. She nods back the way we came, and her dogs overtake us.

'I think it's best if we leave it here,' Kate says. 'I would like you to keep up your tarot practice and your scrying exercises. Aim to learn one card a day and to watch the clouds closely. We will take it from there.'

'Alright,' I say. I want to ask more about sylphs, but my head is buzzing as is. I never expected to meet someone so ancient, so— I'm lost for words. I'm glad Kate is giving me time to internalise everything. 'Oh, one more thing... Do you think we could discuss dreams a bit?'

Kate raises her eyebrows. 'Dreams? Whatever for?'

'I feel like I'm missing something, maybe.' I don't say that this is about Mischief, and it isn't, at least not entirely. 'I just think maybe there's something I've overlooked, you know? Something I can do in my dreamscape that might give me an edge. Some way of, I don't know, exploring it I haven't considered.'

'I'd be happy to help,' Kate says, 'though I'm not sure I'm the best person to ask. Dreams are not my forte. You likely already know more than I do, but— Oh, I know. There's this new shop that opened a few days ago. Why don't you check it out?'

I blink. 'Do they sell information on dreams?' I ask, unsure where she's going with this.

Kate smiles her patient teacher smile. 'They might have something that could answer your questions. They sell a variety of books, for one, as well as many other ingredients and tools.'

'I already have a favourite bookshop.'

Kate laughs. 'Of course, but you can never have too many books, can you?' She winks at me, because she knows my weakness. 'I mean no disrespect to Leverett's selection, but At the Crossroads likely stocks a more modern variety.'

I can't argue with that. As much as I love Leverett's bookshop, his selection is older. He does stock some newer books across different subjects, but it's not the first place I'd go to for modern literature.

'I think I know where that is,' I say. 'Would I have noticed it on my way to Leverett's?'

Kate nods. 'You well might have done. It's at the start of that long main road.'

Then I know where to go. Since I haven't heard back from Zeru and won't do the photoshoot for another few days, I may as well take a look. Maybe Bonnie will want to come, too.

'The owner is human,' Kate continues, 'but they know about the Veiled. I believe they are doing their best to make their shop a Veiled safe space without being obvious about it, and they practice magick themself. They should be a good contact for you.'

I'm getting excited just thinking about it. It would be wonderful to have more people I don't need to watch everything I say around, and who knows what I might find in this shop? Kate wouldn't have told me about it if she didn't think I can get something useful out of it.

'Thank you,' I say. 'I'll go this week.'

I have a skip in my step on the way home. I'm Leverett's partner, I'm learning magick—maybe even the flashier Veiled variation soon—and I have a photography job lined up. This is the most positive I've felt in weeks, and I'm determined not to let anyone ruin it.

CHAPTER
TEN

My dreamscape is empty without Mischief in it. Technically, nothing has changed, but knowing she isn't here and never will be again is a loss I feel every second she doesn't make a sarcastic comment, every second she doesn't yawn because she's bored of our conversation, every second she doesn't paw at me to get my attention. She was a great cat even though she was never an animal to begin with. I miss her.

Which, I know, is part of the problem.

I'm at a loss for what to do with myself now. I don't *have* to enter my lucid dreams every night, but I'm used to my dreamscape being a place of comfort where I can explore whatever I want. Coming here to figure out one thing or another with Mischief is something I've taken for granted.

I can create copies of her, or a mirror image of someone else. It's harder to create people here, but it's not impossible, as evidenced by Mischief creating versions of Leverett only a few weeks ago. But I argued then that sleeping with a version of Leverett here wouldn't feel right, and this wouldn't feel right, either. Whatever copy I might summon isn't Mischief, and I won't pretend otherwise.

'Is there anything I need to see?' I ask my dreamscape. Nothing answers. Mischief would have known and guided me in the right direction, but I have nothing to go on now.

The entirety of my vast dreamscape is right here. I can go anywhere I want and do whatever I want, and instead, all I am is bored. Perhaps it's time to stop entering my dreamscape as often as I do. But Chiara haunts my regular dreams, so I'm not keen on that idea, either. My lucid dreams aren't the same without Mischief, but at least they aren't nightmares.

Part of me can't stop worrying about Mischief, even though I know she's fine—she's *probably* fine, I mean. Messing up in any other job would result in training or even being fired; it sounds like the consequences she's facing are really just that. So, as much as it pains me, I understand why things have gone the way they have. In the gallery, I'm an employee answering students' questions, and every now and again I help them find the right exhibition space or resources for their work. Likewise, Mischief is an employee helping me find answers, too. If I hugged a student or got invested in their private life, HR would likely tell me off, too. At the very least I'd have to watch a few training videos.

Understanding it doesn't mean I like it, though. I've known Mischief for most of my life and have talked to her most nights. Much like my purple-leafed tree, she's been a part of my dreamscape that's never really changed, and I feel bereft in her absence.

I sigh and will myself to the lake that started it all. Its smooth obsidian surface is just as beautiful and mysterious as

I remembered. Are more secrets hiding somewhere in there? But I don't know where I'd start with that. Like most things in dreams, it's symbolic—in this case, it symbolises all the magic that's always been right there but that I didn't know about. Mischief guided me here. She asked me to be careful, but she didn't try to stop me once I'd made up my mind. She didn't try to sway me one way or another. I suppose that's really what guides are meant to do.

I dip my hand under the surface, the not-water like silk around my skin. For a moment, I consider wading back in just to see if anything happens, but I struggle to find the motivation for it. What's the point without Mischief? That other dream guide offered to take over, but I still don't want that.

I will myself to the shadow forest I created specifically for shadow work. There's nothing I want to work through tonight, but the muted colours and deep shadows are comforting.

I feel like I should have something to work towards in my dreamscape, some secret to uncover, but Mischief and I have done it all. I feel lost without her. I don't care to explore.

Until my phone buzzes.

I frown. I've never had a phone in here before; it didn't occur to me to conjure one. I look around, but nothing has changed. The sound has come from somewhere, though. Does that mean there's unexplored territory in my dreamscape after all?

My phone buzzes again, I blink—

And feel disoriented for a moment. I'm on my bed. The

buzzing woke me up.

I let out a deep sigh and cover my face with both hands before I rub my eyes. How annoying—not only did I get woken up from my nap, but I feel more tired now than I did before. Maybe it really is time for me to just… sleep. No lucid dreams. I mean, if I have explored everything and I now can't talk to Mischief, either, what's the point?

I sit up and grab my phone. Kate has messaged me twice.

'Zeru is here,' the first one reads. 'Do you have time to come over this afternoon or shall we arrange a new time?'

I get up so fast I nearly fall off my bed. I'm dizzy from the sudden movement and sit straight back down until the fog has passed, then I reply to Kate to let her know I'll be right over.

Suddenly, I'm self-conscious. Should I take my notebook? Does Zeru expect anything from me and hasn't told me, like a test I don't know I'm taking? Maybe they've come to let me know they won't teach me. Worst case scenario, they've come to tell me that they'll remove my magic. I know I can't do anything useful with it, but I'd like to keep it all the same. Even though it's not really meant for me in this life, and even though I was never supposed to know I have this, giving it up now would feel wrong even though I know I don't have any right to it. But maybe they've come to tell me they'll teach me. I'd love some good news.

I glance at the clock—it's nearly six p.m. Bonnie isn't home yet but should be on her way. I quickly kiss Lady, give her head a quick scratch, and then I hurry next door.

Kate sees me coming and opens the door for me before I

can knock.

'I'm glad you could make it so soon,' Kate says. She looks happy, so hopefully this isn't bad news.

'It's a good thing I saw your text when I did. I was—' I bite my lip. Somehow, admitting to her that I was taking a nap feels terribly unprofessional. 'I wasn't looking at my phone at the time.'

I follow her into the living room and give Zeru a shy wave. They mimic the movement like they're just learning how it works. Today, they're standing up, their head nearly touching the ceiling.

'Thank you for coming, Esta,' they say. 'I have news.'

I nod and sit on the sofa. 'Thank you for deciding so quickly. Kate told me it might take a while.'

'I see your freed magic as a matter of urgency, and my peers agree. In truth, I made my decision shortly after I left, but some of the others are not convinced it is the right one.'

I swallow and brace myself.

'I have decided to teach you,' Zeru says. My heart jumps into my throat. 'We must proceed with caution, however. If you accept, I will teach you what I deem useful or necessary for you. I will push you, but never beyond reason.'

I nod, perhaps a little too keenly. "Never beyond reason" could mean any number of things—maybe they won't push me into exhaustion, or maybe they won't teach me anything they or their fellow sylphs deem inappropriate. Either way, I won't argue. They want to teach me actual magic—I'll take anything I can get.

'Thank you,' I say. 'I appreciate it. Do I... need anything?

Like a notebook?'

'That won't be necessary, though you may take whatever notes you like. Learning magic is a practice of the mind above all else.'

'Then there is just the matter of a suitable location,' Kate says from the doorway. 'I'm afraid this room is too small, and I'm afraid the outside may not be a good fit, either.' She turns to Zeru. 'The humans of this world might pick up on what's going on, even though they might not fully understand it. It's essential that we keep the attention off Esta and anything related to the Veiled.'

She says that last part with a glance at me, and I gulp. I imagine openly practicing sylph magic in public might violate our agreement with the Dreamcatcher.

'But you taught me in the park,' I say to her. 'That was public, too.'

'We attempted small things that are easy to hide,' she explains. 'Zeru can call a hurricane with a thought. While it's unlikely you'll be able to do anything like it, we can't know what their magic might draw out of you. It would be hard to hide if a storm picked up around you. All it takes is the wrong witness at the wrong time.'

'A wide field would be best,' Zeru says. 'Somewhere we won't be disturbed or observed.'

Kate frowns. 'That will be difficult. We have plenty of wide-open areas, but many are private land. The others are public; I can't guarantee no one would see.'

My excitement dies a slow, painful death. Zeru's willingness to teach me won't mean much if we can't find a good location.

I live in the city. Anywhere we might go requires a drive, and Bonnie needs the car at the moment. Unless we do this exclusively at the weekend? But we would still need somewhere to go, and I'm afraid I don't have a mansion with sprawling gardens to spare. Unless…

'There is someone I can ask, but I don't know that he'll agree to it.'

Anton and Saif did say I'm welcome to use their library any time. Their gardens are massive, and the land is private. We wouldn't have any surprise witnesses, and Anton and Saif are Veiled themselves. I'm not that close with them, though. I certainly can't promise anything without talking to them first. Even if they agree to let us use their garden, their mansion is a good hour drive away.

'How easily can you travel?' I ask Zeru, just in case.

'Travelling great distances is no trouble for me.'

Right. Kate did say sylphs can travel on the breeze. Must be nice not having to worry about traffic… unless air currents get busy with too many sylphs flying in the same direction. I imagine a traffic jam of hundreds of sylphs going the same way because someone near the front flew into another sylph. Somehow, I doubt that ever happens.

'I teach Esta non-Veiled magick on Tuesdays,' Kate says, 'though we may have to re-arrange once you're back at work. I believe Esta learns well when she has one day a week set aside for it.'

And suddenly, I feel like I'm at a parent-teacher meeting. She's not wrong, though—once I'm back at work, I won't be able to just drop everything and meet Zeru whenever they have time. It makes sense to reserve one day a week for it so I can keep it free. I'd usually hate losing a weekend day, but if it's for magic, I don't feel like I'm losing anything at all.

'Saturdays or Sundays would be best,' I say.

Until I can slam my resignation on Marvin's desk, anyway, but who knows how long that'll take? Although, since I need to contact Anton about using his garden anyway, I may as well ask about photographing him and Saif. Leverett said he'd ask for me, but I should really do it myself.

'Then I will rely on you to arrange a place,' Zeru says.

'How do I contact you when I have news?' I can't always make Kate pass our messages back and forth.

'Speak my name into the wind. I will listen for you, and I will come as soon as I am able.'

I smile. 'I can handle that. Thank you, Zeru. I really appreciate it. I look forwards to learning magic from you.'

They return the smile; it looks a lot more natural than their awkward wave earlier, like they've used their facial muscles more often and are getting the hang of it.

I turn to Kate. 'I don't suppose you have Anton's number, do you?'

I expect her to say that of course she does, everyone who's anyone has Anton's number, but she shakes her head.

'I'm afraid I myself am not close enough to him to have his number. He has a rather large list of Veiled friends and allies, but he rarely shares private details except with those he trusts and has known for a long time.'

'That's fine, I'll ask Leverett.' Anton may not trust me enough to give me his number, but I'm sure he won't mind if

Leverett calls him and passes the phone to me.

'Then I will take my leave,' Zeru says. 'I will see you soon.'

With that, they vanish. A breeze sighs through the room as they leave, I assume out of Kate's open kitchen window. It would be so cool if I could do that, but turning into wind is probably not in my skill set.

I break into a wide grin and squeal at Kate, who smiles at me in return.

I *will* learn Veiled magic from Zeru. I just need to figure out where.

CHAPTER ELEVEN

The last time I was nervous before a photoshoot, I was still at uni. I found it difficult to take pictures of other people at first—I've never been a people-person—but eventually I got more confident and knew what I was doing. I did a few small unpaid photography favours after I graduated for the experience and the contacts, and I approached them all like a professional who knew what she was talking about, who understood light, how to pose people…

But today, walking up to Sorcha and Poppy's front door, I feel like I did before my first shoot at uni. My head is whirring with everything that could go wrong. What if I don't know how to position them? What if their children won't do as I say? What if I forget how my camera works and I stare at it while they stare at me, waiting for me to hurry up and take a photo already while my mind is blank?

I make myself take a deep breath. I can do this. Sure, it's been a while, and the last time I as much as considered what I'm about to do the Dreamcatcher nearly destroyed my sanity, but *I've got this*. I *know* photography. This is what I've wanted for years now.

I shake out my hands, which sends the camera bag falling down my shoulder and painfully catching in the crook of my elbow, and ring the doorbell. I try to get in the right mindset while I wait. It's sunny today, and Poppy and Sorcha have a large front-facing window. The three lights I brought with me seem like overkill now, but the possibility that I'd start this shoot and the lighting wasn't right when I should have been able to fix it stressed me out, so I brought everything: different lenses, a lightbox, reflectors.

It's *heavy*. Fortunately, it's not too hot today or I'd be a sweaty mess. I once had to take all this onto a train and find a make-up artist with terrible directions; whoever said photography is glamorous didn't see me struggle through Riverstoke that day.

The door opens, and Poppy, I think, beams at me. 'Esta! Goodness, all that looks heavy. Come in, put down your things. Just in here, in the living room.' I'm eternally grateful to her. 'We can't tell you how excited we are. Cass, our daughter, wasn't able to sleep last night. We've never had family photos showing us as we are.'

I follow her into the living room as she speaks. All the houses along our road have more or less the same layout, so I know where everything is without needing to have been here before. Sorcha smiles at me from their sofa. A little girl bounces around the room with a huge grin for me, and a boy frowns at me from the sofa next to Sorcha. He's definitely older, though I don't think he's any older than… I don't know. Eight? He's somewhere between five and ten, and she looks no older than five to me. Not that I have any idea how fairy ageing works. They could both be nearing a hundred, for all I know, although I suppose that wouldn't make them any more mature. They *look* like children, and that's enough to take me out of my comfort zone.

I put my bags down on the floor with a sigh. I'm not used to carrying all this around with me anymore; my shoulder will be sore for days.

I smile at Poppy and Sorcha as I get my camera out of my bag and sling it across my other shoulder. 'Have you thought about what kind of photos you'd like?'

Sorcha shakes her head. 'The only thing that matters to us is to finally have some good family photos, all our wings out and magic in the air.'

'It means so much to us that you're doing this,' Poppy says. 'The last thing we want to do is restrict you. Please, you have full creative freedom.'

I hope it doesn't show on my face how much that worries me. I'm so out of practice that I'm not sure where to start. It's a lovely living room—white walls, light-brown parquet floor, a bright light overhead should the flood of sunlight from the massive window not be enough. But I don't know them as a family at all. Portraits are best when they're natural, at least in my opinion, but I don't know what that means for them. Do they spend a lot of time on their sofa? Do they play board games lying on the floor? I'd hate for my first photography job to look forced, but I don't know what else I can do.

'Did you photograph many families as part of your degree?' Poppy asks with a kind smile.

'None,' I admit. 'All my portraits were of individual people. I experimented with a few other things here and there, but I always came back to portraiture.'

In truth, I loved working with people as much as I hated it. Portraits can be incredible, but I have no control over people being late, or how well they communicate or take direction.

'Oskar isn't quite as excited as his sister, but Cass has been thinking about nothing else for days,' Poppy says. 'I think she'd love it if you started with her.'

The girl stops hopping around the living room and lets out a happy screech. 'Yes! Me first!'

For all my experience of working with people, I've never worked with children. She looks so excited, though. I can do this. I'll just use her energy and let her do her own thing rather than figure out what she should do. Yes, that'll work.

Sorcha looks at her kids. 'Go on, you two. You can let your wings out today. Esta is a friend.'

Oskar won't stop frowning at me, and even Cass hesitates. It's probably not too often that they're allowed to show off their wings when strangers are in the house; this must be weird for them. It's a little weird for me, too, but mostly it's exciting. I've never been this close to fairy wings before; thanks to the camera, I'll get a good close-up look at them, too.

I'm not here to satisfy my curiosity, though. Them being fae isn't entertainment, it's their lives. I can't imagine how they'd feel if I just gawked at them like they're circus animals I paid to see. No, this morning is all about getting some great photos for them, hopefully ones they can treasure for a very long time.

With a proud smile for her children, Poppy arches her back, and bright wings appear. They don't look like they might be a trick of the light as they did that day in the park, when I thought I was just severely dehydrated. This time, Poppy isn't hiding. Her translucent wings look so delicate, not a feather in sight. They don't look strong enough to hold up anyone, let alone allow her to fly. It's not just Poppy's wings that are visible now, either. Her red hair is fuller and more vibrant. Her features are smoother without being blurry, like there's a magical glow to her fine lines: Her eyes are literally glowing a little, her skin is bright with sunlight even through we're inside, as if her skin can't help but attract more sunshine. Even during Anton's party, she didn't look this magical. She's positively radiant.

'Mummy says staring is rude,' Cass says with a frown.

I blush and feel awful. Guess I gawked at them after all. 'Sorry, I—'

But Poppy cuts me off. 'Esta hasn't seen many fairies before, has she?' I quickly shake my head. Poppy winks at me. 'We can't blame her for being overwhelmed by our beauty.'

I sigh in gratitude. 'Your wings are gorgeous. It's an honour that I get to photograph them today.'

And given my terrible behaviour just now, they'll be the best damn pictures I've ever taken of anything.

Poppy beams like the sun. 'Why, thank you.'

Sorcha arches her back, and then her wings unfurl, too, like they've been wrapped around her body this whole time. They look just like her wife's, except the shape is a little different. Poppy's wings have smoother edges, while Sorcha's are more… swirled, for lack of a better word. Sorcha's seem to glitter a little, and every time she moves a muscle, her wings glisten in response like fresh snow under moonlight.

Cass giggles, releases her tiny wings, and lifts a few centimetres into the air. Her brother still eyes me with suspicion.

'Take your time, Oskar,' Poppy says. 'You don't need to rush.'

I nod. 'I have all day, but you don't need to do anything you're not happy with, alright?'

His glare intensifies.

I'm sure his mothers would be disappointed if he didn't come around at all, but I won't force the kid. Hopefully, giving him the option reassures him. Bonnie and I have plans to visit that shop Kate mentioned as soon as I'm done here so I don't actually have all day, but all I need to do is make this look like fun and it'll be fine. No pressure. Initially I wanted to go as soon as Kate mentioned it to me, but Bonnie and I decided we'd go after today's photoshoot. If it goes badly, I can treat myself to some retail therapy, but if it goes well, I can treat myself to a reward instead.

Although, the way Oskar squints at me tells me we actually might be here all day. I suppose that's good. If he's this untrusting of me even after his parents told him it's fine *and* showed me their wings, I expect they won't have to worry about him being careless in public.

'Can we take my pictures now?' Cass sings, and twirls in the air.

I take off the lens cap and shove it into my camera bag, then take a deep breath to try and steady myself. I'm actually doing a photoshoot, with a Veiled family. And I have their—

Consent! I can't believe I nearly forgot. I reach into the camera bag and remove the consent form I brought, just on the off chance I need to prove to the powers that be that I'm allowed to do this.

I pass it to Sorcha and Poppy. 'Would you please sign this? It's a model release form stating what we're doing today, what the images will be used for, who'll be in them, and so on.'

'Oh my, so professional!' Sorcha winks at me. 'Let me just give it a once-over.'

Poppy reads along next to her and grabs a pen. 'Do we both sign it?'

'Doesn't matter,' I say. 'One of you is enough, but both of you isn't a problem.'

If anything, maybe it'll even help if the Dreamcatcher does pay me an angry visit. *See, old friend? They* both *said it was fine, so come at me!*

Actually, no, that's a terrible idea. There's no chance in hell I'll taunt him.

Although, it does remind me of Leverett's advice.

'Could one of you also give me verbal permission?' I feel awkward saying it, like I'm unreasonable. 'I've been advised that the spoken word has power, too.'

Sorcha nods. 'That's wise. Esta Anderson, I, Sorcha Ó Fionnáin, give you full permission to photograph me and my family as our true Veiled selves. You have mine and Poppy Ó Fionnáin's consent.' She smiles. 'Will that do?'

I nod, though really I have no way to be sure. 'Yes, I think so. Thank you.'

Poppy winks at me. 'Can't be too careful.'

Poppy and Sorcha both sign the form and pass it back to me, all while Cass watches with growing impatience. I fold the signed document and put it back into my camera bag.

'Alright,' I say, 'we're good to—'

'YAY!' Cass flies into the air, bounces off the ceiling, and zips around me. 'Can Mister Waggles also be in the picture?'

I've no idea who that is, but I haven't seen anyone else around, so I nod. 'Of course!'

Cass zooms out of the room and, I'm assuming, up the stairs.

'She'll be right back,' Poppy says. With a knowing smile to her wife, she adds, 'She'll be so thrilled to have pictures together. She adores that toy.'

Before Sorcha can respond, Cass flies back into the room with a stuffed toy dog in her arms. I get the secretive smiles now—they are going to get their kids a dog, and neither child has any idea.

'Esta has a real dog,' Sorcha tells her daughter. 'Her name is Lady.'

Cass's eyes brighten. 'Is she cute? Can I see?'

I scroll through my phone for all of one second before I find a picture of her. 'This is her.'

'CUTE.'

I start to take pictures of Cass as she flits and giggles through the living room, happily cuddling her toy dog in one arm while dancing on the spot and throwing excited smiles at me. It's hard to get a clear photo of her when she's rushing around like that, but after around five minutes, I have a few good ones.

'Can I see?' she asks again, this time pointing at my camera.

I swipe through the photos until I land on one I like—her hugging Mister Waggles with a huge grin, her wings glittering behind her and taking up most of the picture.

She beams at me. 'I look like a princess!'

Her mothers crowd around her to have a look, too.

'Oh, Esta, that's perfect!' Sorcha says. 'Come have a look, Oskar.'

He keeps his eyes on me as he carefully comes over, but his eyes lighten a little when he sees his little sister on the screen.

'What's the point, anyway?' he asks with a sharp edge to his voice. 'We can't display these anywhere.'

Poppy and Sorcha exchange a glance. 'We've been thinking about that,' Poppy says. 'Obviously, we can't tell anyone who isn't Veiled that these are real, but people manipulate photos of themselves to look like mermaids and vampires all the time, don't they?'

Sorcha nods. 'I've seen so many of these. Of course, some of them might actually be Veiled, but the point is that you can't tell unless you know.'

'So, we thought why not just tell people that we did a fairy shoot?' Poppy adds. 'Non-Veiled would never know the difference, and if any of our Veiled friends do like the portraits… Could we give them your number? Or do you have a business card we can pass on?'

My heart leaps. My first potential recommendation as a photographer, and all I need to do is say yes.

I offer a shy smile. 'Let's see how the rest of the shoot goes first.' I'd hate to get my hopes up too high just for them to come crashing down when they hate every picture. Except for the one I just showed them, I guess.

Oskar shrugs, but his smile looks a little more honest. 'So… we'll just have these in here on the wall? And we can tell people they're fake?'

Poppy nods. 'Unless a Veiled asks. We can tell Veiled the truth.'

There's a mischievous spark in his young eyes. 'Cool. I guess that's fine.'

I wave at their sofa. 'Would you all sit together for me?'

'Mister Waggles, too?' Cass asks.

'Mister Waggles, too,' I say. 'He *is* part of the family.'

Maybe I can do this again once they've adopted their dog. I'm sure the kids would love that, too.

Cass grins at me again, and all four squeeze together onto the sofa. I was worried it would be difficult to get their wings in the frame, but they know how to move to leave just enough space.

'Are you all comfortable?' I ask, although really I've already taken some photos while they were adjusting. The best photos are the ones that aren't staged.

'Yes,' Sorcha says, and I begin to photograph in earnest.

After several images of me posing them around, I can't think what else to do. This is fine, but the wall behind me is mostly white except for the rustic fireplace and flowers on the mantel. I pose them there, take a few more.

While I work, Cass asks me all kinds of things about Lady,

and I tell her all the funniest and sweetest stories. I ask the kids about their favourite hobbies, the mothers about their favourite memories from when they were little, and after a while, the stiffness and forced poses vanish as everyone relaxes into the chat.

Roughly two hours after I arrive, I think I'm happy with what I have.

I take a few more individual portraits, some cute images of Poppy and Sorcha together, and some of Cass and Oskar together. By the time we're done, I'm creatively and socially exhausted, but I'm also happy. That was *amazing*. I can't wait to do it again.

'Can I go play?' Cass asks when I announce I'm done.

Poppy sends her off, and Oskar follows.

'May we look through them?' Sorcha asks.

We sit together on the sofa as I show them my favourite images. The first few on the sofa look awkward, but the later ones are *good*. I end up showing only two with everyone on the sofa, but we go over nearly every photo against the fireplace. When we look at the paired and individual portraits, there's a constant smile on their faces that makes every Dreamcatcher-induced nightmare worth it.

'Well?' I dare ask when we've gone over a few pictures several times. 'What do you think?'

Sorcha puts a hand on her heart. 'These are wonderful, Esta. Are you sure we can't pay you anything for them?'

After I gawked at Poppy's wings earlier? Absolutely not.

'Please don't worry. That I got to do this at all means everything. You reminded me of how much I love photography. Thank you.' I blush as I utter the confession, but they deserve to know just how much this meant to me. After the Dreamcatcher, I felt guilty every time I looked at my camera because I was denying a part of myself I'd wanted to nurture for so long. Never again.

'We will pass on your details to everyone we know,' Poppy says. 'Do you have a website or a portfolio?'

My stomach twinges. 'No, not right now.' Some professional I am. I'll have to work on both if I want to take this seriously. 'I mean, I do have a website, but it's an old one. I don't have anything like this on there. I don't even know how I'll do it, to be honest. It's not like I can be upfront about working for the Veiled.'

Poppy and Sorcha exchange a glance. My heart misses a beat.

'You can do what we'll do if any non-Veiled ask and say that they're fake, of course,' Poppy says. 'If any non-Veiled try to book you, you can simply tell them you can't fit any new clients. We'll be saying you don't take commissions at the moment.'

'But if any Veiled do find you,' Sorcha says, 'you could mention Shuhalla on your website. It's like a code.'

Poppy nods. 'It won't mean anything to humans, but for us, it's like a safe word. It's only used amongst Veiled, and those few humans we trust.'

My heart swells. My eyes burn. I'm not sure I deserve this, but I'll make sure that I do from now on.

'Thank you,' I say with stinging eyes. 'That means a lot.'

They can probably guess how much by the way my voice

wavers.

I briefly wonder why neither Kate nor Leverett mentioned this to me, but Kate likely felt it wasn't her place since she isn't Veiled herself, if she knows it at all, and Leverett had no reason to mention it.

'No, thank *you*,' Poppy says. 'It honestly means everything to us that we get to have this—that we get to have family photos of us as *us*.'

I promise to send them a selection including all the photos they love later today. My heart feels ready to burst from joy. This is a small thing I can do for the Veiled community. If I can bring the same happiness I've brought Sorcha and Poppy to others, then I *will* make this happen. My photography will be a safe space for all Veiled, and I can give them something real that'll last.

CHAPTER TWELVE

I'm beaming when I get back home. The equipment bag's strap is digging into my shoulder, the camera bag sits around it at an awkward angle and is threatening to slip off and onto my arm, and the sun combined with the effort of carrying everything is making me sweat—but I'm happy. I still can't believe how well the shoot went.

Bonnie hurries over as soon as I open the door.

'How did it go?' She takes my camera bag from me before it can fall.

'So well!' I say with a grin. 'They love the pictures. They said they'll pass my name on, and they've told me how they'll display the pictures around their house, and they gave me ideas for how I can run the website, and—'

Bonnie giggles and passes me a glass of apple juice. 'Can I see the pictures?'

I nod. 'I can't wait to show them off. But first— At the Crossroads?'

Bonnie claps and squeaks, 'Yes! Do you need a shower first, though?'

I'm so high on joy that I want to go right now, but she's right. Drenched in sweat as I am, I'd probably stink out the shop floor.

'I'll be quick.' I grab my camera bag and hand it to her. 'Feel free to look through the photos while you wait.'

Bonnie pouts. 'No, I want to look together. You can talk me through it and tell me which ones your favourites are.'

Everything the Dreamcatcher and the Mara put me through, all the pain with Chiara, all the fear the boggart imposed on me— It was all worth it to get here.

I rush through the shower, throw on some light trousers and a shirt, and hurry back down. Bonnie sets down Lady's water bowl, which she's just refilled.

'Sorry,' she says to our daughter, who's giving us big, disappointed eyes. 'We don't know yet if they allow dogs inside the shop.'

And it's warmed up too much to leave her tied up outside. The heatwave has cooled a lot, but it's the middle of the day and there isn't one cloud in sight. She'd suffer under the merciless sun.

'We'll take you for a walk later, alright?'

She huffs at us and gets comfy on the sofa.

Fortunately, the shop isn't far, and Bonnie and I discuss the kinds of things we'd love to find: pretty crystals, gorgeous tarot decks, herb seeds I can grow at home. Kate and I haven't talked about tools in great detail, so I can't wait to explore the shelves and be surprised.

'Do you want to stop by the pub on the way back?' Bonnie asks. 'I could do with a sundae.'

'Hmm, the big one to share,' I muse with my eyes closed. 'A worthy celebration sundae.'

Part of me is worried I'm celebrating too soon, but I shake it off. Things are going well—great, actually. Chiara is nowhere near me, and as far as I know, I haven't angered any Veiled lately. I refuse to question every little bit of happiness I carve out for myself. I put in the work with this photoshoot, and it's not like making it a business that's also successful enough for me to quit my gallery job will be easy. I deserve to enjoy myself today.

She claps. 'Then we should get cake, too! You only have your first big photoshoot once, you know.'

I laugh. 'No objections from me.'

The shop doesn't look busy when we reach it, but that's no surprise. Most of the places around here are takeaway restaurants, small convenience stores, and hairdressers. It's rare to find a retail shop around here, so far away from any high street. I want them to survive, but it's more likely to be a passing curiosity for most locals rather than somewhere they go regularly.

Wind chimes ring through the shop as we enter. The air con is on, which keeps the chimes moving slightly even after Bonnie has closed the door behind us. Someone I assume is an employee is talking to someone I assume is a customer, but it's hard to tell. Both have their backs to the door, and neither is wearing a uniform.

It smells *lovely*. On the counter, a thin trail of incense dances towards the ceiling—lavender, like in Kate's home. It's become synonymous with safety for me.

'I'll be right there!' the employee calls over his shoulder.

'Take your time,' Bonnie says.

We start looking around the shelves. There are books to the left near the till, and we immediately gravitate towards them. This is definitely the more modern selection I hoped for, but there are so many, and I don't really know what might be useful. There are books on herbs, crystals, sabbaths, the history of witchcraft, different gods and goddesses… In a strange way, it's more overwhelming than Leverett's shop.

'Look!' Bonnie pulls a book off the shelf. It's called *Household Spirits and How to Please Them*. She huffs as she turns it over to read the blurb. 'Where was that before our house caught fire?'

A giggle nearly escapes me, but not yet. The memory is still too fresh.

We leaf through it together. The book talks about different household spirits, variations in different corners of the world, and right there, where I would totally have seen it, it mentions how you should never ever under any circumstance ask a brownie why it's there or what it's doing in your house. Having this book could have saved us a lot of worry and arguing… or it might have done if I'd had some idea of what was going on at the time. I spent so long convinced I was cursed that I didn't even consider other options. Not that a boggart haunting me would ever have occurred to me.

'Hey there!' the employee says behind us. 'Welcome to At the Crossroads! Please let me know if there's anything I can help you find, I'll be right over there.'

Their lanyard has two badges on it, one saying "I'm Bee!"

and one saying "they/them."

'Thank you,' I say. 'We're just having a look.' Kate said this shop is a Veiled safe space, but the other customer is still there, and I don't know how much they know. 'Do you have anything on dreamscapes?'

I can't ask if they have any books on dream guide hierarchy, but what perfectly normal human hasn't wondered about their dreams before? It's not a dangerous question.

Bee considers for a moment. 'Hmm, nothing that specific, I don't think.' They pull a book about deities off the shelf. 'This should have something, though. Look at deities who have to do with sleeping and dreams in general.'

'Ooh, and do you have anything about mermaids?' Bonnie asks with wide eyes.

I give her a look that I hope says, *Surely you can learn whatever you want from Sunny?* but Bonnie shrugs.

'Just wondering,' she says with a glance at the other customer, who's happily browsing herb seed packets.

Bee quickly scans the shelves, then pulls out a book entirely about mermaids and sirens. Bonnie takes it with a gasp and begins to look through it.

'Anything else, just ask,' Bee says, and returns to the counter.

We thank them and get back to browsing. Kate was right, I do like it here, though it weirdly feels like I'm cheating on Leverett's bookshop.

'Wow, look!' Bonnie points to the opposite wall and marches over. 'These are so cool!'

I follow her to a shelf of figurines. They are all labelled with names like Freya, Gaia, Amaterasu, Thoth… Little statues of deities. Next to the shelf is another one with altar cloths and a wide variety of candles in all shapes and sizes.

Kate has implied all these deities are real. I struggled to wrap my mind around the Dreamcatcher and beings like him, but actual gods are even harder to grasp. What do they even *do*? Where do they, I don't know, hang out? Do they just live in cities and villages like everyone else, or do they live in some impossible-to-reach realm like the sylphs do?

My eyes fall on a statue of a woman with three heads and two dogs guarding her. I smile to myself; maybe I should get it for Kate as a thank-you present since she has two dogs. That's close enough, isn't it? I mean, lots of people have dogs, myself included, but… I'm sure she'd appreciate the gesture. I pick it up to check the price and nearly drop it. It's £75. I'm sure it's worth it, but maybe not today.

Bee walks up behind me. 'Do you work with my Mother, Maiden, and Crone, too?'

I blink. 'Huh? Oh, sorry. No. The dogs just remind me of someone I know, is all. She recommended this shop to me, so I thought she might like it, but…' I don't know how to tell them that it's more than I'm prepared to spend.

'Ah, sorry,' Bee says. 'I always get excited when I meet other devotees to Hekate. This figurine is one of my favourites—I have one at home, and a slightly different one out back.'

The wind chimes ring again. I turn around, and the other customer is gone. This seems like as good a time to ask as any.

'So, erm…' I wish I'd prepared a speech now. This'll be terrible if I'm wrong or phrase it badly. 'My neighbour says

115

this shop is a Veiled safe space?'

Bee looks taken aback for a second, but they quickly regain their composure. 'Yes, we are.' A glance to the door—to make sure we're still alone, I'm guessing. 'Are you Veiled yourself?'

'No, nothing like that, we just, erm… We can see them?' I don't know how to phrase our particular skill. 'If there's anything you need help with… Erm…'

I realise how presumptuous that sounds. Bee doesn't know me. I've literally only just walked into their shop, and I already assumed they must need help with Veiled business.

Fortunately, Bee doesn't look offended. 'Does this offer come from both of you?' they ask. Bonnie nods eagerly. 'Alright, give me a second.' They walk to the till and pull back a door/curtain-thing. 'Jirina? Can you watch the shop floor for a moment?'

I freeze, and Bonnie and I glance at each other. I didn't realise there was someone else here.

A young woman in a flowy skirt and corset top comes out. 'Sure.' She gives me and Bonnie a curious glance as Bee thanks her.

Bee waves us over. 'Follow me!'

It feels weird to walk behind the counter and into the back, like we're about to enter an otherwise forbidden world. If we're about to talk Veiled, that's not far from the truth. I even notice a sign above the door that reads Veiled Safe Space.

'Isn't that a little… I don't know.'

It's not like any non-Veiled would think twice about it, would they?

Bee winks at me. 'I do tarot readings back here, so

everything that happens behind the curtain is confidential. That makes this a safe space. And the curtain functions like a veil. So, that's my explanation when I'm asked, which isn't often. People don't pay much attention to signs.'

I nod with an awed glance over the room we enter. We passed through a small corridor first. I figured we'd enter a storeroom, but instead, this feels cosy. The walls are painted a red so dark it's almost black. A round table is at the centre with nothing but a cloth depicting the moon phases on it. On a shelf behind it, I recognise different tarot decks, a crystal ball, and something large and square covered in a black sheet. Bee's other figurine of Hekate is there, too, and it's larger than the one they're selling. I don't see any incense smoke, but the smell of lavender and something earthy is strong back here. The ceiling lamp above the table must have a dimmer switch, and it's turned right down.

'I didn't know storerooms could be so comfy,' Bonnie says.

'It's very important to me that my clients feel safe,' Bee says. 'Hang on, let me grab another chair.'

They disappear around the corner, and I hear footsteps above us soon after.

Bonnie gives me a confused look. 'What exactly are we going to talk about here?'

I shake my head. 'I don't actually know. I didn't plan this very well.'

Bee returns and places a third chair at the table, then sits. 'Please, sit. Tell me what brought you to the Crossroads, how you know about the Veiled, and what you want from today.'

My heart beats a little faster. This feels like a job interview I didn't prepare for.

Bonnie launches into an explanation, covering my lucid dreams and the void lake, the Dreamcatcher—everything up to Kate suggesting we check this place out. Bee doesn't interrupt once.

'We don't really know what we can do to help,' I add. 'I took some Veiled Pride photos of a fairy family this morning, but, er, I don't know how that would fit into what you're doing.'

Frankly, I haven't the faintest idea what they *are* doing. Kate wasn't very clear on that.

Bee's face lights up. 'That's such a lovely idea! I'm sure they appreciate it. And Veiled Pride—I love that. I don't mind putting out some business cards, if you have any?' They wink again. 'One small local business supporting another small local business.'

Right, note to self: I really must get on those business cards. That's twice now I've been asked today. I wonder if Poppy or Sorcha would let me use one of their close-up portraits for the design? I don't have a logo, so an example of my photography is probably the best idea.

'I'd love to bring you some once I have any,' I say.

'Happy to help,' Bee says. 'What do you want from me exactly, though? I get the feeling you want some sort of collaboration.'

I blush. 'Come to think of it, my neighbour just said you're doing your best to make your shop a Veiled safe space and that you practice witchcraft, too. Sorry.' My blush deepens. 'I jumped to conclusions.'

'Ah, so you practice, too?'

I shake my head. 'No, sorry. I meant my neighbour does. I just try to study the Veiled and help where I can.'

Bee slowly nods to herself. 'I... see. Hmm. I'm afraid I don't have your natural talent of seeing the Veiled, so you probably have an advantage over me there. But I have been practicing witchcraft for a little over ten years now, and I've been devoted to Hekate for most of them. I know a bit about various occult topics, too, like demonology and the Goetia. Maybe I can help your research? You asked about dreamscapes earlier, but it sounds like you're a natural lucid dreamer, so you likely have an advantage there, too. I'm happy to answer any questions you might have, though! Maybe I can teach you tarot or scrying? All forms of divination are my speciality.'

Now it's starting to make sense. Kate must have thought I could learn divination from Bee.

Bonnie raises her hand with a coy smile. 'Can I get in on that?'

'Of course! The more the merrier. Do you both have decks?'

I nod at the same time that Bonnie shakes her head.

'Not to hit you with the hard sales pitch, but I happen to sell a few decks. Maybe you'll find one you like. I could teach you what I know once the shop is closed for the day, so from five p.m. onwards?'

Bonnie and I exchange a look. 'We'll have to talk about our schedules first, I think. It's a little complicated on our end.'

With Kate teaching me on Tuesdays, Zeru hopefully teaching me at the weekends, and me going back to work soon-ish, my diary is getting kinda busy, plus Bonnie still has her internship and will start her final year at uni after that. Finding a good time for us all might be difficult.

'No rush,' Bee says.

We get up and are about to walk back to the shop floor when I think of something else.

'You said you work with Hekate. Do you know much about other deities?'

Bee grins. 'I'm by no means an expert, but I've read up on lots of different pantheons. I've petitioned different deities on the behalf of past clients for any number of things, too, so I know my way around.'

'Do you know who dream guides would be ruled by?' I bite my lip. I got carried away there. 'I m-mean, since I spent so much time in the dreamscape and all, I can't help wondering if there's a deity overseeing it all, you know?'

Bee thinks for a moment. 'That depends. Every pantheon has their own deity ruling over dreams or sleep.' They look at their watch. 'I'm doing a tarot reading in ten minutes. Sorry to kick you out, but could you come back another time? It's just me and Jirina working here and the shop is mine, so if we're open, I'm here. Come by whenever.'

I thank them, and Bonnie browses the tarot decks before we leave. Maybe they can point me in the right direction in regards to dreamscapes and who rules what. I thought I'd seen everything worth seeing in my dreamscape; maybe Bee can show me how to explore farther afield.

CHAPTER
THIRTEEN

'Esta, darling!'

I hurry over to Anton, who pulls me into a tight bear hug. Leverett takes his time getting out of the car and following me; he's come along as moral support for my first magic lesson and to catch up with his friends. By the time I went back to Leverett to ask for Anton's number, he'd already contacted him and was about to pass Anton's permission on to me. So, we've talked about me using his sizeable lands for my lessons, but I haven't had a chance to offer him my less-sizeable photography skills yet.

Anton's suit today is louder than his voice, the bright-green fabric complementing his blond hair. He looks like spring, and exactly as I remember him. His husband, Saif, on the other hand, looks like he's wearing pjs, and I love that about him—about both of them. They appear to be mismatched from the outside, but it's obvious they couldn't fit better together.

Anton holds me at arms' length. 'Oh, we heard what happened with Chiara, it's just awful! We are so glad to see you're alright.' He hugs me again.

There's something about Anton that just puts me at ease and makes me feel cared for. He adores looking after his friends and making them feel welcome, so it's probably that. I also get the same vibe I might from a loving grandparent, though I wouldn't dream of calling him that. He's several hundred years old, but I don't think he'd appreciate being called old by anyone's definition. Saif has the same calming effect on me, except rather than feel like I won't leave their home hungry, like I do with Anton, Saif makes me feel like I'm wrapped in a blanket by a fire on a rainy day with a good book in my hands.

I don't try to free myself from Anton's hug. He'll let me go when he's ready and sure I don't need any more protecting. Over his shoulder, I make eye contact with Saif, and we exchange patient smiles.

'Thank you,' I say. 'And thank you for letting me use your garden, I don't know where else we would have gone.'

Anton pulls away. 'Of course!' He puts a hand on his chest and smiles at Saif. 'Our little Esta is learning magic, my love. I still can't believe it.'

I giggle. It's odd how I feel more fawned over by them than I do with my own parents. I wonder if I'm too old to ask Anton and Saif to adopt me. Anton would probably do it, too.

'Welcome back, Esta Anderson,' Saif says. 'We will be inside, so don't worry about having an audience.'

I keep my relieved sigh to myself. I don't know how today will go, but there's a non-zero chance I'll make an idiot of myself. I'd rather keep my failure between me and Zeru.

'I'll be sure to have some food and cold drinks ready for

you when you're done, my dear,' Anton says. 'Come, Leverett. Let us catch up.'

Leverett gives me a quick kiss. 'Don't push yourself too hard.'

I nod and kiss him, too. 'I know, I know. It'll be a miracle if I achieve anything today.'

'I'll be waiting to hear all about it.'

He follows Anton and Saif into their mansion, and I'm all alone with the breeze. Despite what they said about leaving me to it, I can just imagine Anton sneaking a few peeks out several windows to see how I'm doing. I can also imagine Saif asking him to give me privacy.

'Erm… Zeru?' I awkwardly mumble into the air. 'I'm ready.'

For a moment, nothing happens, and I feel like an idiot. Then, the breeze around me picks up a little, and Zeru appears before me like all they had to do was step off the wind current.

'Hello again, Esta,' they say, then look around the gardens. 'Yes, this will do. It was a good idea to come here.'

I stand a little straighter. Not even one full minute into my first lesson and I'm already getting praised—go me.

Hopefully, I can get praised for more than common sense today.

'We shouldn't get interrupted,' I tell them. 'The owner is giving us as much time as we need.'

Inside Kate's living room, Zeru seemed unnaturally still to me. People have small mannerisms and fidget all the time, but Zeru doesn't. They're in their natural element today. Zeru's movements aren't awkward out here, but graceful and elegant. Despite their size, I can believe that a breeze could easily pick them up and carry them away. The air around them seems to shift, like it can't help being attracted to its elemental. Zeru seems more vibrant, too—nothing like Sorcha and Poppy in their full fae-ness, but there's an otherworldly *air* to them. I wouldn't be shocked if they broke into dance and the wind shifted with them, like they're the breeze come to life.

'Tell me how you summoned the wind before,' Zeru says.

I try to remember. 'We were outside. Kate asked me to focus on the breeze, so I closed my eyes and did that. She, erm…' Probably best to come clean now. 'She told me I should be able to feel my magic inside me, like a sphere of energy or something like that. We tried, but I haven't felt anything even remotely like it.'

'Kate didn't know any better,' Zeru explains. 'She tried to teach you regular Veiled magic as a non-Veiled herself. The energy she described is what Veiled sense within themselves. We sylphs do not.'

'So… it wasn't just me being bad at it?' Hearing otherwise seems too good to be true.

Zeru attempts a smile. It looks kind. 'No, Esta. You tried to find a magic inside yourself that you don't possess. You couldn't have found it.'

I let out a relieved gasp. 'You don't know how happy that makes me. How do you feel your magic?'

'I am an elemental. My magic is not something I need to feel, it simply is. How do you breathe?'

I stare at them. How do I *breathe*? I just *do*. I'd die if I didn't.

'I don't think about it,' I say. 'It's subconscious? Involuntary? I don't know, it just kinda happens automatically.' If that's how sylphs feel magic, I'm not convinced it's something I can learn. 'I can hold my breath for short amounts of time, but I will need to breathe eventually. I'll die otherwise. Is magic the same for you?'

Zeru watches me, unblinking, like they're trying to figure something out just by looking at me, or like they're deep in thought and don't know how to make it show on their face.

'Are you asking if I'll die if I don't use magic?'

I bite my lip but nod. Not sure now if that sounds insensitive.

'In a sense. The magic comes naturally to elementals, Esta. Much like you don't need to think through every movement required to fill your lungs with air and empty them again, we don't need to think about calling the wind or rustling leaves with a breeze. We will the air to move, and the air responds. Like all elementals, we cannot exist safely outside our element. We have but one natural habitat. We cannot adjust, only work together or suffer and finally perish.'

I nod as I let their words sink in, though in truth I'm not entirely sure what they mean. I can't exactly survive in lava, either.

'If it's so natural to you, how do *I* learn it?' I ask. 'I don't know how I'd teach someone to breathe who's never done it before and never needs to do it.'

'And yet that awareness will serve you well. It's a good first step in understanding.'

I'm not so sure, but I nod.

'Tell me about the time you used magic in self-defence. What happened?'

125

I don't really want to relive that moment, but if that's what it takes, I'll be honest with Zeru no matter how painful the memory is. 'A vampire kept me prisoner. I thought I saw a chance to run and took it, but I was wrong. She was faster, obviously, and flew after me. She grabbed my wrist, bit into it, and I panicked. The magic shoved her down the stairs.'

'Then you now know two ways in which our magic can manifest—through subconscious will, and through strong, uncontrolled emotion.'

I half expected Zeru to pity me for what happened, maybe to say they're glad I'm okay, but they don't. I didn't realise how much I needed that: for it to just be something that happened to me, something that doesn't need to derail my present.

'Are there any other ways?' I hope there are. I don't know if I'll ever be able to summon a breeze as naturally as Zeru does, and I'd rather not have to be in a life-or-death situation every time, either. The latter would make my lessons a nightmare, and I'd prefer to stay done with those.

'Watch,' they say. 'Tell me if you observe any changes.'

I'm about to ask what I'm supposed to be watching, but there's a calm kind of focus in their eyes that shuts me up. Instead, I pay attention. I don't notice anything different at first, but then...

A slight breeze on my arms.

The nearby shrubs rustle as the wind sighs through them.

Another breeze strokes my face and swirls down my neck, and I close my eyes in appreciation.

'Are you doing that?' I ask. 'The breeze, I mean.'

Zeru smiles. 'Yes. Very good, Esta. This is the third way:

conscious effort.'

Now *that* sounds like something I can practice.

'How is that different to Veiled magic, though?'

Granted, I don't have that kind myself and can't speak from experience, but it seems like it would be the same.

'The Veiled you refer to need to use conscious effort to use their magic no matter how small the spell. It's also possible for a Veiled to use magic by accident if their emotions are strong enough, though it would require more of a... how do you say? Loss of control?'

I nod like that's definitely something we say all the time. I get what Zeru means, though: For a Veiled to lose control of their magic, they'd *really* need to lose it. Anger isn't enough, it would need to be blind rage. That it takes less than that for sylphs is unsettling. Might explain Zeru's usual calm demeanour, though.

'Veiled witches cannot use their magic in the same natural way we do, simply by existing. For Veiled witches, magic is a skill, a talent that can be nurtured much like painting—anyone can learn it, but some have more of an affinity for it. For an elemental, magic is as much a part of who we are as your breath is for you. You might liken it to another sense.'

I have a feeling some Veiled witches might take offence at that, but they aren't here and I understand Zeru's explanation, so I won't get nitpicky over it. It's not my argument to start, anyway. Frankly, I don't want to.

'And when I called that small breeze in the forest with Kate, that was conscious effort?'

Zeru goes still for a moment. 'I believe it was subconscious effort.'

My heart skips a beat. 'I can do that?'

Zeru pauses again. They are a great teacher, but they're not the right person to get excited with.

'We will do an experiment. Sit. Repeat the steps you took in the forest.'

I quickly sit, drop my shoulders and close my eyes. Last time I felt like I was meditating. I do the same thing now, focus all my senses on the breeze around us. Now that Zeru is no longer influencing it, the breeze is only small, but it is there. I feel it on my arms, my ankles; through my clothes and caressing my covered skin. It smells fresh and cool. I can hear it in the rustling leaves around us, though the sound is only faint.

I don't know how long I sit like that. I don't open my eyes; I do nothing except focus on the breeze and will it to move around me, and Zeru doesn't interrupt me. After a felt half an hour, they say:

'Open your eyes. Look at the grass.'

I do as they say and nearly break into hysterical laughter. The grass around me *swayed*. I did that!

'If you were a sylph, you could have done more,' Zeru says. 'I do not say this to hurt you, Esta, only to help you realise you may never progress past this.'

I deflate a little, but I'm also excited that I did that much even though I've managed it before. But they're right, I can't use this in a fight. I doubt most opponents would even feel something so slight in the middle of an argument.

'And conscious effort?' I ask. 'How do I do that?'

Zeru hesitates again. 'It will not be easy to learn. You may not accomplish the results you want.'

'I don't care,' I say. 'I want to try.'

Zeru nods. 'All you need is a connection to the air and the will to move it. You already have the connection, though it is faint. It may not hear you.'

My heart sinks a little. 'Because I'm human?'

'Because you are human.'

Well, it's not like I didn't see that coming. 'Show me anyway? I can practice at home.'

'Feel the air all around you,' Zeru says. 'Realise it is everywhere, including inside you. Do not treat it like a lifeless object, but rather as a force with its own energy.'

I close my eyes again. In a way, I've always seen the breeze as more, so it's not difficult for me to wrap my head around what Zeru said.

'Once you are consciously aware of the air, will it to move.'

'Erm... Like, out loud?'

'To begin with, yes,' Zeru says, and my confidence crumbles. It felt weird enough to say their name earlier, but to speak a whole command? 'If you can learn this, you can advance to silent applications of will. For now, this will be easier.'

I swallow my pride, blush, and say in a breaking voice, 'Rustle that bush?'

I've never felt more silly.

'Intention is vital in all magic,' Zeru says.

So, in other words, I'll have to say it like I mean it.

I take a deep breath in, allow myself a moment to focus

again, and whisper, 'Rustle the leaves,' while staring intently at the closest flowerless shrub.

And I would love to say that it worked. That I called the magic and it responded. That I felt like there was some point to all this. But instead, nothing happens. Not one leaf falls to the ground to humour me.

'Are you discouraged already?' Zeru asks.

I quickly shake my head, but the energy drains out of me before I've finished the movement.

'You are exhausted,' Zeru says. 'We will return here next week Sunday.'

'No, wait!' I want to beg them to stay, but Zeru shakes their head. Deep down, I know it's the right decision, but I really wanted to have something to show for my first lesson. Something more encouraging than the same tiny grass shuffle I managed with Kate. I know it's better than nothing, but it's so far away from what I wanted. I know I deluded myself, but I didn't think I'd be this bad at it.

'You agreed to do as I say,' Zeru reminds me. 'We will stop for today. I will see you again next Sunday. If you want to practice in the meantime, I will not stop you, but you must promise not to overdo it. Neither your body nor your mind are used to this kind of exercise.'

Begrudgingly, I nod. 'I promise. Thank you for today.'

'You show promise, Esta,' Zeru says. 'Do not give up.'

And with that, they dissipate like fog and I'm alone again.

CHAPTER
FOURTEEN

Leverett pulls me into a hug and kisses me when I join him, Anton, and Saif in their sitting room.

'How did it go?' he asks.

'We didn't watch, as promised,' Anton says, which isn't suspicious at all, 'but we *are* curious.'

I sigh and let myself fall onto the sofa next to Leverett. 'It went badly. I didn't really achieve anything.'

Anton waves me off. 'You're too harsh on yourself, my dear. It was only your first lesson.'

'Patience and perseverance are kind teachers, Esta Anderson,' Saif says with a smile.

I nod, but I'm still disappointed with myself. 'I suppose. I just wanted to achieve *some*thing, you know?'

Leverett puts an arm around me. 'You will.'

I lean into him, already feeling a little better. I feel better still when Anton says:

'Leverett told us all about your photography business! Oh, Saif and I would adore new portraits of us together. Wouldn't we, my love?'

Saif nods. 'It has been a rather long time since we've had paintings commissioned. It will be nice to have new portraits.'

'Do you have any examples on you?' Anton asks. 'We would just love to see some of your work.'

I nearly say that yes, I do, in fact I took some just yesterday, but I catch myself in time.

'No, sorry. I did photograph a family yesterday, but I don't know if they'd be comfortable with it. I'll have to ask. And, erm… It's not actually much of a business yet.' Something about the word *yet* makes me feel like a massive fraud—or like I'm in way over my head. There's a huge gap between *I took a few pictures* and *I have a legitimate business.* It makes me feel like I'm trying to fly before I can even crawl.

'Just you wait,' Anton says with a wink. 'To tell you the truth, many of our friends have been looking for someone just like you, but as you can imagine, there aren't many who would photograph the Veiled knowing what we are. We can get regular portraits any time, of course, but it's not the same.'

This makes me wonder something I haven't considered until now: Why aren't there more Veiled photographers? Surely they'd be perfect for the job if they *want* photos?

I ask Anton and Saif.

'For the same reason there aren't many Veiled retail workers, for example,' Saif says. 'Most Veiled have been around for a long time, or they were born into families who have been. Art is not a rare hobby amongst us, but there is no need to create for profit.'

Well, more for me, then. If they want to pay me to do it for them, then I won't question it.

'When would you want to do this?' I ask.

I try to stay professional, but my head is whirring. If it can wait a little, I can have a website ready, followed by business cards. I'll have something to give them to hand out. Of course, I'll be here every Sunday for the foreseeable future anyway, but— No, there's no need to rush. It'll be fine. Anton will be recommending me and my camera before I know it, and I'd rather put together a good website and business cards with links I'm proud to share than rush through the process and regret being hasty.

'Well, why don't we do it next Sunday?' Anton asks. 'You'll already be here, after all. Does that give you enough time to prepare?'

I nod, maybe a little too keenly. 'Yes, that's great. Thank you.'

I smile in gratitude, but really I'm prepared to fall to my knees before them. Chances like this don't come around often; I will not waste this opportunity.

That's assuming Anton and Saif will like what I do. Their expectations are no doubt high, and I am not that experienced.

'Please have a think if there's anything specific you want,' I say. 'You have so many beautiful backdrops here, we can do this shoot anywhere. I'll have a think, too, but I'm happy to take whatever images you want.'

Maybe I shouldn't have said that. What if they want something more... intimate? Gods, what if they want photos of them biting each other? I don't even know how I would handle that. They *are* vampires, though. There must be a reason they don't just go to a regular photographer—after all,

133

no one would know they're vampires unless their fangs come out.

The good news is, I now have all week to stress about it. Wonderful.

'We'll defer to your expertise, my dear,' Anton says. 'Whatever you think is best.'

Not gonna lie, I'm a little relieved. Although… who knows who they'll put me in touch with? Maybe the next vampire will want vampire Pride photos, fangs and claws and blood and all. What if the next vampire has a human blood bag? I'm not sure I have it in me to tell a vampire no, especially for that reason. Maybe I will one day, but right now… Where's the line? It's nothing unusual for vampires, after all, even if the tradition is dying out. Never mind where their line is—where do *I* draw mine?

I suppose I won't know until it happens. I meant what I said: I want to take Veiled Pride photos that my clients will treasure for a very long time, without any judgement from me. I just didn't realise everything that might entail, and I doubt I realise the full extent now. Maybe it would be better if Anton and Saif wanted photos of them biting each other. I'd rather navigate this with people I know than be surprised with complete strangers.

Then again, I might never be able to look them in the eyes again after a shoot like that, so maybe it wouldn't be all that ideal.

'I'll be sure to bring my equipment next week.' If nothing else, I shouldn't need my heavy lights in this beautifully bright mansion. 'Could I use your library before we leave?' I glance at Leverett. 'Would you mind?'

Leverett smiles at me. 'Not at all. Anton, Saif, and I can continue our conversation while you read.'

'Actually…' I look at Saif. 'I'd appreciate your help finding some books, if you have them.'

He inclines his head. 'I'll help however I can.'

'Take as long as you need,' Anton says with a nod to us both. 'We'll be here when you're done.'

I follow Saif out of the room and one door to the right. The wonderful smell of old books greets me as we enter.

'How can I help?' Saif asks.

'Do you have anything on dreamscapes?'

Saif watches me with calm curiosity. 'What could my books possibly have to offer you, a lifelong lucid dreamer and expert on the subject?'

I shrug so I don't come across as too interested. In truth, I don't even expect to find anything, but I'd love something to help me understand Mischief's situation even if there's nothing I can do.

'Before we talked it out with the Dreamcatcher, Kate helped Bonnie enter my dream so we could face him together. Something like that never even occurred to me before that day. It's made me curious what else is possible, you know?'

Saif stills. 'Oh my, that is unexpected.'

I shrug again like it's no big deal. 'I'm not really an expert, either. I've always just done it, but I've never actually looked into it. I don't know how any of it works. And the way the Dreamcatcher and the Mara could interact with and influence my dreams… It's made me curious, is all. My dreamscape isn't as simple as I always thought, that much is clear. I thought if anyone knows something, it's you.'

Saif smiles at me. 'Flattery won't get you answers, Esta Anderson.' He doesn't sound put off, though. I think he's teasing me, in his own calm way.

I wave him off. 'It's not flattery. I mean, just look at all these books. How am I supposed to navigate this without your help?'

Also, in my head at least, Saif knows everything. He may even be smarter than Kate. If she's ever too busy to teach me or goes on holiday, I imagine Saif could easily take over. Zeru seems like a great teacher, too, but I don't know them that well, and I find Saif's home library comforting. I'd rather be in here if given a choice. I suppose I don't really know Saif all that well, either, but there's something about him that makes me feel like I've always known him. We're not related, but he's my favourite uncle.

'There is likely more knowledge on the wider dreamscape than you think, and not as much as you hope,' Saif begins. 'It is not a subject many have studied due to its ethereal nature. Take yourself, for example. All humans have the potential to lucid dream, but many struggle to do it once, let alone repeat their success whenever they wish. You, on the other hand, do so with ease, and even you didn't suspect it goes beyond your own unconscious.'

I slowly nod. 'You said "wider dreamscape"… Does that have anything to do with Bonnie entering my dream?'

Saif stills again. I get the feeling this is, well, not classified knowledge as such, but probably not where he thought today's chat would go.

'Has either of you visited the other's dream again since that first time?'

I shake my head. 'We only managed it then because of the tea Kate made her. We've tried a couple of times, but...' If only I knew what ingredients Kate used. Maybe they're herbs I have in my garden or something I can buy from At the Crossroads. I could learn how to brew my very own dream-share potion.

'Esta.'

I look up. Somehow, Saif using only my first name has the same effect as someone else calling me by my full name.

'Kate won't tell you how she brewed the tea,' Saif says. 'It is an advanced magic I'm surprised she is capable of. I mean her no offense, of course. You and Bonnie haven't been able to replicate the journey because the wider dreamscape is not meant to be traversed by mortals. You can try again and again, and you will fail every time.'

The tone in his voice tells me we're not arguing about this, but I have so many questions. If the wider dreamscape isn't meant to be travelled, how did a *tea* allow Bonnie to hop on over? How did Kate know what to do? Why did she have this recipe in the first place?

'What exactly is the wider dreamscape?' I ask.

'Hmm, how to explain it... Imagine an ocean so vast there is no end. Your dreamscape is a small island in that ocean. Bonnie's is another. The tea Kate gave you acted like a raft that allowed Bonnie to sail to your shores. The precise method Kate used ensured the raft was sturdy enough to carry her consciousness, and that it wouldn't be swallowed by the waves. Otherwise, however, the islands aren't linked. As I mentioned earlier, the wider dreamscape—this ocean—is not meant to be travelled by mortals. What Kate did is not impossible, but it is extremely rare and difficult. If you tried to replicate the results without her knowledge and skill and experience, it could have disastrous consequences.'

I swallow. No toying around with the dreamscape ocean—got it.

'What would have happened if Bonnie had fallen off the raft?' I ask. 'Can that happen?'

Saif nods, and my stomach sinks. 'Kate's tea helped her stay on, so to speak, but if you attempted the same without the correct preparation, your consciousness would be forever lost in the aether.'

'But it *is* possible to prepare?' Saif shakes his head even as I speak. 'If we're comparing it to an ocean, isn't it possible to—'

'No, Esta Anderson. Nothing good would come of it. Neither you nor your sister have the means to traverse the dreamscape without being lost. I mean no disrespect; I only want you to understand how ill-advised an idea this is.'

I decide to let it go, at least for now. There's probably nothing worthwhile to explore anyway. If the dreamscape is as vast as Saif says, I have no chance of finding Mischief or her boss, and I have no intention of peeking into anyone else's subconscious. That's private and none of my business.

'Alright,' I say. 'I probably have enough to do anyway. Learning magic isn't easy.'

Saif gives me a patient, and relieved, smile. 'It is not, but it should prove to be a worthwhile endeavour. Having said that, you are already experimenting with forces that weren't meant for you in this life. Perhaps you should stop there and count yourself lucky to have so much insight.'

I return his smile. He makes a good point: I've stumbled upon enough forbidden knowledge for one lifetime.

'By the way, there's something Kate mentioned that made me think of you.'

Saif cocks his head. 'Oh?'

'A library.' I let out a small laugh. 'That one isn't meant for regular mortals, either.'

'Ah, yes. The sylphs' second natural habitat. I am familiar with it.'

Of course he is. Although... Does that mean—

'Have you been there?'

Kate said it's invite-only, that access is restricted even then, but if the sylphs gave anyone permission to browse the shelves of secret knowledge, I wouldn't be surprised if they gave that privilege to Saif. He doesn't strike me as someone who would abuse the power.

Saif nods. 'I have been granted access only a small handful of times. It is not a responsibility to be taken lightly.'

I can't imagine what kind of knowledge Saif would have wanted that he can only get there, and it's not my place to ask. Even without having seen the place, the sylphs' library strikes me as a kind of sacred space. I would be afraid to move in it for fear of accidentally ruining an ancient tome.

'Is it as beautiful as I picture it?'

Saif nods with a secretive smile. 'It is magnificent beyond even your lucid dreams, Esta Anderson.'

And that tells me everything I need to know. It's a shame I'll never see it in person, but that's okay. It's a special kind of sacred place, not a public library.

'I will find you some books on dreamscapes and related subjects,' Saif says as he gently moves towards his shelves. 'I trust you to take good care of these books. Return them when you're done.'

I stare until he's disappeared behind a shelf. 'You mean I can take them home?'

The rustling of books fills the quiet. Then:

'Yes. You will be here a lot, and I know you won't disrespect these books.'

And when Saif places a small pile before me on the table, I feel like he has gifted me the most wonderful treasure.

CHAPTER
FIFTEEN

'I'm *exhausted*.' I sigh as I fall onto Leverett's sofa. I didn't realise how much Zeru's magic lesson tired me out until I sat in the car. Apparently, I fell asleep before we'd left the property. I vaguely remember Leverett suggesting we go to his first—I think he wants to discuss something—and I missed the rest of the drive after that. I didn't even know there was parking behind his shop.

'Can I make you a tea?' Leverett asks.

I sit up and at least try to look awake. 'If you don't mind? I'd love some cinnamon.' That should invigorate me enough to drive the three minutes home. I have no issue with staying here, but Bonnie asked for an emergency movie night, and I'm not the kind of sister who would say no to that. If she needs me, I am there.

Leverett busies himself in the kitchenette. I close my eyes, and a felt second later, I smell cinnamon and lean against something warm.

'Hm?' I open my eyes and am surprised to feel Leverett behind me, his arms closed around me and me lying between his legs, snuggled against his chest.

'Sleep,' he says.

It's tempting, but I shake my head and make myself sit. Not enough to leave his arms, though.

I take the tea and drink half.

'I can't, Bonnie has asked for an emergency girls' night. Thank you, though.'

He kisses the top of my head, and I let myself melt into him a little.

'Is she alright?'

'She didn't say what's wrong.' I put the tea down and close my arms around his back but don't dare close my eyes. 'I'm sure it's nothing pizza can't fix.'

He chuckles. 'I hear it solves everything, same as tea.'

I laugh, but it comes out more like a drowsy sigh.

'Speaking of comfort food,' he says. 'I talked to Anton and Saif about your request earlier. We discussed how I might approach biting you.'

Suddenly, I'm wide awake. I'm not sure how to feel about him telling them what I asked. I trust Anton and Saif, but this was a personal request, and an intimate one. Then again, it's normal for vampires to drink from humans, so it's not like they discussed an embarrassing kink.

Leverett strokes my shoulder and side. 'I told them I was the one who wants to try. They don't know it was your idea.'

I wrap my hands around the tea mug; being so sleepy has given me a chill.

'And what did they say?'

'To be careful, but they were encouraging.'

I wonder if this is the vampire equivalent of the sex talk— *remember, it's perfectly natural to want to drink each other's blood, as long as you clean the wound after.*

'That's good, right?' I ask. 'We don't have to rush, though.'

I tilt my head back as much as his chest allows, and he kisses me.

'If you like, we can try it now.'

I blush. '*Right* now?'

He chuckles. 'Only if you're comfortable. The truth is that there's very little I can do to prepare myself. Your blood will taste overwhelmingly good. I have mentally prepared myself for this truth as much as I can, but I won't know how my body will react until I taste you.'

So, there's risk either way. I'm not surprised, but knowing he might bite me *now*, tonight, is so unexpected. I'm not against it, I just didn't see it coming so soon.

'No, I trust you. I want this, too.'

His eyes darken. 'I want you to be in full control. You tell me where to bite you. If you change your mind, tell me to stop and I will.'

I hope he's right. I can't wrestle a blood-crazed vampire off me—I couldn't even push Chiara away from me.

'I, erm… What's easiest for you? Can I stay like this?'

My heart is hammering, but lying as we are now feels safe. I don't need to do anything except trust him, and that's not difficult.

'Yes.' Leverett strokes my hair with one hand and my side with the other. He's trembling a little. 'Move up a bit.' I do as he says until my head is right next to his. 'That's it. Try to relax,

143

if you can. I won't hurt you, Esta. You have my word.'

I nod, but I'm shaking a little, too. Leverett kisses my temple, trails his lips down to my neck. No fangs yet. He holds me tight with one arm while the other caresses my shoulders, my face, my breasts. I feel his breath on my neck and try not to tense. Any second now.

'Are you ready?' he whispers, his voice husky. I imagine his eyes completely black.

'Yes.'

'Hold on to me, if you need to.'

I try to nod without moving my head too much. Leverett kisses my neck again, gently runs his tongue over my skin—

And then I feel it. A small scrape of something sharp.

In my head, it's Chiara tormenting me all over again, her grin as she toyed with me, the malice in her eyes. I break out in cold sweat.

'*Stop.*'

Leverett draws his head back and wraps his arms around me. He kisses my head again, his fangs so far away from my neck. But I still feel them.

'Ssh. It's alright.' He folds me into his chest, and I cling to him like my life depends on it. Chiara isn't here. I'm safe.

But I can't stop shaking.

Leverett gently rocks me in his arms until my breathing has calmed a little and I feel like I can talk without crying.

'I'm sorry,' he said. 'I should have waited longer.'

I rapidly shake my head. 'No, no, I should—' My nose burns again. 'This isn't fair on you.'

He was expecting blood. What does it do to a vampire to

144

be denied it?

He shakes his head against my hair. 'No amount of your blood would make your fear worth it. We will wait until you're ready. Or we don't need to try this again, ever. Alright?'

I want to argue, but what am I going to say? That I want him to bite me against my will?

'No, we'll try again,' I say. 'I want to. Just… not tonight.'

I refuse to let Chiara take this win. I just need to prepare myself better, or at all. Tonight was only the first attempt. We can build up from here.

I hate that all I can see now when I think of trying again is Chiara's hateful grin.

'I wish I could stay,' I mumble against him, 'but I take my sisterly duties very seriously.'

Leverett chuckles, kisses the top of my head again, and lets me sit up. I take a moment to gather myself, then finish the tea and look at him.

'You're really not angry?' I ask. 'Or disappointed?'

He takes my hand and kisses that, too. 'I could never be disappointed with you, Esta. That you were prepared to try at all means more than you know.'

Leverett sees me out. We kiss again at the door, and for a moment, we just stand together, his forehead to mine. It makes me feel better than his reassuring words do. This doesn't mean we're not okay. He isn't upset with me, and he stopped when I told him to even though his fangs must have ached. If anything, I trust him even more now.

'Pass me the ham?' I ask Bonnie as she starts frying the

mushrooms and sausages.

'Here you go,' she says, her words swallowed by the sudden sizzle of oil.

I grab a knife and chopping board, then remember the most important topping and go back to the fridge. 'How much cheese do you want?'

My sister throws me a look over her shoulder. 'Erm, all of it, Esta.'

Naturally. I return to my spot next to her and start tearing the ham to pieces.

We've decided that, since we seem to be needing a lot of movie nights lately, it'll be better for our bank accounts to make our own pizzas, at least every now and again. I stopped by the shop on the way from Leverett to buy some extra toppings and two large pizza bases, and Bonnie just got home herself from walking Lady when I parked in front of our house. Roughly twenty minutes later, and the kitchen smells *good*.

'So, how did it go?' Bonnie asks as the sizzling calms down a little. 'I figured if it had gone well you'd have texted me while you were still at Anton's, so I didn't want to ask until melted cheese was imminent.'

I quickly set the oven to preheat since we forgot that, and sigh.

'Oh, you know. Fine, except for how I'm completely inept and disgraced myself and my family.'

I smile at her to make it clear I'm not that gutted, but my words come out sadder than I intended. I *am* gutted. I expected nothing but I wanted everything, or at least a gust.

Bonnie cracks some pepper and salt onto the mushrooms and stirs. 'Are you being too impatient with yourself again?'

'I know, I know.' For a moment, I'm not sure if I should tell her what really bothers me, but we've always told each other everything and that's not about to stop now. 'And, erm… I asked Leverett to bite me, but—'

Bonnie drops the wooden spoon and turns to me with wide eyes. 'I'm not even gonna pretend that's slang. You asked him to bite you? As in, drink your blood?'

I nod and pretend the ham I'm shredding is Chiara's face.

'I couldn't do it. I panicked.'

Bonnie puts her arms around me and her head on my shoulder. 'Because of what happened?'

I nod again, hating that my eyes burn. It's not that big a deal, and Leverett was lovely about it. I don't know why I'm crying.

Bonnie squeezes me. 'Oh, sister. I'd probably be scared, too, you know? It sounds like a big step. Hey, look at me.' I do. 'Did he hurt you?'

I quickly shake my head. The last thing I want is for her to think Leverett treats me badly.

'Good, then I won't need to beat him up.'

I sniffle-laugh through the tears. 'That's my emergency, anyway. What's yours?' I reach around so I can half hug her with a hand that smells of ham and squeeze her back as much as I can.

Bonnie returns to the frying pan, gives everything one last good shake, then removes it from the heat.

'Mine's complicated.' She takes a jar of pizza sauce out of the cupboard. 'I mean, not complicated, but… Just a bit

147

different to what I was expecting. That's on me.'

I take one of the pizza bases and spread half the sauce on it with a spoon. 'Different how?'

'What comes to your mind when you think of mermaids?'

'Uh…' Not that long ago, that would have been an easy question, but now? I've learned very recently how little I actually know. 'They… live in the ocean? And… Wait, *do* they sing people to their deaths? That's sirens instead of mermaids, right?' If it's mermaids, I've been a terrible sister.

'Yeah, that's sirens,' Bonnie says. 'Mermaids can sing, though. Sunny sings to herself all the time, she has a beautiful voice.' She sighs and stays silent for a few seconds. 'I, um, thought… God, this sounds terrible. Tell me to shut up any time if you don't want to know, alright?'

'Okay.'

For a moment, we both just put toppings on our pizzas: ham, mushrooms, and sausage meat in no particular order. The slices will be too heavy to pick up, especially once all the cheese weighs them down, but it's everything we need tonight.

'So, Sunny said she might never feel like sleeping with me.'

I spread the cheese without looking up once, like we have this conversation all the time. 'And how do you feel about that?'

We carefully place the pizzas in the oven, slam the oven door shut, and then we sink onto the sofa next to each other.

'Fine, I guess? You know I'd never make her. I just wasn't expecting it. We've been on so many dates now. We've kissed, even slept in the same bed once, but she never made a move. We, uh… We actually have had sex, and I thought she enjoyed it, but she hasn't initiated. So, I asked why, and she said it's just not something she does or feels.' Her eyes water. 'What if I made her do something she didn't want? She didn't tell me not to or anything, but I've never been in this kind of relationship before, where my partner has no strong feelings around this.'

I move over a little and hug her. 'Did she say she didn't like it?'

Bonnie lets herself fall against me. 'No. She said she did enjoy it in the moment, she just doesn't feel like she needs it.'

'Are you okay with that?'

They seemed so happy together, and frankly, they are an incredibly cute couple. I'd hate for them to break up over something like this. My sister and I have never been that similar where sex is concerned, though. I slept with one person before Leverett and never understood how anyone can sleep with a stranger, but Bonnie had more of a wild phase and likewise doesn't understand my reservations. We've always been respectful of each other. Then again, we're not a couple.

'Yeah, I think so,' Bonnie says. 'I'm just not used to it, you know? And you and Leverett have…?'

I nod. 'That's different, though. I'm in love with him, so of course I'm attracted to him *now*. I wouldn't be if I didn't feel emotionally safe with him.'

Bonnie slowly nods, sits up, and fidgets with her hands. 'I really like her, Esta. I want us to work.' She lets out a teary laugh. 'Is it too early to say that I think she's the one?'

I giggle and break into a grin. 'No, that's exciting. When you know, you know. Why don't you invite her over? I've barely spoken to her. Why don't we have that BBQ before the heatwaves turn to rain?'

Bonnie giggles, too. 'Alright, I'll ask her. Thank you.'

I give her one last hug and jump up to check on the pizzas. I don't think either of us remembered to set a timer since we were both feeling all the things.

'Oh, but you should probably discuss boundaries with her next time you talk,' I say before I enter the kitchen. 'You want to make sure you're both on the same page.'

Bonnie stands, too, and follows me into the kitchen. 'Damn it, I wish I could make us some strong cocktails, but I'm driving in the morning. Can I interest you in a hot chocolate instead?'

'After food? Not sure chocolate goes with pizza. I do insist on cake, though.'

Bonnie rifles through the freezer, finds an apple pie, and then we settle in with our sort-of homemade pizzas. For now, we both feel better. Hopefully, it'll last.

CHAPTER
SIXTEEN

I'm not quite sure yet what I'm going to do when I become lucid in my dream that night, I just know I want to try *some*thing. Everything Saif said has me excited. I'm not an idiot—I won't try to jump into someone else's dreamscape, but Bonnie managed to get into mine, so there must be some way to explore this wider dreamscape. Saif compared it to an ocean; I feel like I'm in a dense jungle on my little island, and I have no idea which way to go to find the shore. I didn't even know there *is* a shore until recently.

I have no intentions of throwing myself into strange waters this time. I just want a glimpse, to get an idea of what it looks like. Will it look anything like my void lake? Maybe that's where the lake got its appearance from—a smaller version of the incomprehensible larger whole.

If Mischief were here, I would have asked for directions, but that's not an option anymore. Without her guidance, I haven't the faintest idea of where to start.

I cross my legs under the purple leaves of my tree and ground myself. My hands on the yellow grass; my skin pressed against the rough bark on my back; the breeze on my arms, face, neck. I've never realised before how quiet it is here. Mischief and I have always talked a lot, but now, there's only silence. I will some birdsong into existence and amplify the sounds of wind until it positively wooshes in my ears and rustles the purple leaves above me. It's just strong enough for me to hear it but not so loud I don't hear the chirping of non-existent birds.

I let my mind wander. I could ask that other dream guide for help, but I doubt they'd lead me to where I want to go. It likely goes against dream guide protocol to let me glimpse the wider dreamscape.

Mischief would have shown me. At least like this, on my own, no one can blame her for what I'm trying to do.

Bonnie managed it—with a tea made by my friendly neighbourhood witch, yes, but I know it's possible. There must be a way to do it without any help, but it can't be so easy that millions of dreamers wade into the depths by accident every night. So, it must be hidden.

I fly into the air and take a moment to look around. My dreamscape looks like it always has from up here, but then I wasn't expecting a door or an arch beckoning me through. Would have made things easier, though.

I cautiously fly higher and higher until my dreamscape is just a small dot below me, but other than that, nothing changes. I don't suddenly see other dreamscape-shaped blobs in the distance. I don't suddenly find myself in rough obsidian waters. I'm literally just higher than I was.

Disappointed but not surprised, I will myself back down to

my tree.

If this shore is hidden, it could be anywhere: in a cave, through the void lake, inside my hopes and fears. Didn't I feel like I was floating through space when I entered the void lake? That was nice. Maybe I already entered the greater dreamscape that time and didn't realise it.

Stepping back into the void lake, though, is very far down my list of things to do again. Last time I jumped in, it unlocked Veiled Vision. Who knows what it'll do if I go for another swim?

Although, it does beat searching every corner for some hidden door that probably doesn't exist.

I fly all the way to my void lake just in case I spot something new after all, but there's nothing. I half expect to be on to something and therefore find the lake dried up or just straight-up gone, but it's still there and as beautiful as ever. It still looks more like an oversized scrying mirror than a lake, too: smooth obsidian, the illusion of faint stars twinkling on the surface if I tilt my head just so. Rather than wet, it's soft to dive into, like satin or velvet.

I land by the shore and take a few steps in. It feels lovely on my feet and ankles once I've willed my shoes away, like a comforting blanket after a hard day at work.

I decide to be brave and just do it already. Chances are, the gods of dreams wouldn't allow this if I was actually on to something, but then again, it could be a double bluff. Maybe they are so convinced I won't find anything that they're happy to let me tire myself out.

Or—and this is the more likely option—I'm overthinking

it and the void lake really is just a void lake. I mean, it already let me see the Veiled as they are. How many secrets can one not-lake hold?

Still, I walk in until all of me is covered in darkness. It doesn't feel overwhelming or scary but soothing, like this is a safe space. Like I'm exactly where I need to be.

What am I missing? I silently ask my dreamscape.

I probably imagine it, but I think I hear a soft purr. It's not wrong—I do miss my dream guide kitty. That's not what I meant, though.

Anything else?

That's likely not clear enough, so of course I'm not getting anywhere. I decide to put all my bets on this one chance and be much more specific.

Where is the wider dreamscape? Where is its entrance?

I let myself float, try to pay attention to anything that might change in case there's a brief flash of a location or a person or even coordinates. I make myself as light as I can so the dream current can sweep me up and carry me to wherever I need to go.

But nothing happens.

After a felt hour and my request repeated a few times, I give up and will myself back to the surface. Turns out, it was right there; I didn't even leave where I entered the void lake.

I spend the rest of my dream time trying to think of locations that might make excellent hiding spots and visit as many of them as I can. First, I go to the mountains where my fears live, because hiding something where I'm least likely to look seems like a safe bet. I don't find anything. I search the memory of the house I grew up in, my shadow forest, even the small herb garden that I think symbolises my friendship with Kate.

Nothing.

When I try to climb my purple-leafed tree and finally start digging around the roots, I give up and admit that I may be losing my mind a little. I thought if this mysterious shore isn't hidden anywhere I wouldn't go, maybe it's hidden where I always am, but no. And now I've made a mess of my poor tree. I hug the trunk, apologise, and will the soil around the roots back to the way it was before I assaulted it.

I guess I'm just not meant to find the wider dreamscape, which is fair enough. That, or there's nothing to find in the first place, at least not through anyone's personal dreamscape. Maybe the tea Kate made wasn't a map but more like a portal or something like that.

Disappointed, I accept defeat. There's nothing else I can think to try, so all I can do is drop it.

The next week passes in a blur. I'm determined to be a good student and to impress Zeru with something, anything. I practice as much as I can every day, with zero results. It would be disheartening if I had time to dwell on it.

The last time I was this busy with my photography, I was still a student. I went over the pictures I took of Poppy and Sorcha's family and send them the best ones. I took notes for my shoot with Anton and Saif; I want them to love my work so they recommend me to everyone they know, sure, but they've been so kind letting me use their garden and their library that the least I can do is a fantastic job with their portraits. To no one's surprise, I can't find any examples of vampire photos. I didn't seriously expect to find something, but I *was* curious how many studios or individual photography artists have taken the fake-fangs-and-blood approach just to hop on the craze. It's surprisingly few. So, my website *will* stand out to everyone, Veiled and non-Veiled alike. That's not a problem, though. It's common sense to have a unique selling point.

What is a slight problem, however, is how incredibly unprepared I am for my little business to progress. I've spent most of this week setting up my website, trying to understand technology, designing a business card for myself and ordering a trial batch of one hundred, and worrying repeatedly that I've messed it all up somehow. I've printed another one hundred copies of the model release form, too, even though there's no way I'll need that many in one go and can print more whenever I need them.

By the time I'm ready for my next lesson with Zeru, I've done more business admin than magic practice, and I'm still not completely happy with everything. I paid extra for the shipping on my business cards just so I'd have them ready today. My website looks empty since I only used three examples so far—one portrait of Poppy and Sorcha each, and one of them both together—but it's getting there.

And then, I got carried away and created a Friendspace group to match my website. I regretted it almost right away since most of my business will come from recommendations, but it's up now and not doing any harm. Besides, it's as empty as my website.

If the Dreamcatcher and the Mara have any issue with all this progress, they can argue with Poppy and Sorcha about it, too. I have their full permission, and we even agreed on which pictures to showcase on my website together. They are my Friendspace group's first followers, and already left a recommendation.

I gave Anton the link to my website and the group when I arrived so he can have a look while I embarrass myself with Zeru, and then I made my way into his garden.

I'm stretching my back and wrists when the air behind me shifts.

'Hello, Esta. Have you recovered?' Zeru asks.

I turn to smile at them and nod. 'I've practiced a little, too. Don't worry, I haven't pushed myself too far.' Honestly, I'm starting to know my limits quite well now.

'I'm glad to hear it.'

It occurs to me that Zeru wears the same loose clothes as every other time I've seen them. They must be there just for my comfort so I don't have to see them naked—I don't imagine they need clothes when they're in their natural form, but I haven't asked. They're not naked now, anyway. Their feet are bare, but the material covering their arms, legs, and torso looks light and billows a little in the breeze, yet I can't see any stitching or hems as such. I think it's one piece, like a massive, airy poncho. I don't look too closely; I've stared at enough Veiled lately, and it's not like their fashion choices are any of my concern. Maybe they've used magic to only appear clothed?

'I still haven't been able to do anything, though,' I admit. 'But I feel good about today. I'll have more time to practice next week, too.'

Unless I'm suddenly inundated with photography jobs. That'd be a nice problem to have. My Friendspace group has been up for a few days now and as far as I can tell, no one except Poppy and Sorcha knows it's there, but I've been too much of a coward to share it anywhere yet. Not until I'm sure that I'm happy with it.

'Let us pick up where we left off last week,' Zeru says. 'Do you remember the three ways to call our magic?'

Photography aside, I've thought about little else all week.

'Subconscious will, emotionally charged outburst, and conscious effort,' I say.

'Very good. I want to see if I can help you call on your magic today. Stand here with me.'

My heart races when I stand closer to them. I tried to call my magic alone all week with no success, but it sounds like Zeru will do more than advise me.

'This is a simple test,' they say, 'to see if your magic responds to mine. Since you have already used magic in self-defence, I am confident we will see some results this way.'

I gulp and nod. 'What do I need to do?'

'Are you comfortable taking my hands?'

I hold both of mine out, and Zeru takes them. Their skin is soft, strangely smooth and slightly warm, like an early-summer breeze.

'Focus on my magic, if you can, and allow yourself to let go. Do not be alarmed if your blood begins to race or your heart rate increases; those may be signs that your magic is responding to mine.'

I brace myself. A small storm picks up around us before I can really prepare myself, and I gasp. It's not difficult to relax into this; it feels wonderful.

I don't feel anything within myself, though. I didn't ask what happens if my magic doesn't respond, but I think I know the answer: If Zeru can't draw it out with their own, what hope do I have? Maybe it's proof that I need to be in danger first. Maybe I can only ever use it in self-defence as a knee-jerk reaction. It wouldn't be my first choice.

'Relax, Esta,' they say. 'It will be easier if you let go.'

That's easier said than done while they look into my eyes. I feel too awkward looking straight ahead at their chest, but I'm not sure where else to focus, so I close my eyes. I allow myself to feel the wind against my skin, tousling my hair and ruffling my clothes. Some branches creak nearby, although this storm isn't that strong.

There's a tingling in my arms, as if it's coming from inside my veins. I try not to get too excited; it could be nothing.

'Do you feel anything?' Zeru asks.

'I do, but I don't know if it's related. It's like mild electricity in my limbs.' The current spreads from my core into my legs. It flows through my arms into my chest and makes my heart soar.

'Very good, Esta. This electricity you speak of is your magic.'

My heart skips a beat. My *magic*! I can *feel* it, just like that!

'Direct it to flow towards your palms. Collect it there, if you can.'

I picture the tingling move from everywhere towards my hands at the same time. My palms begin to itch; I resist the urge to scratch. Zeru guides my hands away from theirs and points them in front of me.

'Now, command it to leave your palms in a burst. Keep your hands open—that's it. Push the magic away from you. Imagine you can see it, if it helps.'

I picture a massive air blade cutting the grass ahead of us in a long sweep, a wall of invisible magic rushing over the lawn until it dissipates several metres ahead of us.

Instead, the sudden force of my magic rushing out of my palms shoves me backwards. I stumble and fall onto my butt, but I don't care. I used magic—*without* needing to be in mortal danger first.

An excited giggle escapes me as I get back to my feet. 'Why didn't we try that first?'

Zeru smiles at me. I think they look proud. 'Because it's important that you can use your magic without my interference. Now that we know you can—'

Zeru stills even more than usual. I freeze, too, because I've never seen the sylph like this before: interrupted; startled.

Worried.

'Allow me to speak for you, Esta,' Zeru says.

I frown. 'What do you—'

Three sylphs step out of the air and into Anton's garden. Their faces and postures are passive, but I get the feeling they haven't come to congratulate me.

'Explain yourself,' the sylph in the middle says. 'What

happened here?'

I glance around the garden, unsure what they're on about. We haven't exactly destroyed the lawn, and the worst the shrubs have suffered is a few fallen leaves. But then something clicks, and I remember what Zeru said before:

Not all sylphs agree that I should be allowed to learn magic.

'I have conducted a standard test with Esta,' Zeru says, their voice calm and their posture as passive as the newcomers'. 'I wanted to determine the potential of her skill, as we have done many times before.'

'In very different situations, Zeru,' the sylph says. I get the feeling they're the one in charge while the other two are merely here for backup. 'Intervention such as this is not necessary here.'

I feel like I should justify myself somehow, defend my right to learn, but I stay silent. Zeru asked to speak for me, and I trust that they know a lot more about this than I do. If nothing else, they seem to know these other sylphs and will know how to talk to them.

I should probably be grateful they're having this conversation where I can hear it, too. There's nothing stopping them from arguing on the breeze or in their library where I can't follow.

'Esta is unable to use considerable amounts of magic,' Zeru says. 'There is no harm in teaching her. Or do we no longer teach the willing?'

The other sylph strides towards Zeru. The breeze increases with their step; something tells me that means they're angry.

'Not like this, and not here. That she was able to do this

much should prove to you that our fears are valid.'

They and Zeru glance at the general area where I unleashed my magic, though I don't see any sign that I did anything to it. The slight thrum in my butt is better proof that anything happened, though I don't particularly want them staring at that for confirmation.

'If you felt this much, you will also know how little she used,' Zeru says. 'You know that my intervention was necessary for even so little.'

'We felt its unnatural touch, yes,' the sylph shoots back. 'You said it would take her months to do half this much. Do you see now how quickly she is progressing? Do you not see it is too fast?'

I clear my throat and step out from behind Zeru. 'I really barely did anything. I would hardly call this too fast.'

The sylph shakes their head at me. 'You comment on issues you don't understand, human. This magic was not meant for you.'

Part of me wants to get angry, but instead, all I feel is sad. They are right, and I know it.

'Amphorn's concerns are valid, Esta,' Zeru says, and I feel like they've slapped me. 'However, I believe they are also unnecessary. If Esta truly isn't meant to have this magic, our lessons will ultimately be futile. However, since she can evidently use some, there must be a reason.'

'And what if that reason is to start another war?' A pale imitation of a smirk twists Amphorn's otherwise passive face. 'Or was your last failed experiment not enough of a lesson to you?'

Zeru stills again. Thunder rumbles overhead and stops as soon as it's begun.

They collect themself and say, 'As you said yourself, this is an entirely different situation. Esta has no desire to destroy us.'

'We only have your word for that,' Amphorn says. They turn to me. 'We have come to issue you a final warning, human: Stop learning powers you were never meant to have, or we will take said powers from you.'

Before I can even begin to think of a counterargument that won't make me look worse in their eyes, they are gone.

I look at Zeru. 'I *don't* want to start another war. You believe me, don't you?'

Zeru doesn't move for several seconds, then they nod. 'I do.'

My shoulders slump in relief. I don't know what Zeru will do about my lesson, but I'd hate for them to think that I want to hurt anyone.

'I'm sure Amphorn is just being mean to you, too,' I say. 'Whatever you did in the last war, I'm sure you did whatever you thought was right.'

A slight smile appears on their lips. 'Thank you; although, that is not what they meant. I was not here when humans first fought the Veiled.'

Somehow, I doubt they mean here, in Eastport, but I don't ask. If they wanted me to know more, they'd have volunteered the information. Whatever happened, it seems to be a source of regret for Zeru. I can leave it be.

'You have made good progress today,' Zeru says. I smile at

their kind words; it's just what I needed to hear after everything Amphorn threw at me. 'I believe it is best if we end our lesson here and if you don't practice until our next lesson in one week.'

My smile grows wider. 'You mean you'll still teach me? After what they just said?'

I already got Mischief in trouble. I would hate to cause problems for Zeru, too.

'Yes. Give me time to talk to them. If we have not reached a satisfying conclusion in one week, I will let you know, and you will not need to come here.'

'Thank you.' I bite my lip and glance up at Zeru. 'You won't get in trouble because of this, right?'

They pause for too long. I'm about to object, say I don't need lessons after all, I'll be fine, but Zeru says:

'I thank you for your concern, but my mind is made up. I once had the chance to teach humans magic, and I hid from it. This opportunity is as much for me to teach you something I believe you're meant to have as it is a chance for me to redeem myself.'

My heart skips a beat. 'I thought I'm *not* meant to have this? Isn't that the main issue?'

'Many believe this to be the truth, for good reason. You must be aware that the Veiled are watching you, at least to some degree? Many are worried about the consequences your very knowledge of their existence might force on them. Amphorn and those who fear like they do believe that your magic being freed is a perversion of the natural order, that it will set Chaos in motion. They are too afraid we can't weather

164

the storm you might bring to consider the good you might do instead.'

I shiver. When they put it like this, how can I argue? I don't know what effects my using this magic might have, but I do know it's nothing but a leftover from another life.

'How can you be so sure of the opposite, then?' I ask. 'How do you know I won't do what they're afraid of?'

I'd never start a war or even a minor argument on purpose, but what if it slips out by accident? What if me pushing Chiara down the stairs has set worse things in motion that I don't know about?

'Because one thing is certain: You are more than a small light in a large universe. None of us can deny you have power. Think about the first time you used magic: You didn't know you had it, and you still managed to catch a vampire off guard. No mean feat, wouldn't you say? I would rather teach you control and responsibility. Of course, that's assuming your magic has any room to grow at all. You are incapable of doing any real damage right now. Regardless of your intentions and your ability, you may invite Chaos to this world, but consider that Chaos is necessary for progress. Change is often painful. It is not always negative, however.'

I'm not sure how to respond. What if it hadn't been Chiara that time? What if I'd lost my patience with another human? Would they have shrugged off a fall down the stairs like she did? A human would have broken something. A human could easily have been injured worse.

'And what if it does grow?' I ask, my voice small. 'What if I accidentally call a hurricane and destroy someone's house?'

That Zeru stays quiet again for a moment tells me everything I need to know: There's a chance. It may be small, even severely unlikely, but it's there. How can I take the risk?

'Trust my guidance, Esta. I believe it's no coincidence that you have acquired this magic in this life. I would teach you how to use it wisely so you might prove those who are afraid of you wrong.'

I suppose I do have a week to think about it, though I'm not looking forward to it. I trust Zeru. They are a good teacher, and so is Kate. Neither would let me do something stupid, but they can't always be there. I also know that my magic hasn't just leaked out of me in some normal everyday situation, though. As long as no one tries to kill me—as long as I don't have any reason to panic—it'll be fine. Even then, I panicked somewhat when Leverett's fangs touched my neck, and my magic didn't react. Because I trust him and knew I was in no real danger? Or perhaps I've exhausted my supply of emergency gusts.

'Alright,' I say. 'I do trust you. Thank you.'

Zeru and I go our separate ways, but as I walk towards Anton and Saif's mansion and my next photoshoot, I keep wondering if Amphorn isn't right.

CHAPTER
SEVENTEEN

'How did your lesson go today, my dear?' Anton asks as he leads me towards wherever Saif is waiting for us.

I force a smile, not wanting to get into the whole thing with Amphorn. 'It was fine. Sorry if we knocked some leaves off your plants.'

Gods, I really hope I haven't destroyed some rare flowers Anton has carefully cultivated. I didn't do any actual damage, but if I had, I'm not convinced I could pay for it. I can just see Anton spending big on some exotic plants just because he likes them.

He looks over his shoulder at me. 'But you did knock some leaves off?'

'Yeah. I did.' My smile still feels forced. I don't particularly want to talk about it, which isn't fair, given that I managed to use my magic. I didn't think it would come with a threat.

'Oh, darling, we're so happy for you. Is that why those other Veiled showed up? I saw them from the window.'

My smile grows a little more earnest; I feel somewhat reassured knowing that Anton is keeping an eye on me. Like a parent staying up until their child has returned home safe. So, if nothing else, those sylphs probably wouldn't get away with attacking me while I'm here.

It seems I was also correct in my assumption that Anton would totally spy on my lesson from a window.

'Yes, that's why.' I try not to sigh. 'Tell me about what you have in mind for this shoot. Have you and Saif had a think about what you want?'

I know they said it'd be completely up to me, but in my experience, people absolutely have an idea. I doubt Anton, being the creative force of nature that he is, hasn't thought about it.

'We do have a few ideas, my dear. Come, just in here.'

I follow him into a room on the first floor, grateful that he doesn't push for more details on those sylphs or my progress. Anton can read a room better than anyone; that doesn't mean he won't ask about it once he can sense I'm no longer on edge, though.

My excitement returns when Saif and I greet each other. This seems to be another sitting room; smaller than the one I've seen before, but still a good bit bigger than my bedroom. The colours in here are a little more muted: light walls, cream sofas, light wood panelling and furniture. An ornate rug lies under a coffee table, and long light-green curtains adorn the two large windows.

'This'll work well,' I say as I let my eyes wander. I can pose them along the wall, maybe on the sofa, just opposite the window for optimal light. 'Where do you want to start?'

'Would you prefer Anton to talk you through his vision

before we begin?' Saif asks.

I nod. 'I can plan better that way. Are there any rooms that are off limits? How would you feel about taking a few pictures outside?'

I remember a beautiful gazebo behind the house, a small fountain, even a maze. I've stayed away from that side of the mansion out of worry Zeru and I might actually break something; I'd rather rustle a bush than risk destroying a small structure. I hope the flowers are still in bloom—it was so colourful when Anton held his party. So much potential for absolutely wonderful images.

'Ah, yes, that would be fine,' Anton says. 'Why don't we take a few in here to warm up and then move outside?'

Saif gives him a look, but Anton doesn't say anything more. It sounds like he's holding back, but I won't push him. It does seem out of character for him, though.

'No problem,' I say. 'Why don't you sit on the sofa together?'

I start to pose them, and we all easily melt into the process. Anton and Saif look adorable like this: smiling together and at each other, holding hands, an unmistakable air of familiarity and trust between them.

'How long have you been married?' I ask as we make our way down into the garden.

Ahead of me, Anton and Saif smile at each other. 'Two hundred years this year,' Anton says.

'These images are an anniversary gift, of sorts,' Saif says.

Now my smile is real. 'Congratulations.' I won't charge them for these, though if I say so now, Anton might argue. I'd much rather make it a surprise.

But damn, that's a long time. So much longer than Leverett and I can be together. I shake my head at myself; this is not the time to dwell on my mortality.

'What's your favourite part of the garden?' I ask. 'Is there anything you bought or designed together?'

'Do you remember the large gazebo at the back?' Anton asks.

I nod. It's the one I thought of earlier, though I remember they have a smaller one inside the maze.

'We bought it for our wedding.' Anton turns around to look at me. 'We had the ceremony inside the gazebo.'

'Right, then let's take a few images in there, if that's alright?' A place so emotionally valuable to them would make a great background.

Or I thought it would, anyway. We do take a few nice photos inside, the sun bright and the moving shade from the leaves overhead, but Anton still seems distracted.

'Would you like to go through the ones we've taken?' I offer, hoping it'll tickle out of him what he really wants to suggest.

We sit in the gazebo together, and Anton makes cooing sounds at every other photo. Saif regards them with quiet love, too.

'Oh, Esta, darling, these are wonderful,' Anton says. 'Thank you.'

I wave him off. The beautiful garden and natural light did a lot of the heavy lifting.

'Is there anything else you'd like?' I ask.

I was half expecting Anton to ask for some delicate private moments, but now I'm here, I can't see him asking for it. I hope he has something, though. It doesn't feel right that I've only been here a short time and feel like we're as good as done. I should have more ideas. I saw some very sweet and romantic couple shots during my research phase this week, but I don't know how to ask them for any of that. How do I ask them to cuddle on a sofa? To be adorable and lovey-dovey with each other? I don't know what they're like in their everyday life. Maybe that's just not something they do; if that's the case, it'd be awkward to suggest it for this shoot, and it wouldn't represent them very well. I'd hate for them to take an image just to be nice and then feel weird about it every time they see it.

'There is one thing we were wondering,' Saif starts.

Anton immediately holds up his hands. 'Please don't feel you can't say no, my dear! We would never expect you to do this if you're uncomfortable.'

'O…kay?' Maybe I should be just a little worried. 'What is it?'

'In all our years together, we haven't had one portrait of us as vampires,' Anton explains. 'Of course, you understand this isn't something you can just ask any photographer to do. We couldn't keep our fangs in each other long enough for a painting without it being uncomfortable for both of us, and while we could fake it for the sake of an image, we'd know it's a lie.'

I swallow. 'You… want me to photograph you biting each other?'

'Only if you're comfortable, Esta Anderson.'

Am I comfortable with this? It's not like they're asking me to photograph them having sex, but it's still a terribly intimate and personal moment. I can't call myself a Veiled Pride photographer if I say no, though. Really, this is no different to Poppy and Sorcha letting out their wings, just with fewer sparkles and more blood. If I want to do this properly, then that'll need to be part of it, too, or my unique selling point is a lie.

Anton waves the idea away. 'We've made you uncomfortable. Please, forget we brought it up.'

I shake my head. 'No, no, not at all. I just didn't expect it. Honestly, sooner or later I'll probably be asked for this anyway. I'd rather it's with you two.'

Well now, that just sounds dodgy. I do mean it, though. If I get up close and personal with a vampire couple, I'd prefer it to be Anton and Saif over some strangers.

Anton smiles and takes my hand. 'Are you sure, Esta?'

I return his smile and nod. 'Of course. I'm sad it took you two hundred years to get something like this.'

'Nearly three hundred,' Saif says with a smile for his husband. 'For a century we'd said we didn't need to get married to be happy, and then one day Anton just proposed.'

Anton giggles. 'It took me by surprise, too, don't you know? I didn't have anything to give him when I asked. It just slipped out.'

I hope we're still talking about the question. I chuckle and wave my camera at them.

'Where would you like to take these?' I ask.

'We have a small winter garden at the far end of the house,' Anton says. 'We don't have much furniture inside, truth be told, as we don't use the space much at this time of year, but you should have excellent light.'

I nod and let them lead me there. I didn't notice it during the party despite the all-around, ground-to-ceiling windows, but then we didn't come this way. I was too fascinated with all the Veiled all around me.

Anton wasn't kidding. There's a small seating set that consists of one round table and four chairs, and a large cream sofa with one pot of large green plants to each side stands along the back wall. The ceiling is glass, too. It's nice in here, but it certainly doesn't look used.

'I'll have some flowers planted in a month or two, ready for the colder months when nothing grows outside,' Anton says. 'Is the light good enough?'

I smile and nod, wondering what on Earth I'm going to do. I decide it's best to just ask.

'How would you... Do you have a favourite... How do you want to do this?'

I blush. This feels terribly unprofessional, but I've never asked two vampires how they usually bite each other before, or if they like to sit a certain way for it.

'We will keep it family friendly, of course!' Anton says. I wonder at that but won't question it. 'I will bite Saif's wrist, and he will bite my neck.'

I nod like that's totally what I expected. 'Alright. Uh... Go ahead.'

I blush harder still when, a few moments later and with my

173

subjects sitting on the sofa, Anton sinks his fangs into Saif's wrist and a tiny moan escapes him. It doesn't feel sexual, though—it's actually kinda sweet. Like anyone kissing their lover's hand.

I still feel awkward as hell, though, as I take the pictures. I don't know what to zoom in on.

And I try *really* hard not to make eye contact with Saif. If I do, even for a second, our friendship will be forever ruined. Turns out, no amount of research this week could have prepared me for this.

'Can you, uhm, get a little closer to each other?'

Anton pulls back, a thin trail of blood running down his chin. I quickly sneak a cheeky picture of his smile as he looks at Saif like this. It's nice, but something's missing, and I can't put my finger on what.

'Let's swap,' Anton suggests, and Saif nods.

But the moment Saif leans in for Anton's neck, I can see how difficult this is going to be. Either way, someone's neck or someone's head is going to be in the way. It'll be near impossible to pose them in a way I get both men into the frame, or even just their faces.

I'm too far out of my depth here. I really don't want to mess up their shoot. As long as I have a few pictures I can show them, it'll be fine. We don't need to go over all the bad ones.

Even if that's most of them.

I try to get around them to snap a few pictures from different angles, but it's difficult because there's a wall in the way. And a sofa. And my own inability to do this well.

And all that aside, there's the ease with which they bite each other. Not even a hint of difficulty. Definitely no panic. I'd be lying if I said my mind wasn't at least a little on jealousy when it's supposed to be focussing on work, but they look so... Fuck it, yes, they look good together. It's a sweet moment. Their love and respect for each other is obvious in such a gentle way. This is what I want with Leverett.

'Oh, Esta, darling, you look positively heartbroken!' Anton says.

I blush, shake my head, and quickly get back to shooting. I focus on Saif since Anton looks worried now, and— Gods, no, my eyes are burning. Why am I crying? Why now?

Saif extracts himself from Anton's neck, and Anton scoots over to pat the seat between them.

'Come here, my dear. Tell us what's wrong.'

'Perhaps we shouldn't have asked for this, my love,' Saif says. 'Esta can't have seen many vampires bite each other. We're sorry if this was overwhelming.'

I vehemently shake my head and let Anton take my hand.

'It's not you, or this,' I say. 'It's—'

How do I explain? *Should* I? I'm supposed to be doing a photoshoot for a client; if I vent about my love life, it would be beyond unprofessional. Pretty sure it's too late to be worrying about that, though; they did call off the shoot because I started crying. And who better to understand than two vampires?

'Leverett talked to you about, erm... him biting me, right?'

'Yes.' Anton squeezes my hand. 'Why don't you two talk while I make Esta a tea?'

I'm about to object, but Anton isn't interested. He's out the door before I can say anything.

I sigh and sink back against the sofa. 'I'm sorry. I'm usually more professional than this.'

Saif gives me a wise smile not unlike Kate's. 'I'm relieved we didn't make you uncomfortable. How long ago is it now that you've learned of us Veiled?'

I quickly do the maths. It was at the very start of my summer break, so it's not hard. 'Nearly two months ago.'

It doesn't feel that long ago. Because I stepped into my void lake at the beginning of July and it's now August, it still feels like it was only a month ago at most, but it's almost September. Just a little more and it'll be more than two months.

But Saif shakes his head. '*Only* two months, Esta Anderson. I believe you are a fast learner, but you need to acknowledge just how much you've learned in that time. Your old worldview, shattered and reassembled into something else entirely. My husband and I admire how well you seem to have adjusted, but that doesn't mean you aren't allowed to struggle. You fit well into our world; this is a credit to how open-minded you are. Remember the you from three months ago. Would she have let a vampire bite her and enjoyed it?'

I want to say yes, of course, but I imagine we both know that wouldn't be true. I didn't even know vampires existed three months ago. I don't know what I would have done if someone I don't know had approached me and kindly asked to bite me, even if I had proof they were a vampire and even if it had been an emergency. We're not talking about a stranger, though. We're talking about Leverett.

176

I sigh, because it's complicated. 'Probably not.'

Saif nods. 'You have suffered great trauma through Chiara's actions. Sharing your blood with the vampire you love is a beautiful thing, but you mustn't rush it. You will know when you are ready.'

I sigh and resist the urge to lean against Saif. 'It sounds like you're giving me The Talk.'

His quiet laugh makes me feel better. 'It's important you hear this from someone you trust than go out into the world and regret it.'

'You're doing better than my parents. They never gave me The Talk because, and I quote: "You had the internet. We figured you'd find everything yourself when you were ready."'

Arguably the worst parenting decision they ever made.

Anton returns and hands me a cup of Earl Grey. 'We told Leverett it might be too soon, you know, but he's an idiot in love. We remember what it's like in the early days. We know he wouldn't do anything stupid, and we know he didn't hurt you. He's not someone who would.'

I take a sip of my tea and thank him.

'It was me. I panicked.' I felt absolutely rotten about it before, but after hearing what Saif had to say, I actually feel better. I understood it as something deeply intimate, but if I follow his comparison to sex, then... what Chiara did... Maybe I should give myself more time. Maybe I will know when I'm ready. Or maybe I need therapy; not the first time I've wondered that.

'Take your time,' Saif says. 'Intimacy is better when it isn't rushed.'

Anton takes Saif's hand and gazes at him. 'You will only share your first bite with another vampire once, my dear. Take your time. He understands.'

I smile. 'Thank you. Would you like to look through some of the photos before I leave?'

I appreciate everything they've said and how lovely they've been, but I mustn't forget why I'm here. Hopefully, there's something useful amidst the pictures I took.

But my heart drops as I flick through the images, trying to find something I'm happy with. There are one or two nice ones outside, by the gazebo where they got married. Anton's smile with blood running down his chin is alright, but Saif isn't in it. Everything we took in the first room is boring and generic.

'Send us your favourites, my dear. We will take it from there.'

Anton doesn't sound disappointed, but he must be. His standards are so high, and today's images are not up to them. He's too sweet to complain, though, as is Saif.

I thank him again for the tea, and then I excuse myself. The air is heavy as I walk back to my car, almost suffocating. It's still hot outside, and everyone is ready for the heatwave to break. Judging by the dark clouds rolling over, it won't be long. I just hope it can wait until I'm home.

I close the car door with a heavy sigh and deflate into the seat. Due to Anton's connections, this was the most important photoshoot I could have had, and I've blown it. I'm sure they'll still like some of the photos, but I know I could have done better. Why couldn't I save my unprofessionalism for a much smaller client? I sigh again. That wouldn't have been good, either; no one deserves bad photos, and especially not when they're such vulnerable ones.

I quickly check my phone to see if I've missed anything. My heart leaps when I see I have a notification from my photography group—my first comment besides Poppy's review. Excited, I open it.

My heart immediately drops again.

`'Leave Veiled business to the Veiled, human. Know your place.'`

My heart pounding, I quickly delete it. I knew this would happen, but so soon? When I haven't even shared the page yet? I've no doubts whatsoever that some Veiled must have searched for me online out of curiosity. It makes sense they'd find my Friendspace group sooner or later. But it's really not what I want to see today.

After today's shoot, though, I have no counter argument, and it takes me a few minutes before I feel steady enough to start the car.

CHAPTER
EIGHTEEN

Bee is busy with a customer when I arrive, so I busy myself with the bookshelves.

I feel a little better after my disaster shoot yesterday. Anton and Saif spoke some sense, or rather some patience, into me, and I'm determined to make this week better. The images I took for Anton and Saif weren't *all* bad, either, just most of them. I have maybe three or four alright ones, which isn't great, but it's what happened. It's not nothing, anyway.

In truth, I haven't gone over all the images I took again. I've been too embarrassed to face them and haven't even shown Bonnie; not that I would show her the more intimate ones. Pretty sure that's a line I shouldn't cross.

'Hello again!' Bee says, and I jump a little. 'Sorry, I didn't mean to scare you. See something you like?'

I roam over the book spines, but nothing jumps out. I was only killing time with it, and then I got caught up in my regret.

'No, just browsing. I've got something for you.' I take out a pack of twenty business cards I set aside for Bee. 'They just arrived late last week. You said you could place them on your counter, so here I am.'

Bee gasps and takes them, turning one over in their hand and reading the info on it: my website, my photography group, and an email address I connected to the website. I'm too introverted to put my phone number on there. And what if the next threat is over the phone? I wouldn't know how to respond, so I'd rather not. I know I'll end up meeting any client anyway, but my phone number still feels too private, even if it is for my business.

'Oh wow, look at these! They look great!' Bee turns it back over to admire the image on the front: Sorcha's sparkling fairy wings. To the non-initiated, it'll just look like a great Photoshop creation, but I'm hoping that Veiled will see them for the real thing. 'Did you take this?'

I grin. After yesterday's failed shoot, Bee's reaction is a balm on my soul. 'I did.'

'Wow. This is amazing. Come with me.'

I follow them to the counter, where they rummage around a hidden shelf and pull out a small wooden holder. They place it in front of the counter and carefully put my business cards inside.

'How's that?' they ask.

I well up a little. That's my business cards, for my tiny but hopefully growing photography business. In a shop. Like a pro.

I slowly nod first at the cards, then at Bee. 'Looks great, doesn't it?'

'Aww, hey. Come here.' Bee hugs me, and I'm happy to let them. I'm not usually much of a hugger, but Bee has this comforting energy I don't mind leaning into, much like Anton and Saif. Their shop is a safe space, after all; I just didn't realise that includes emotional customers. 'They look wonderful, Esta. I'll be handing one to everyone I think would like one.' They wink at me. 'And I'll be following your group. Can't wait to see what you do.'

'Thank you,' I say. 'I needed that.'

I owe Anton and Saif an apology, and I absolutely owe them another shoot. Now that I've got my business cards on display, it's important I get my shit together, and not leaving yesterday's shoot as it currently stands is part of that.

'Since I'm here…' My eyes flick to the sign at the counter advertising tarot readings. 'Do I need to book you to do a reading?'

'It helps, but we're not too busy with them yet. My apprentice is doing one right now, but she's free after that! Want one then?'

I nod. 'Yes please.' I kinda hoped Bee would do the reading, but their apprentice is probably that young woman who was here last time, and she seemed nice. Not that we spoke much, or at all.

Maybe it's silly, but after the photoshoot, that message that awaited me afterwards, and the sylphs' warning, I'd feel a lot better to be told I'm not about to unleash destruction upon the world. I could do a reading myself, but I remember what Kate said about not doing it when I'm too emotional, and I haven't practiced that much. I'd rather have someone unbiased do this.

I browse the shop without really looking for anything while

Bee charges a customer. I listen up when I hear:

'Oh, and take one of these! She's an excellent new photographer in the area, I think you'll like her work.'

I swear I can hear their wink.

My heart flutters, and I turn around with a shy smile. They're talking to a young man with long hair and the bushiest beard I've ever seen. At least, he looks like a young man. He could be a thousand-year-old chaos goblin.

He gives the card a once-over and nods more to himself than to Bee. 'Alright. Thanks.'

He leaves, and this time Bee winks at me for real. 'See? They'll be flying off the counter.' They wave me over and whisper, 'Werewolf,' when I'm close enough.

'Thank you,' I whisper back.

Well, now I *really* need to get my shit together. I know nothing about werewolves. Who knows what kind of pictures he might want? I cannot mess this up again. It would be my first "real" shoot—the first job with a stranger who didn't book me just because he knows me. My first organic client. Unless he never actually contacts me, that is. That's a possibility.

Bee's apprentice comes through the hanging curtain followed by a middle-aged man. She gives me a shy smile and waves.

'Do you mind doing another reading?' Bee asks.

'Alright.' She looks at her client. 'I'll see you in one month, Mr Peterson.'

Mr Peterson shakes her hand with a lot more energy than the young woman seems to have in her entire body and excuses himself.

'Did it go alright?' Bee asks.

'Yes. I'm getting used to it now, and he's patient with me.' She turns to me. 'You want a reading, too?'

I nod. 'If it's not too much trouble.'

She seems so fragile, I wonder if Mr Peterson's handshake bruised her. Her smile is warm, but she doesn't look confident, at least not completely.

'You're in good hands,' Bee says. 'Jirina is a natural, you'll see.' They wink again and hurry off to help another customer.

'Follow me,' Jirina says. Her demeanour has changed now her last client has left. She seems a little more at ease as she leads me into the back. 'Is this your first reading?'

I blush but remember that it's not odd to admit it here. 'From someone else, yes. I have my own deck, but I haven't practiced too much.' Thank the gods that Kate can't hear me.

'I'm glad,' she says. 'Then I won't need to explain too much. Yesterday I had a client who only wanted a reading to tell me how wrong I am, I think.'

My heart drops for her. I bet she deals with confrontation in a similar way to how I do, which is to say badly.

'Take your time,' I said. 'I'm not going anywhere.'

I mean, technically I should go over the photos I took yesterday, but I'm still working my way up to that. I'll feel a lot better about it after this reading, I'm sure.

Jirina inclines her head and nods to the round table and chairs. 'Thank you. Please, have a seat.' She pulls a deck off a shelf on the wall. 'Is this deck alright? It's my favourite. I can read a little easier with this one.'

I smile when I recognise the images. 'I have the same one. It's so beautiful.'

Her smile grows. 'Are you ready?' I nod. 'What do you want to know?'

Oh, right. I should have seen that coming, but I haven't got one specific question prepared.

'What will happen if I— No, wait.' I was going to ask what'll happen if I keep building my business, but that's too specific. I'm afraid that she'll draw something I won't like, and it'll get into my head. I have just three more weeks left before I'm back at work, so I decide to focus on that. It's a nice little window. Nothing too life-altering can happen in three weeks, unless I find another void lake to step in. 'What should I know about the next three weeks?'

Jirina nods and shuffles the cards. I'm relieved to see that she's as unskilled at it as I am—if it's good enough for her, it's good enough for my own home readings.

After around thirty seconds, she splits the deck by letting the cards fall onto the table in their pile. They separate just once.

'Looks like we have two cards. This one'—she takes the one from the middle, where the deck split—'and this one.' She takes the one from the top and flips the first one over. It's Death, my favourite.

'Oh, please, don't be alarmed,' Jirina says quickly. 'It's not as bad as you might think.'

I smile and hope it'll help her relax. 'I actually find this reassuring. I'm aiming for big change.'

Her shoulders fall back. 'I'm so glad! It looks like you'll have just that. Something new will be born from something that will pass.'

I really hope this is related to my photography, that I can quit my gallery job to grow my business. One thing ends and another begins—that would fit beautifully.

With both of us reassured, Jirina turns over the second card. My heart sinks. It's The Tower.

'Oh, erm…' Jirinia gives me an apologetic glance like it's her fault. 'This likely fits into your first card. Maybe the thing that ends, uhm, won't end easily.'

I gulp. It's easy to be optimistic about the Death card. Rebirth is a good thing, if initially painful. But this? Hard to find the positives in utter disaster. Maybe—*maybe*—I go back to work and Marvin and I have a massive falling out? Maybe he makes sure I get fired for it. Maybe he's plotting my demise even now. Asshole; that sounds just like him.

And while I want to believe that, my gut isn't having it. Besides, I asked about the next three weeks. Marvin is just beyond that, so it's unlikely to have anything to do with work.

'Does it mean anything that they're both Major Arcana cards?' I ask. I'm sure Kate told me something about it, but I don't remember.

'The Major Arcana signifies important turning points in life. For both of your cards to be Major Arcana cards, a lot must be about to shift for you.' She gives me another apologetic smile. 'That doesn't have to be bad, though!'

I raise an eyebrow at The Tower.

'No, it's fine,' I say. 'I'm not too surprised big things are happening. I just hope it's nothing too unexpected, you know?'

The Dreamcatcher hasn't shown up to remind me of our agreement yet, so the two shoots I've done must have been fine. That doesn't mean my photography can't be heading towards disaster in other ways, though. It might not have anything at all to do with my business plans, though I'm not sure what I'd prefer: a storm coming for my photography...

Or Amphorn bringing a literal storm to me.

CHAPTER
NINETEEN

'How did your shoot go?' Leverett asks as I enter his shop and follow him upstairs.

I raise my eyebrows at his back. 'Anton hasn't told you anything?'

I figured they'd have caught up over it, whether Anton calls Leverett to update him or Leverett calls him, so I'm surprised they haven't discussed it at all. I'm surprised, but grateful.

Leverett looks at me over his shoulder. 'We don't have the same need to talk every day like humans do. He hasn't called me, and I haven't contacted him. To be frank, we've seen each other more times in the last few weeks than we've seen each other in decades.'

I follow him upstairs. That makes sense; even I'm terrible at catching up with most people, and I haven't known anyone for hundreds of years. I imagine I'd start to feel suffocated quite quickly if I had to catch up with any one person outside of my immediate family every day over several decades or even centuries. Gods, I don't call my parents every day *now*.

'I'm glad, to be honest,' I say with a sigh as I sink onto

Leverett's sofa. 'It wasn't great.'

He sits next to me and opens his arms in invitation. I take it and snuggle against him. Here, cuddled to him like this, I feel safe, like I can tell him anything and he'll make me feel better just by being here. At the very least, I won't feel worse.

'What happened?' he asks.

'I got in my head. It was so much easier with my first shoot. I don't want to say this wasn't fun, but...' I sigh again. 'I don't know. It just wasn't quite right.'

'And you've brought your camera tonight to get my opinion, or to use me as a test subject?'

I glance at my camera bag. 'Both? I don't know. I don't feel right asking for your input on the ones I've already taken. I don't know if Anton and Saif would be alright with it. They are, uh... private images.'

Leverett doesn't stop stroking my arm, but he does slow down. 'What did they ask you to do?'

Despite myself, I laugh. 'Okay, nothing like *that*. They just asked for photos of them biting each other. Honestly, they were so sweet together.' Like I hoped Leverett and I could be, though I don't say that. I'm putting enough pressure on myself over this as is. 'It was all me. Something just didn't click.'

'Can I help?'

I start to nod but change to a shrug. 'I don't really know. I thought maybe, if I took some photos of you, of *us*, maybe I'll figure out what's missing.'

He chuckles. 'What kind of photos do you want? Am I overdressed?'

I slide my hand under his shirt. 'I mean, if you want to take this off, I won't stop you.' He kisses my head with another chuckle, and I lean into him. 'I want my photography business to empower the Veiled. Not in any political sense, obviously, but on a personal level. I want my clients to be comfortable with everything we do. I want them to look at the results and see themselves, not the disguise they have to wear to fit in with us humans. It was so easy with Poppy and Sorcha: They have their sparkly wings and that otherworldly glow to everything, even their hair. What do vampires have?' I kiss his chest. 'No offense. It's just that fairies can make it so… visually obvious. Does that make sense?'

Leverett nods against my hair. 'I can see how it would be difficult to photograph fangs when they are buried in someone's neck. They would look like regular photos of two people kissing, wouldn't they?'

I sit up. 'Yes! That's part of it. You can turn to fog, which I'm guessing is specific to being a vampire, but a cloud of fog doesn't look very interesting.' I bite my lip. 'Or does it? Can you tell each other apart like that?'

'Only by scent,' Leverett says. 'Although, turned vampires appear slightly differently. Anton and I shift into black fog, but Saif's form would be more grey.'

That's not a huge difference, but it's something. Nothing I can use to ensure my next photography job won't be a disaster, though.

'And you're so quick when you change,' I say. 'It would be hard to get the timing just right.'

Honestly, *impossible* is a better word for it. Every time I've seen Leverett turn into fog, it was instant. I'm not convinced there's a camera in the world that could capture the exact fraction of a second their bodies change.

'What if we turned more slowly?' Leverett asks. 'Would that work?'

I lean back to stare at him. 'You can do that?'

'There is much you don't know, my love.'

My heart skips at hearing the term. Also, he may have just solved my problem.

'May I see? If you don't mind?'

Leverett kisses me, vanishes in front of my eyes…

And partially reforms a few feet away. His legs are gone, but his torso comes out of the fog, like he's hovering in mid-air hidden by clouds. It's not a hard line where his body begins but soft and faded, like any solid object behind fluffed cotton pads or tulle.

'I take it you're impressed?' he asks.

'I— How long can you hold that?'

'As long as you need me to.' He nods towards my camera bag. 'Do you want to see how it looks?'

Gods, do I *ever*. I jump up and retrieve my camera. I take a photo of him from every angle just to see how it comes out.

'What happens if I touch your, uh, fog? Do you feel it?'

He watches me with an amused smile. 'I do. It's as much a part of me as my solid body. I could grab you and throw you on the bed while shifted into fog, for example, and there'd be nothing you could do about it.'

Oh damn, I'm feeling warm suddenly. I smirk at him. 'And if I punched you?'

He laughs. 'You could try. It may not look like it, but we're more agile and flexible as fog. We can shift around you like air, but we have full control over ourselves. You won't be able to grab my legs like this, but I could kick yours out from under you.'

Alright, that's a little scary. I'm not scared of *him*, but I'm glad Chiara never tried that. I don't know if my magic would still have done anything to her. It might have dispersed her briefly, but she would just have re-collected herself. If she'd had any inkling whatsoever that I was about to use magic on her, I wouldn't have got away. Good thing it surprised me, too.

'Can we take one together?' I ask.

Leverett holds out his hand. I take it, and he pulls me towards him.

'What do you have in mind?' he asks, his eyes darkening.

I hold the camera as far away from me as my arm can reach and hope I won't drop it when I take the picture.

'Kiss me.'

His eyes go nearly entirely black. He cups my face with both hands, tilts my head up, and presses his lips to mine. I almost forget to press the shutter button.

It's really awkward to do this without a tripod or at least a shutter remote.

'Have a look,' Leverett whispers against my lips.

The camera was too close to us, courtesy of my short arms, but apart from that, the photo looks good—a little like I've gone to town with Photoshop, applying a cloud filter over just his lower body, though some of his fog moves up my body, too. Leverett, however, looks like he's materialising out of a cloud. I smile. I look so happy with him; his own smile while he kisses me is cute and hot at the same time.

This one image is so much better than anything I did with Anton and Saif. If they let me try again, we can have some fun playing around with their fog forms. I won't need to worry about not getting their fangs into the frames like this. They can be their vampire selves, and to everyone else, it'll just look like I'm decent at Photoshop.

I beam at Leverett. 'This is just what I wanted.'

I think back to the photo of Anton having a thin trail of blood on his chin while he smiles at Saif. If I could ask him to show his fang a little more, to partially shift into fog… It would have been a fantastic image.

'Do you want to try some more?' Leverett asks.

I kiss him. 'Thank you.'

His smile turns dark. 'Hold on to your camera.'

'What—'

All of Leverett shifts into fog. Within seconds, I find myself hanging in the air. A surprised gasp escapes me. It's *weird* to see nothing but a puff of smoke between me and the hardwood floor. I hear a soft laugh from near my ear and remind myself to relax. I'm not about to fall. Leverett has me.

I do kinda wish I could hold on to something. I'm entirely defenceless as Leverett carries me on invisible arms into his bedroom and lays me onto his bed. I'm relieved to have a solid surface under me again; I trust him completely, but it's a strange experience all the same.

A strange experience, and a thrilling one.

My breath catches when Leverett rematerialises straddling

me.

'Sit,' he orders, a husky growl in his voice. 'Wrap your legs around me. That's it. Hold on to me.'

I do everything he says.

'Stay very still.'

Unsure if it's safe to nod, I give him a look that hopefully says, *Do whatever you want with me.*

Leverett's arms close around me. His eyes blacken completely, and his fangs extend.

I'm about to become a puddle.

'I won't hurt you,' he says. 'I have extended my nails into claws. Don't wiggle too much or I might cut you by accident.'

And yet, I feel completely safe.

'You can stretch your arm to take a photo. I'll adjust if needed.'

I didn't even consider this when I was at Anton and Saif's. I knew vampires could grow their fangs and nails, but it didn't occur to me for one second to ask them to do this, and now I could kick myself. They could have held each other with their claws at full length, like they're cocooned in each other's potentially deadly embrace. It could have looked so good.

I carefully take a few photos from different angles— partially to experiment, partially because my grip on my camera isn't great so it slides around in my hand a little. I picture blood trickling from Leverett's lips, from two small puncture wounds in my neck. I picture nothing but love and trust in our eyes—that's not too difficult since that's how we're looking at each other now. But gods, that would be a great vampire Pride photo.

'Happy?' Leverett asks.

'I think so.'

He retracts his fangs and claws. His eyes stay dark. I fall back onto the bed once I'm sure I won't cut myself into ribbons, and Leverett lies down next to me. We go over the photos together. Again, I really wish I'd brought my tripod and shutter remote. My head is buzzing with photo potential, and that's just for Leverett and myself. It'll be so much easier when I photograph other people.

I give Leverett a shy smile. 'What do you think?'

He pulls me to him and kisses me. 'I think they're the most beautiful photos I've ever seen. Print your favourites for me?'

I break into a grin. 'I love them, too.' I kiss him once, twice. 'Thank you. This has helped immensely.'

He smiles. 'I'm glad I could help.'

I look over tonight's photos again, and something else strikes me:

Unlike all the photos I took of Anton and Saif, which were well lit, all of these are dark. It's evening approaching nighttime, and we didn't turn on any of the lights. The curtains are permanently drawn in Leverett's bedroom. My aperture was a tiny bit too small, so all the images have the tiniest blur to them, which gives them a slight ethereal quality. The shadows are longer. If Anton and Saif let me try again, I'll definitely suggest going over at night. I wonder what the light from a few candles might do? If I take a light or two, attach a soft box to one, I could enhance the shadows just so while giving everything a faint, smooth glow. My next shoot with them will be incredible.

And I have Leverett to thank for it.

I kiss him again. 'There's one thing I noticed when we went over these.'

'How beautiful you are?'

I blush. I don't know how to reply to compliments.

'How good they could have looked with bite marks.'

Leverett stills. His eyes had lightened a little, but they go black again now.

'I know, we don't need to rush,' I say. 'But I'd like to try. Please?'

A low growl comes from his chest at my last word. I didn't mean to effectively beg him to bite me, just to try something that didn't work before.

'Are you sure?' he asks.

I nod. 'Yes.' I feel good about it. No part of me is worried or scared. It'll be fine this time, I'm sure of it.

'Tell me if you want me to stop,' he whispers.

Leverett kisses me, first gently then more demanding. He lies over me, and for a moment, we just make out. He can probably smell when I'm, erm, relaxed enough, and I appreciate that he's taking his time. Now I just need to stop thinking about it and disappear in the moment with him. Leverett knows just how to touch me, how to stroke and kiss me, to make it easy.

He kisses his way down to my shoulder, makes a detour to my breasts, slowly licks up my neck. I moan. It'll be fine this time. I'm excited to finally find out what it's like.

But then his fangs touch my neck, and tears shoot into my eyes. I try to block out the memory of Chiara, but when I close my eyes, she's right there instead of him.

Leverett strokes my face. 'It's alright. Look at me.'

I stare into his beautiful eyes until they're all I can see. Chiara isn't here. I'm safe. Still, a tear runs down my cheek, and I hate myself for again letting one bad experience ruin what Leverett and I might have had.

He strokes my tear away. 'Are you feeling better?'

I nod. 'Yes. Thank you. Sorry.'

Leverett rolls onto his side and pulls me into his arms. 'Don't be.' He strokes my hair, over and over again, and slowly my breathing steadies and my heart calms. I will defeat this. One day, he will bite me, and I will enjoy it.

But I guess tonight is not that night, and I fall asleep in his arms more disappointed than I care to admit.

CHAPTER TWENTY

It's ridiculous and unfair that, so close to the end of my summer break, I feel like I need a break. But the sun is warm, the breeze is wonderful, and the smell of sausages fills our garden, so I'll take today off from everything, thank you. No angry Veiled. No failing at magic practice. Not one bit of negativity at all. Just friends and barbecue.

'Can you help me carry the rest of the meat out?' Bonnie asks Sunny.

'Of course!' Sunny sing-songs, gives Lady's head a quick affectionate scratch, then follows Bonnie into the house.

Head scratches aside, our rottweiler watches the BBQ like it's the most precious treasure in her life.

I sit back with a relaxed sigh and with both eyes firmly on my dog. I need this. I'd like to think I've earned it.

'Thank you for coming,' I say to Leverett.

He sits next to me on the low wall halfway up our garden and puts an arm around me.

'Social gatherings are not my natural environment.' He smiles. 'But this is nice. It's not often I get to relax with friends.'

I kiss him, closing my eyes for a second. Lady whines at the barbecue and licks her lips. Usually, she's well behaved around food, but she deserves a breather, too, and I think she knows it. I've taken the brunt of the attacks, but my dog and my sister have put up with a lot, too. Today is for all of us.

'I feel bad that I barely know Sunny,' I admit. 'She and Bonnie have been dating for weeks now and I've barely talked to her. I'm excited to get to know her better.'

Because, as bad as that sounds, all I really know about her is that she's a mermaid and a diving instructor. I don't even know if that's her full-time job. Bonnie has been so busy with her apprenticeship, and when she and Sunny have been out together, they've gone elsewhere. It hasn't left us many opportunities to get to know each other. So, today is like a double date without any of the pressure or hassle of leaving the house, at least not for me and Bonnie. I know we're both wondering if she and Leverett will get along, and we're all a little tense about not mentioning the Veiled. With a mermaid and a vampire in our garden and making up half the people here, we'll have to be extra careful not to slip up.

Not that there are any neighbours close enough in their own gardens to overhear anything we might say.

There are little things we've done to make the day more enjoyable for Sunny and Leverett. We've set up a paddling pool so Sunny can sit in water if she wants, and Leverett has brought a blood bag and emptied it into a glass. Since he hasn't drunk blood for so long, he wants to get himself used to it slowly so mine won't overwhelm him when we make it that far.

'Let's chuck it all on,' Bonnie says as they return. She lays out the sausages, steaks, pork belly slices, and corn on the cobs until there's no room left for anything else. Lady and I are salivating at the smell and the sizzle as the meat hits the grill.

Sunny lets herself down into the paddling pool with a contented sigh. 'Thanks for this,' she says to me. 'I really do appreciate any opportunity to show off my bikini,' she adds with a look to my sister.

'How often do you swim?' I ask. I grew up believing that, if a mermaid wanted to walk on land, she needed to pay some brutal price to an evil sea witch first, but that's clearly not the case.

Quietly humming a melody to herself, Sunny splashes some water on herself and paddles her feet. 'As often as I can. I'm one of those maniacs who goes swimming even in winter.' The look she gives me suggests it's a joke... I mean, she *is* a mermaid. Makes sense that she swims in every weather, doesn't it? I don't know her well enough to know if it really was a joke, though, or just her answering my—in hindsight—unnecessary question.

I blush, unsure how to respond, and decide to assume she's just answering my question. 'I know we don't get a lot of snow here, but isn't that cold? Or do you not, erm, feel it?'

I imagine it's very different when you're a mermaid, but I still shiver at the thought.

'It's a family tradition! I've done it since I was a child. We make a big deal out of it.' She winks at me, then laughs. 'I'm basically half fish, Esta. The water is my home no matter your above-water-level temperatures.'

'Meanwhile, Esta gets cold in a heatwave,' Bonnie says as she flips the steaks.

'I'm a little chilly now, actually,' I say with a smirk. 'Might put a cardigan on.'

Bonnie shakes her head at me while Sunny stretches like she's sunbathing, but Leverett pulls me closer. It's almost seven p.m.—still warm out, but definitely not so warm that I'd be happy in a bikini.

'Help me serve?' Bonnie asks me.

I hurry over and hold up plates while she puts two sausages and a steak on each—she plates, I hand out the food, and then we repeat the process. Lady whines when we're all sitting and she hasn't got her own.

'Sorry,' Bonnie says. She puts a sausage on a spare plate and sets it down in front of Lady. 'Here you go.'

Sunny crinkles her nose slightly and stops humming to herself. 'You're letting her eat off a plate? Isn't that unhygienic?'

'This dog has slobbered us awake more times than we care to remember,' I say. 'Besides, if washing-up liquid can deal with raw chicken juices, it can deal with puppy spit.'

Bonnie nods. 'You can't get an affectionate dog and then not let her be affectionate, that's just mean.'

Lady barks in approval, her tail wagging as she devours the food.

Sunny frowns. 'Not sure that's the same, but whatever, she's your dog.' She turns to me. 'Bonnie says you're a hot-shot celebrity photographer?'

I hold up my hands and shake my head. 'Not quite. No celebrities and certainly no hot-shotting, but you do need a password to get in.'

Bonnie must have mentioned who I want my clients to be, so this won't be news to her girlfriend.

Sunny cocks her head. 'Does your camera work underwater?'

I shake my head again. 'There are special bags you can get to protect your camera, but I don't have one and I don't know how reliable they are.' I'd hate to lose my camera because I stupidly held it underwater. The bags aren't too expensive for what they'd allow me to do, but if it doesn't work perfectly, it'll cost a lot more to replace the camera. I'm still crossing my fingers and toes for an influx of clients, so that wouldn't be ideal.

'Shame,' Sunny says. 'My parents would love some underwater pictures. My whole family would. We love to pose!' She's humming to herself again whenever she's not speaking; it seems she's recovered from us letting Lady eat off a plate. Bonnie mentioned Sunny sings to herself all the time, but I didn't expect it to be literally all the time.

I sigh. 'Yeah, I'd love that, too.' The fact that I can't swim aside, it'd be easy to have fun with this. Mermaids could do all sorts of neat spins and whatnot underwater, but we'd have to be far away enough from the shore no one could accidentally see them shift, and that screams *major health risk* to me. 'I'll let you know if I ever get one. If you have a pool, I can maybe work with that?'

'How is that any easier for your camera?' Bonnie asks.

I bite my lip. I was still thinking about my chances of drowning. 'I guess it's not. Oh well.'

'Don't worry about it,' Sunny says as she splashes her feet and playfully splashes some at Lady. My daughter looks confused but not upset. 'I just thought it'd be neat.'

'Anton loves the photos you sent him, by the way,' Leverett says.

My lips pull into a thin smile. 'I thought you didn't catch up over this?'

Leverett chuckles. 'Usually, we don't, but he wanted to reinforce his opinion that you have nothing to worry about.'

'He's probably just saying that because he knows how I felt during the shoot,' I say. 'I still need to schedule a new time with him.'

'Why not this Sunday?' Leverett asks. 'You'll already be there for your lesson.'

I start to shrug but stop myself. Why *not* this Sunday? The truth is I'm worried it'll go just as badly next time. I don't think I'll get another do-over, so that's extra pressure. I do have much better ideas now, though, and it'll be nice to have something positive when the lesson no doubt doesn't go anywhere again.

'I'll message him,' I say.

Anton decided it would be easiest to communicate if I had his number. I sent the best photos from the last shoot that way, just for them to decide which ones they want, and I can let them know if I can't make it one Sunday or ask if I can use the library on a different day.

Sunny whistles. 'That's right, Bonnie mentioned you're

doing *that*! I can't believe you're taking extra lessons during your summer break. I could never.'

Despite myself, I smile. 'It's the only time I can do it, really. I don't know how easily I can keep it up once I'm back at work.'

I know Kate will be flexible if I'm too exhausted to still meet for weekly lessons, but I don't know how tolerant Zeru will be. Not that I'd want to drop my magic lessons, but if I'm too tired for anything, that's that. Kate has been telling me for weeks now not to push myself too hard.

'*Oh*, before I forget!' Sunny jumps out of the paddling pool. She dashes towards the house without shaking off the water first, so she leaves wet footprints over the path. Being soaking wet outside of water doesn't seem to be as inconvenient to her as it would be to me. I and Leverett look after her in confusion, but Bonnie wiggles her eyebrows at me. Sunny hurries back and passes me a small card. 'Bonnie said you've been, erm, struggling after your ordeal and some other stuff, so I thought I'd give you this. It's my therapist's number and email address.'

My heart skips a beat.

'She's one of us,' Sunny says. 'She's great at guiding people, very nurturing and supportive.'

I shove it into my trouser pocket. 'Thank you.'

'No problem,' she says. 'She was great when I talked to her. I only saw her a handful of times, but I felt so much better after. I, uh…' She laughs awkwardly. 'This is embarrassing, but when I was sixteen, I got caught in this strong current while out diving in the ocean. You'd think I'd know better, right?' She rolls her eyes at herself. 'My dad and brother were there and got me out, but I was terrified to swim in deep water for a while. Super awkward for someone like me, as you can imagine.'

'Gods, that must have been awful,' I say. I suppose if this therapist could help a mermaid not be afraid of deep water, she can help me to not be scared of vampire fangs.

She scoffs, every trace of the melody in her words gone. 'The gods have little patience for people like me who can't even do something so simple.'

I want to say something to make her feel better or lighten the mood, but I don't know what to say. I have no experience with this myself.

'I wouldn't know,' I eventually say. 'I don't know any.'

Sunny shrugs. 'My family isn't devout, exactly, but they still leave offerings to Varuna and invoke him like you might invoke God or Jesus. He's been our guardian for generations, but I just can't do it anymore.'

Bonnie raises an eyebrow. 'And your parents don't mind you discussing that?'

'Why would they?' Sunny shrugs again. 'Lots of people worship the old gods.' She laughs, and adds in her bright sing-song voice, 'Paganism is on the rise again, baby.'

So at least that's one thing we can easily discuss. Some of my neighbours might judge us, but it doesn't call anyone out as not being human.

'Are you and your friends religious?' Bonnie asks Leverett.

Lady whines for more food. Bonnie swears and quickly puts some slightly charred steaks aside. She gives one to Lady, then waves the tongs at us.

'Anyone want any more meat?'

We hold out our plates, and Bonnie moves the rest of the sausages and beef. We each take a corn on the cob, too.

'To answer your question,' Leverett says, 'we're not religious, no, though one of my friends differs slightly. Saif doesn't worship outright, but he's had… shall we say, his own past experiences and friendships.'

Well, that's intriguing. No part of me is surprised to hear Saif may have befriended a god or two.

Sunny gets back into the paddling pool, lies on her tummy, and props herself up on her crossed arms on the edge as she hums a new tune to herself. She rests her head on her arms and looks up at us. 'But there are no typical patron deities?'

Leverett shakes his head. 'You'll find my family is made up of strong individuals. I daresay some of my older distant relatives worship themselves before any god, if that answers your question? We aren't raised with any one common belief system. We are free to cultivate relationships with whomever we wish.'

Sunny rolls onto her back and lets her hair hang over the side. 'I've never met one of you, that's all. I hope that's not a rude question.'

It makes me wonder how vampires are raised. We've never really discussed it, but then we've never had a reason to. Given how long vampires can live, it makes sense that Leverett's parents, Anton's parents, and Saif's parents are still around, too. Well, probably not Saif's—he was turned, after all, so unless someone turned his whole family, they're long gone.

206

Will I ever meet Leverett's parents? Has he told them about me?

'This must be a weird conversation for you two,' Sunny says to Bonnie and me. Lady whines at her, and Sunny pets her head with a content smile. 'God means something pretty different to you, right?'

Bonnie sits next to her besides the paddling pool. 'Doesn't really mean anything to me. My mother didn't care enough to raise me any which way, and I've no idea what my father believes since I don't know him.'

I shrug. 'I remember going to church for Christmas when I was very young and things like that, but that's it. Although, I've been learning a few interesting things lately.'

Sunny giggles. 'I'll bet! How do you decide where to focus? Is it just based on what you're interested in?'

'I guess?' I say. 'That, and I have a great teacher. She decides a lot of it.'

We stack our empty plates. Lady throws them longing glances.

'Anyone want dessert?' I ask. 'We made a strawberry cheesecake earlier.'

'I'll help,' Leverett says. 'Let's give Bonnie and Sunny a chance to sit.'

Bonnie smiles at him. 'Thank you, sir!'

Leverett and I stroll to the kitchen with the now-empty plates. I decide to just ask since we're alone while I get the cake out of the fridge.

'I don't think you've ever mentioned your parents.'

Leverett stills, if only for a second. 'We're not close. They hold rather old-fashioned views and have barricaded themselves somewhere in the Alps, last I heard. They haven't kept track of me in years, and I haven't made an effort to stay current with them. There's nothing to say, Esta.'

I nod. 'Alright. Sorry, I didn't realise it'd be painful.'

'Not at all.' He pulls me in for a quick kiss. 'The relationship between vampires and their children is often difficult, for various reasons, and that's before turned vampires enter the conversation. It's not something I kept from you on purpose but rather something I don't think about myself.'

'I'm not that close to mine, either,' I say as I cut into the cake and carefully move pieces onto smaller plates. 'We're not estranged or anything, like Bonnie is from hers, I just don't call as often as I should. We're not on bad terms, we're just also not on fantastic ones. *Anyway.*' Time to change the topic to lighten the mood. 'Saif knows a few deities, huh?'

Leverett chuckles. 'It'll be better if you discuss it with him, but yes, I believe he does.'

I make a mental note to ask him on Sunday, if we get a chance to chat after my lesson. Maybe I'll ask him while we do the shoot? Which I still need to arrange, so I guess I'll do that tonight.

'Can I stay with you tonight?' I ask Leverett. 'I think Sunny is staying here.' Hopefully, she won't get water everywhere if she decides to have a shower or a bath.

A dark smile spreads on his lips. 'You don't need to ask, my love. You're welcome in my home any time.'

I lean into him and breathe deep. Tonight was good; it was nice to relax and just chat with friends. I needed this, and judging by Bonnie's carefree laugh carrying into the house from outside, she needed it, too.

So, I focus on everything good coming my way, and I leave no room for doubt:

I'll redo the photoshoot with Anton and Saif this Sunday, and it'll be every bit as beautiful as the images already look in my head. We'll have a very interesting conversation about Veiled deities. And before all of that, I'll ace my lesson and summon a real breeze, without Zeru's help, because Zeru will have talked down the other sylphs and convinced them that I'm allowed to learn.

Everything will be plenty boring and frustrating and stressful once I'm back at work. Marvin the Arsehole being my new manager doesn't help matters. So, until then, I will enjoy what's left of my break.

Surely I can go three weeks without getting in serious trouble?

CHAPTER TWENTY ONE

I don't really expect Zeru to show up this Sunday. I haven't heard anything from them, but since I've now scheduled a new photoshoot with Anton and Saif for today anyway, I figure I might as well see if Zeru has got anywhere talking to the other sylphs. I also want to talk to Saif about his divine connections if there's time, so whether Zeru can teach me or not, today should be a great day.

I greeted Anton and Saif first to let them know I'm here, but I still hope I can at least talk to Zeru. Even if they haven't reached a conclusion, it'd be good to know what's being said since it's about me. If anyone is coming for me, I want to know before it happens this time.

I say, 'Hey, Zeru. Do you have time?' and then I sit and wait.

I cross my legs, close my eyes, and allow myself to relax. The breeze is getting chilly, though it's still early September. The Eastport weather can be unpredictable at this time of year—we could have torrential downpours for an hour and then go straight into another heatwave. Personally, I welcome our cooler-weather overlords.

'Hello, Esta.'

I open my eyes and smile at Zeru. 'Hello. I wasn't sure if I'd see you today.' I get to my feet and brace myself for whatever they have to say.

'Neither was I. Arguing with other sylphs is an interesting challenge, especially when both sides are right.'

'I get it,' I say. 'I have questions, too, though. You said there must be a reason I can access my magic, and I want to believe that, but what reason could there possibly be when it was an accident?'

I want to believe it because it'll make me more likely to keep my magic. If there really is no reason whatsoever, it's hard to argue against Amphorn. It took effort to free my magic, and Mischief only went looking for it in the first place because my life was in danger. If Zeru is right and there's a reason I can use it, wouldn't I have had it from birth?

Zeru is quiet for a while. They watch me with their calm, unflinching demeanour, until I'm no longer sure if they heard me or are just considering what to tell me.

'Do you believe in fate?' they finally ask.

I blink. Wasn't expecting that. 'Uh… Not really?' But then something clicks when I remember what Saif told me before, during Anton's party. 'Is this about that prophecy that I'll guide the Veiled out of hiding or whatever?' I sigh, because that sounded terrible. 'I don't mean to brush it off like you no longer needing to hide wouldn't be a huge deal, I just don't believe I'll have anything to do with it. I've spent a lot of time convincing the Dreamcatcher that I don't want anything to do with another war between us humans and the Veiled.'

In reality, it was only a few days, but days seem a lot longer when you can't sleep without graphic nightmares.

'Do you believe that is the only possible outcome?' Zeru asks. 'War? Progress through violence?'

'No, of course not, but—' I shrug. 'What do I know? I'm not the right person to ask about things like that. I studied photography, not politics or whatever the right subject would be.'

'Whether you'll try to achieve freedom for the Veiled is irrelevant, Esta. Your involvement alone is enough.'

I frown. 'How?'

'Think of it as a pebble thrown into a pond. You acted as the pebble when you stepped into the void lake in your dreamscape. You can try to control some of the resulting ripples, to guide them into your desired direction, but you will never control every wave you create, no matter how small. You might place an obstacle onto a path you don't wish to tread only for someone else to force their way around regardless.'

'But I don't mean to—' I sigh again. 'I see your point. I didn't know what would happen when I stepped into the void lake, but I didn't expect any of this. Me using magic might have similar effects.'

Zeru nods. 'I'm glad you understand.'

I sit back down on the grass to ground myself. 'That's it then? No more lessons?'

'On the contrary.'

I look up. That's also not what I was expecting. It sounded

like Amphorn's mind was made up, like there's nothing Zeru could say to convince the other sylphs.

'The consequences of your actions, intentional or not, may be good for the Veiled, or they may lead to war. There are also a vast number of possible outcomes in between. Many of us, myself included, believe you can access your magic for positive reasons, but the opposite is equally likely. Your path is not fixed; we don't know your outcome or the effects your life will cause, only what has happened so far. I do not believe you wish anyone harm, but those who don't know you believe the risk is too great.'

'So, all I can do is my best?' That sounds doable, but I was trying my best with Chiara, too, and she still kidnapped me to eventually kill me.

'Yes. While none of us can be certain what you will do, what your very existence might cause, we all agree that your magic is not powerful enough to do any harm on its own. As long as you struggle to summon a breeze, we don't perceive you as a danger. You have refrained from practicing magic this week as I asked. This has earned you the benefit of the doubt with many who previously spoke against you.' Zeru *smirks*. The gesture is so human, so out of place on their face, that it looks even more sassy. 'While we all agreed, some did not agree happily. But we all saw reason in the end.'

I stand again and smile. 'Thank you for speaking for me. I'd have no other way of defending myself without your help.'

My heart sinks. So, that's it? I'm helpless again? At least the Dreamcatcher and Chiara were *right there*, and I could *try*. But I have no way of reaching the sylphs without Zeru's help. I can't go to their library and ask to be heard. It's frustrating.

'This, too, has gone in your favour,' Zeru says. 'You cannot harm people you cannot reach in any way, at least not seriously.'

Huh. Guess that's one way of looking at it.

'So, what are we doing today? Can we practice, or do you need more time to talk to the others?'

'Paralda has given you leave to continue under my guidance.'

My heart jumps into my throat, and I let out an excited squeal. 'Thank you! Who's that? I don't think you mentioned them before.'

Or maybe I just forgot. I *am* bad with names.

'Paralda guides. You might see them as our leader, though the truth is more complicated and far simpler than that.'

I bite my lip. If they're the sylphs' ruler, I probably sounded disrespectful. 'Then, if you have the opportunity to thank them for me, please do.'

Zeru smiles. 'If an opportunity presents itself, I will pass on your gratitude. Shall we begin?'

I nod, eager to get started. I haven't already forgotten what Zeru said, though—I'm allowed to continue for now because I very much seem to be unable to do anything big. I might continue with these lessons until I die of old age and not make any satisfying progress, or I might suddenly have a breakthrough just to be subject to the sylphs' scrutiny again.

'Do you remember what I told you to do last week?' Zeru asks.

'I think so.'

'Then please proceed. Take your time. I will alert you if half an hour has passed without progress.'

I sink back into my relaxed meditation pose and breathe out. It doesn't matter if nothing happens today; at least that way, I don't need to worry about the other sylphs retaliating. Zeru made it sound like most of them are fine with me practicing now, but how quickly would that change if I summoned a small hurricane? *I* would be stunned. Gods know how they would react.

Instead of actively trying to achieve anything, I merely focus on the wind's caress on my skin. I sigh into it; this is bliss and I will enjoy my thirty minutes of uninterrupted silence. After this, I will enjoy my photoshoot with Anton and Saif, and after that, I will enjoy my chat with Saif. I have so many ideas now I can't wait to get started. There haven't been any more threatening messages. No one has called me to book a shoot, either, but that's alright. I didn't expect to be fully booked within days of leaving my business cards with Bee. These things take time. I'm sure the right clients will find me eventually.

A deep sense of calm spreads through me from my core. It spreads from my head, a soft shift of velvet blanketing my mind first. It's lovely. As the feeling of peace spreads down my neck and through my body, I can't remember the last time I felt this calm. Probably before I stepped into the void lake, to be honest. There haven't been many reasons to be completely at peace since, but I won't let it rattle me. As I said to Zeru, all I can do is my best. And when the next trouble finds me, I will address it with reason like I did with the

215

Dreamcatcher.

I feel a yawn coming on, but I will it back down. If I let it slip out, there's a real chance I'll fall asleep. I focus on the breeze on my skin again to let me stay just aware enough. The rest of me feels so light I'd be floating if this were a dream.

Slight currents of electricity zap through my veins. My magic? I acknowledge it, am grateful I can feel this much, but I don't try to make it do anything. Maybe that's the secret. Maybe, if I treat it like a scared cat and let it sniff me first, it'll come to me when it's ready.

So, instead, I let myself fall into the feeling. I don't feel any grass or soil against my back or on my neck, but there was a jolt in my stomach like I fell over, like that time I passed out when I was younger—I was aware of it happening without feeling anything. I almost feel like I did when I stepped into the void lake and just floated through space until I woke up: incredibly light and paper-thin. Like the slightest breeze could pick me up and carry me away.

It feels wonderful.

Thank you. I don't know if my magic can hear my thoughts like Mischief did, but this feels right. Even if I never achieve anything magical, I'll forever remember this feeling.

'Esta. Look.'

I slowly open my eyes. I blink like I've been asleep for hours; the midday sun is too bright for a moment as my eyes struggle to adjust. It's also disorienting that I am, in fact, still sitting up.

And around me, there's a breeze like a small, soft whirlwind. I feel it more than I can see it, but some leaves and blades of grass spiral on my current. It dances on my skin and through my clothes, twirls my hair.

'Did I do that?' I whisper.

'Yes. This is all you.'

Tears burn my eyes, and I gasp. The small whirlwind dissipates, and the leaves and grass glide towards the ground. It's not quite the hurricane I was worried I'd summon by accident, but it's a start.

And I don't know what that means for me.

'What happens now?' I ask.

'We will work on your control,' Zeru says. 'Do you know why your breeze vanished?'

'Because I got distracted. Or because… I got excited? Because I let strong emotions get in the way?'

Zeru gifts me a smile, and my heart swells with pride.

'Very good, Esta. It is part distraction, part emotion. We sylphs are logical creatures, and our magic reacts in kind. As I explained—' Zeru stills, and I brace myself. I fully expect the opposition to arrive.

'Do you need me to stay out of it again?' I ask.

Zeru nods. 'That would be best.'

The same three sylphs as before step out of the air before us, like a mirage brought on by an invisible storm.

'Amphorn,' Zeru begins. 'There is no need to worry. I have it under control.'

Amphorn frowns. 'It no longer matters. We have been asked to bring this human with us for examination.'

My blood runs cold. That sounds bad. I imagine lying naked on a table while aliens dissect me, though I know that's not fair. Zeru wouldn't let them, and they're not after my insides. They said before that they might need to remove my magic, but I don't know what that involves.

'Of course,' Zeru says. 'I will take her myself.'

I glance at Zeru. 'Huh? I'm actually going?' I try to keep the worry out of my voice, but I can't shake the feeling that I'm about to be kidnapped again. 'Where are they taking me?'

'It is not as bad as Amphorn made it sound,' Zeru says. 'We didn't believe you to be capable of even minor magical feats, but you have just proven that you may be capable of more after all. We simply need to assess you to fully understand your potential.'

I hug myself. 'And remove my magic if you don't like what you find?'

'This power is not yours, human,' Amphorn says. They sound perfectly calm and unbiased, so I probably imagined the smug tone.

'My name is Esta,' I say with a little more force than I intended. If they're going to try to take my magic from me, they can at least call me by my name.

'Please don't be alarmed,' Zeru says. 'I will speak for you, and many more of us are on your side. Please know that we don't cause harm unprovoked. We are not asking you to come with us to hurt you.'

I resist the urge to scoff. They may not intend to hurt me right now, but what happens if they don't like my "potential"? If I go with them now, I'll only have myself to rely on inside their home. There'll be nowhere for me to run. Zeru said it themself: As elementals, sylphs are forces of nature, and forces of nature can really fuck shit up. There are plenty of natural disasters every year that destroy lives.

'Esta,' Zeru quietly says. 'Trust me. There is no need to be alarmed. We have been asked to bring you to our home; there are only very few sylphs and what you consider deities who have the authority to issue a command like this. None of them would harm you without good reason.'

I gulp. What do I know what they might consider a good reason? But I do trust Zeru.

That doesn't mean I can't have a backup plan.

'My friends who let us use this garden expect me to do a photoshoot after this lesson. I can't just disappear without telling them the shoot is cancelled.' We'll have to reschedule again, but that's hardly my biggest worry right now. 'Can I quickly let them know I need to leave? They'll worry otherwise.'

All three sylphs stare at me for a moment as they consider my request. Zeru, however, stares at them with the same look of deep consideration. I don't know what it means. Maybe they don't believe the others? That doesn't make me feel any safer.

'Very well,' Amphorn says. 'We give you one hour to speak with your friends.'

I nod. 'I won't need that long. Thank you.'

The three sylphs disappear with a gust of wind. I want to crumble to the ground. Zeru just said it—this is basically standard. Nothing to worry about. I'm probably just scared, that's all; I can quite happily admit that I am. The Dreamcatcher found me in my dreamscape, but it's still his turf. Things could have ended very badly that time. Chiara abducted me and brought me to her basement. That nearly ended in my death. Now, Zeru is going to take me to the sylphs' nearly impossible-to-get-to library, and rather than joy all I can feel is fear. If this goes badly, I've no idea how to get back out.

'I will wait here,' Zeru says. 'Thank you for agreeing to come with me. Your cooperation will not go unnoticed.'

My neck feels stiff when I nod. 'I'll be quick.'

I want to run to Anton and Saif, but my legs don't feel strong enough. My knees are shaking, my feet too heavy. Something feels very wrong about this, though I don't know what.

'Anton? Saif?' I call as soon as I shut the front door behind me.

They materialise before me in an instant.

'Esta, my dear, what's wrong? You sound terrified!'

I hurry to tell Anton and Saif everything that happened, from my unexpected progress to the sylphs' intervention. Anton looks as troubled as I feel, but Saif regards me calmly.

'Can you please tell Leverett?' I ask.

I don't know why it matters. I just know that, when Chiara took me, no one knew where I had gone. This time, I want as many people as possible to know. Not that any of them could just wander into this elusive library, but at least they'll know where I am. It'll be an advantage if there is something they can do.

'Of course,' Anton says. 'How long will you be gone?'

I shake my head. 'No idea. Oh, and can you ask Leverett to

let my neighbour know?' I turn to Saif. 'Is there anything you can tell me about this place?'

He thinks a moment. 'It is a haven of knowledge and learning. Sylphs are not rash creatures, Esta Anderson. You will be safe as long as you don't antagonise them, and even this they would counter with logic.' He pauses. For a second, I think he'll say something else, but then his chest falls and he remains silent.

'Thank you.' A nervous laugh escapes me. 'I'm afraid we'll need to do this shoot another time. You *will* get your anniversary photos, I promise.'

I hope I haven't jinxed it.

Anton pulls me into a hug. 'Don't you worry about that now! You come right back here the moment they let you go, you hear?'

I do feel a little better as I hurry back to Zeru. This time, I wasn't taken by surprise. I've done all I can to protect myself, even though it's not much at all.

I'll be fine.

CHAPTER TWENTY TWO

The wait is agony.

Zeru left me in this seemingly infinite white space with invisible borders. If there are walls or any other structures, they blend into each other. I tried to walk around, but before long I hit the invisible barriers, like concentrated wind gently but firmly pushing me backwards. There's nothing to do here.

I certainly don't see any books.

I can't believe I've made it to the sylphs' wonderful, secret, magical library and won't see one book. I know I'm not here to sightsee or enjoy myself, but it just adds insult to injury. Being allowed to roam the library, even if only a small part of it, would have helped take my mind off things.

I don't believe I'll get hurt while I'm here, but I don't believe I'm just here to talk, either. I can't get the way Zeru watched the others out of my mind. Like they were lying and Zeru was trying to figure out how. But that trail of thinking won't get me anywhere, so I drop it. All I can do is be honest and not dig myself in deeper.

It's impossible to guess anything about this place. All I

know is that this is a library… isn't it? Maybe I'm wrong about where they took me. Come to think of it, neither Zeru nor Amphorn said where they were taking me, just that I am to be assessed.

There's no clock here, and my phone doesn't work in this strange place, so I don't know how long I've been waiting.

I really hope this isn't one of those situations where ten minutes pass for me but an entire year passes back home. Zeru said they live much longer than we humans do, but they never said anything about time literally passing differently in their home realm.

I don't know what to expect when someone finally comes to talk to me. Will I be taken to a hearing, like in court? Is there actually a bustling city outside of this space? Maybe I haven't left Eastport at all. Maybe this is some kind of parallel plane, or a pocket realm of some kind.

The sheer whiteness of this space is starting to give me a headache. With no objects at all to focus on, my vision soon feels fuzzy. At least it's neither hot nor freezing; the temperature is quite pleasant, actually.

I almost weep for joy when Zeru appears beside me. I resist the urge to throw myself into their arms.

'What's going on?' I ask.

'Follow me,' they say. 'I will confront the others, and then I will take you home.'

I pause. 'Just like that? What about the assessment?'

Zeru is quiet for too long. I was right; something is wrong. 'It will be done another time. You must have questions for those who would take your magic from you. I believe you have the right to ask them.'

I follow Zeru farther into the white nothingness. I only know we're moving somewhere because I have to walk to follow them. Visually, nothing changes. It's disorienting.

'Will Amphorn try to, I don't know, hurt me?'

'Not while you are under Paralda's protection.'

I blink. 'Your ruler is on my side?'

Zeru's shoulders move up and down like they're chuckling, though they don't make a sound.

'Paralda is unbiased, but they do not believe this matter warrants violence of any kind. They may choose to assess you themself when the time is right.'

'Hang on, "when the time is right"? So, it wasn't Paralda who ordered me to come here? Then who did?'

Zeru hesitates again. 'You can ask Amphorn all your questions yourself in a moment. They are in a better position to answer truthfully.'

I huff. 'You really think I can count on them to tell me the truth?'

'Of course. We have no reason to lie, Esta. We understand it is a human habit, but we sylphs rarely see the need.'

I bite back my response that "rarely" isn't "never." I guess I'll judge for myself soon enough.

'Don't be alarmed,' Zeru says. 'You won't fall.'

'What do you—'

With a wave of their hand, the white space disappears, and we're outside—*outside* outside.

We're *in a cloud*.

My knees lose all strength when I make the mistake of

looking down and see nothing but water very far below. I grasp Zeru's arm for safety. I wanted the maddening white place to change into *some*thing, but I preferred it to this.

'You will not fall,' Zeru repeats. 'I have brought you into our natural habitat. My magic keeps you safe.'

To Zeru, being so high up in the air must be relaxing. I let out a whimper that sounds like agreement and panic at the same time.

'Why *here*?' I ask.

'We thought it best to settle their concerns here,' Zeru says. 'Or rather, I wasn't given a choice. I was outnumbered.'

I nod. 'Alright. Let's get this over with.'

I let go of Zeru's arm, but I also stubbornly keep my eyes ahead. It doesn't help much since all I can see ahead of me is sky. I want the white space back. At least there, there was zero chance of me dropping into an ocean.

Amphorn and their two friends step out of the cloud, looking as calm as ever. I'd have preferred evil grins. Their faces are a little too relaxed given that I'm *hanging over the fucking ocean.*

'What is the meaning of this?' Zeru demands. I've never heard them so forceful before. It's unsettling, like all hell is about to break loose. It seems I'm not the only one with questions, though that doesn't comfort me right now.

'We apologise for the deception,' Amphorn says. 'We thought it best to resolve the issue before it has a chance to escalate further.' They look directly at me. 'We truly are sorry. We would not wish to resort to such means if we didn't believe the future of your world to be at stake.'

'What does that mean?' I ask. 'What are you going to do?'

'No less than we have been commanded.'

Zeru steps in front of me. 'Paralda has given no such order. She is under their protection.'

I'm beginning to hate the sylphs' habit of staying silent while they think. Their faces give nothing away. Zeru, at least, seems to have had more contact with humans or other Veiled and has adopted some facial expressions, but these three may as well be the same blank canvas as the space I was in before.

'This order did not come from Paralda,' Amphorn finally says. 'Another shares our concerns.'

'No one stands above Paralda,' Zeru argues.

'No air elementals do,' one of the other sylphs, who hasn't spoken so far, says. 'But there are some who stand above even them.'

I don't know what they could possibly mean, but Zeru freezes. And that tells me everything.

'Do you mean whoever sent the Dreamcatcher and the Mara after me?' I swallow. This is a dangerously thin line— one glance below reminds me just how thin—but this is my chance to get answers. Who knows when I will get another?

'You don't need to know her name,' Amphorn says. 'Only that she has seen what your involvement might bring, and she cannot allow it.'

A breeze picks up around me. I find it comforting for all of one second before I remember where I am. Are they going to throw me off this cloud? Even if we weren't above the ocean—my mortal enemy—I could never survive a fall from such a height.

'We have come to offer you a final chance to choose for yourself,' Amphorn says. 'She wants you gone. We offer to remove your magic instead, and with that, all knowledge of the Veiled. This is necessary.'

Zeru pushes me behind them. 'Then you allow fear to guide you. Do you not know better than that?'

'Fear can save lives, Zeru. Think what it might have done for Aither had they not chosen to ignore it.'

Zeru goes unnaturally still. Even the breeze around me dies.

'Do not speak of situations you have no right to judge. You weren't there. We tried, as ever, to let logic guide us. You seem to have lost sight of that.'

I've no idea what they're talking about, but I get that Amphorn hit below the belt, and I get that Zeru can hit back just as hard.

'What will you choose, human?' Amphorn asks.

I want to choose survival, more than anything, but I don't see how that's an option if I ask to keep my magic. Besides, if I couldn't learn how to use it, why would I keep it? It'd be nothing more than a once-interesting bauble that's collected dust over the years. These sylphs are good at making it look like I have a choice, but I doubt I do.

'I…' Damn it, there must be something I'm missing. 'Isn't there another way? Can't you take my magic without taking my memory?'

I can't believe I'm even suggesting it, but it seems like a fair trade to me, if a painful one.

'I'm afraid not,' Amphorn says. 'She demands that you're no longer a threat. Erasing your knowledge is the kinder solution.'

Compared to death, they mean. How can I argue with that?

'Will you allow *me* to speak?'

My head darts around. Kate is behind me, walking over. *Kate*. How the hell is she here? How did she even find me? Part of me wants to think that of course she's here, she's Kate, she can do anything, but this isn't the same as teaching me magick. It's not even in the same neighbourhood. She found me in the *sky*, and she's walking on clouds and air to speak for me. As much as I respect and love her, I don't understand.

What's even more baffling is that the three sylphs before me stiffen, like they didn't expect to see her here—which is probably true, but I doubt their reasons are the same as mine.

'We're deeply sorry,' Amphorn says, 'but she has spoken. Surely you can see the threat this human represents?'

To my horror, Kate nods. 'I see the threat she might have represented if she were somebody else. She has my guidance, however.' She cocks her head in a manner not unlike her dogs. 'Or perhaps you believe my guidance to be insufficient?'

I don't know if sylphs can feel mortified, but I'm feeling it on their behalf. It seems like the right response somehow, like the very idea that Kate's knowledge might not be good enough is deeply offensive. She *has* been a great teacher. This goes beyond that, though, I just don't know how.

'Kate was the one who contacted me about Esta,' Zeru says. 'I agree with her assessment. Esta should be allowed to keep her magic and her memory. Her teaching has prepared Esta well.'

And yet, I don't feel well prepared at all in this moment.

Whatever is going on between Zeru, Kate, and Amphorn isn't anything she trained me for.

Amphorn attempts a smile. On their face, it looks like mockery. 'Kate, is it? As I said, we are sorry, but we can't go against her instructions, even if what you say is true. Please, step aside.' They turn their eyes on me. 'We trust that you have made your decision?'

I look to Kate. 'What do I do?'

She smiles at me. 'What do you want? Leverett and I offered you a similar choice once: to keep your memory but lose your sanity, or lose your memory but keep your mind. Today, more than that is at stake.'

I hesitate. 'I don't want to lose anything, but if losing my magic is the only way, I... I can sacrifice that but keep the rest.'

Kate nods and turns back to the sylphs. 'Esta is under my tutelage and my protection. Paralda themself has spoken for her. We will not bend to the will of one ruled by fear.'

Amphorn grimaces; I'm not sure what the expression is supposed to be, but I doubt it's joy.

'You forget your place,' Amphorn says. 'This is neither your decision nor your jurisdiction.' A strong breeze whips up around them. 'Stand aside. The human has made her choice, and we will honour it.'

'Don't move,' Kate tells me without looking back.

I don't think I could have even if she'd told me to run. I understand what she said about not letting fear rule you, but right now it's gluing my feet to the cloud, and I don't know how to fight it.

'Step aside,' Amphorn repeats.

'No. You have no right to interfere in this way,' Kate says. I don't know how she can sound so calm, like she's in perfect control. 'You will allow her to leave with me. You will not harm her, and you will not harm me. Zeru.' Next to me, they look at Kate. 'Take Esta home. Await us there.'

'As you wish.'

Zeru places a hand on my shoulder and gently encourages me away. I begrudgingly let them.

'We can't just leave her!' I argue.

But Zeru nods. 'Kate can handle herself.'

I decide to place all my trust in Zeru. We turn around—

Amphorn appears before us, more breeze given shape than solid form.

'We regret this necessity, human,' they say, 'but it's the only way.'

They raise both hands. My limbs freeze until I can't move a single muscle.

'Stop this!' Zeru shouts. 'Don't you see this is irrational?'

The breeze around Amphorn turns into a whirlwind. I can't even scream or beg or tell them to fuck off. They shape the wind into a wall. It rushes towards me and Zeru without as much as a flick of Amphorn's wrist. I wish I could at least close my eyes so the last thing I see doesn't have to be ocean.

But suddenly, I'm behind Amphorn and their wind barrier. Kate stands where I was only moments ago.

'What—' I barely have time to gasp.

And then the wall of air rushes into Kate. She falls, and the clouds swallow her.

CHAPTER TWENTY THREE

The last time I lost someone, I was twelve. It was my granddad. We weren't close and I can't say I miss him, but I cried during his funeral. In the years since, he's sometimes crossed my mind, but only as a vague memory and never with any sadness attached.

Kate's death hits me so much harder.

I hide under my duvet and hug my pillow to myself. It's too wet to really get comfortable with it; I've cried a lot today. Lady lies next to me, her eyes full of uncertainty about what's going on. All she understands is that I'm hurting, so she wants to comfort me.

It's been two days since Amphorn threw Kate off the cloud into the ocean. It feels longer. Zeru took me home after Amphorn and their friends left in what looked like stunned shock, but it's hard to tell with their expressionless faces.

I've only left the house once since then: That evening, Bonnie and I went to Kate's house to check on her dogs. The plan was to bring them over to ours. We could mourn Kate together, but...

Her dogs were gone, too. I don't know how. That, more than anything, confirms that Kate really is dead, though I don't know why or how.

And I *tried*. This whole time I've shut myself in, I've tried to make sense of it.

Kate told Zeru to take me home and wait for her here. She didn't say how long she'd be, though, and it's been several days. If she were alright, if she were alive, she'd have at least let me know that she's fine by now. She has my number; she would have texted. The other sylphs, including Amphorn, seemed to respect her. They meant to kill me. Somehow, Kate switched our positions on that cloud so the wall of wind hit her instead. That's not even the newest point on my long list of things I don't understand. That goes to her dogs being gone.

If Kate really is dead, where did her dogs go? Bonnie and I searched the whole house, but there's no sign of them. It's possible that Kate brought them somewhere else before she came to help me, but that means she suspected that she wouldn't make it back. Bonnie didn't notice any unfamiliar cars parked before Kate's house, and I don't know who would have come.

I've realised how little I really know about Kate. I don't know if she has children. I don't know if her parents are alive, if they live nearby, if they're on good terms. I don't know any of her friends and have never seen anyone visit her. She's been my friend for years, my teacher for a few short months, and I know next to nothing about her.

None of that explains why she would have known that

something might happen to her or how—*how*—she came after me in the first place. I know *I* was up there because of Zeru and their magic, but I don't understand how Kate found us and then followed us. Maybe I wasn't in the clouds at all? That certainly seems a lot more plausible, but that implies it was just some impressive trick of the light, and that doesn't make any sense, either. I *saw* Kate fall.

I've seen her fall many more times since. Whenever I close my eyes, the memory is there.

There's so much I wanted to ask her. About magick. If she knows who exactly is after me, 'cause it sure as fuck sounds like she doe—like she *did*. If she *knew*.

Kate is gone, and she took her answers with her.

I waited, like she asked. I even prayed for some sign that she's alright. I've made myself watch the news, clinging to a blanket, wondering if anyone's fished her out of the sea or if she's washed up somewhere. I know it's extremely unlikely, but in a horrible, morbid way, I'd find it much easier to accept her death if I could just see her body. Amphorn made sure that will never happen, though. She's probably sunk to the bottom of the ocean by now.

Lady has spent a large part of the last few days with me. I've left my room a few times, mostly to get something to drink and because Bonnie insists I eat. It's comforting to be around her. She and Leverett make sure I don't shut myself away completely, though neither has made me leave the house. Leverett has held me while I cried into his chest. Bonnie sat with me while I stared at the TV screen without seeing anything. Lady won't leave my side.

I wonder if she misses Keano and Bruin as much as I miss Kate.

Lady sticks her nose in my face and whines. I put the pillow I've been hugging behind me, open my arms, and she snuggles against me. Her warmth and love are too much; I start sobbing again.

I just can't believe that Kate is gone. We were supposed to have a lesson today. What will happen now that I can't uphold my end of the deal with the Dreamcatcher and the Mara? Maybe Kate died to protect me from Amphorn just so the Dreamcatcher can destroy me after all. I don't know if Zeru will still teach me magic, and even if they are, they never agreed to teach me about the different kind of Veiled or regular non-Veiled magick. I can't keep my promise, and the reasons are completely out of my control. I don't really care what the Dreamcatcher might do, though. I only know I want Kate back.

I keep wondering how Kate could have been there, in the sky with us. With everything else that's happened, I can try to force some sense or explanation, but not with this. Somehow, Kate found me. She argued for me. She stood there and said I deserve to keep my magic, that I'm not a threat and wouldn't hurt anyone. Kate has believed in me since before I set one foot into the void lake. She did all that to help me when she didn't need to.

And now, she's dead because of it. I know it was an accident, but knowing they meant to kill me instead doesn't help. If anything, it makes it worse, because that means Kate is dead because of me.

I sob. Lady whines at me with a worried look in her sad eyes. I hug her.

Kate is *not* dead because of me. She's dead because of Amphorn. The Dreamcatcher came after me—fair enough, I did overstep. The brownie turned into a boggart and haunted me—fair enough, that's on me. Chiara kidnapped me and tortured me—not really fair enough, but her problem was still just with me. Kate had nothing to do with this. I don't even care whose fault it is. I only care that Kate did not deserve to be punished on my behalf.

I don't care what problem my secretive enemy has with me; what happened to Kate wasn't an accident, and it wasn't my fault. It was murder. That they killed the wrong person doesn't matter; it was murder all the same. I won't pretend to know the first thing about Veiled politics or whatever decisions they make in the shadows, but I do know her death was unnecessary.

I'm so tired of not being able to do anything. If the Dreamcatcher had decided not to trust me and take my sanity after all, he easily could have done it, and I couldn't have defended myself. It was sheer luck that I managed to get away from Chiara—Mischief didn't know that her idea would work. We were both guessing, both grasping in the dark. And now, Amphorn has gone somewhere I can't even follow them. How am I supposed to demand answers when I have no way of reaching them? I doubt they'd come if I spoke their name into the wind.

Because Amphorn has answers, I'm sure of it. After what they did, they owe me—no, they *need* to answer for what happened. Amphorn killed a human. Surely sylphs don't see some twisted logic in that?

I sit up and rub my eyes. They're sore from crying, and I've a feeling they'll hurt a lot more before I'm done. I cry when I'm angry, and the more I think about what happened in that cloud, the more furious I get. Amphorn can't just get away with this. My secret would-be assassin can't keep getting away with this.

And I am done being defenceless.

I hurry downstairs, my dog in tow and still whining at me. Bonnie isn't home, and I don't care how deranged I look when I rush into my garden and shout:

'Zeru! Talk to me, dammit!'

My voice did get quieter by the end. It's not that rare to hear people shouting where we live, but I never thought I'd be one of them.

A breeze picks up around me, but Zeru doesn't manifest. I don't blame them; it *is* the middle of the day. Any neighbour looking out of their window at the wrong time would see them.

'Hello, Esta,' I hear on the breeze. 'How are you feeling?'

'Pissed off,' I hiss. 'My friend is dead. I want justice.'

'You want revenge. It is not the same thing.'

The breeze picks up around me like Zeru is trying to comfort me. On any other day, I would have appreciated it, but today it just feels patronising.

I shake my head at the air. 'I want justice. My friend is *dead*. You can't tell me it's fair or alright that Amphorn doesn't have to face any consequences!'

'It is not. I'm looking into it.'

I pace up and down the side of my apple tree so fast I may wear tracks into the grass.

'That's not good enough.' My nose burns as I say it. I take a second to breathe, but it just makes it burn more and brings tears to my eyes. 'I want to be there. Don't you need a witness or something? I was there. I can tell them what happened.'

Zeru is quiet for a long while. The only reason I know they're still here is because the breeze hasn't let off.

'Please, Esta. Let us handle this. I will call for you when and if the time is right. I understand how you feel, but remember that Amphorn is guided by fear. Do not let your own grief and anger override your reasoning.'

I take a step back, feeling like Zeru slapped me. That's not even remotely the same thing.

Is it?

Lady has followed me and whines at me again. She sounds so worried, and it's my fault.

I sigh and sink against my tree. 'Fine. Promise you'll let me speak for her? She's spoken for me so many times. The least I can do is repay the favour.'

The wind briefly picks up, then gently dissipates, like Zeru sighed in relief, too.

'I promise I will do what I can.'

The breeze disappears completely, and I take a moment to pet my dog and ground myself. I don't want to start a fight. I don't even really want to argue about it. If they still want to take my magic, fine. It's not worth losing anyone else. It's not worth what I've already lost. Honestly, it's hard to care either way when my friend is dead. Kate has done so much for me. I can't just sit here and do nothing, especially when she only got involved in all this because of me. Zeru is right, I mustn't let anger cloud my judgement. Deep down, I know this, but it's hard not to get angry all over again when I think about what happened. My heart begins to race again when I remember how Kate argued on my behalf and Amphorn just shut her down like her input didn't matter, when she's the one who—

I make myself take a deep breath. If I throw myself into this while I'm angry, I'll only make things worse. I don't want that. But I do need to do something or I'll lose my mind. I'm tired of feeling like I'll mess up, like someone else will come after me when I haven't had a chance to recover from the last incident. I want justice for Kate, and I want to be left alone. I want peace. Surely that's not too much to ask? If I can't even make beings of pure logic see that, what hope do I have? No, I'll have to approach this like Zeru would: with rationality.

I just hope I won't lose my patience when I see Amphorn again.

I make myself take another few deep breaths until my heart is calm and my head is focussed.

Then, I get up and grab my car keys.

CHAPTER
TWENTY FOUR

I feel somewhat insecure when I pull up in Anton's driveway. I'm still angry, too, but mostly I'm *just* insecure. It takes me too long to realise it's because I didn't call ahead. Anton and Saif are not expecting me today, which explains why he sounded surprised when I asked to be let in over the intercom. I rest my head against my steering wheel. If I was too distracted by my anger to call Anton first, how will I ever make a good argument against Amphorn? Of course, if Amphorn hadn't killed Kate in the first place, I—

I slowly let out a shallow breath. Zeru is on it, they said so themself. I trust them. But that doesn't mean I can't get things moving on my end. I'm done being idle.

Anton opens the front door just as I'm about to knock.

'I'm sorry I didn't call first,' I say by way of greeting. 'I hope I'm not interrupting anything today?'

I don't know what Anton's or Saif's schedules are like. I don't think they have jobs, do they? But they could have any number of other commitments. I should have thought for one second before driving off in anger.

'Nothing important, my dear. Do come in and tell us what happened. You sounded terrible on the intercom.'

'Is Saif around?' I ask as Anton ushers me inside.

He nods. 'He's already upstairs and serving tea. Come. Let's talk.'

I feel a little better now I'm here. Anton's massive mansion somehow feels like a cosy safe space, and I put it down entirely to the two men living here and their library.

'Hello, Esta Anderson,' Saif says as I enter the sitting room on the first floor. 'To what do we owe this pleasure?'

Anton waves for me to sit, and I gratefully accept the cup of tea Saif prepared for me. I feel like I've gone to my uncles' to pour my heart out.

I take a shaky breath in. 'Kate is—' I choke. Take a moment and try again. 'Kate is dead. A sylph tried to kill me and got her instead.'

Saif looks surprised, but Anton hurries to sit next to me and takes my hands in his.

'Oh, Esta, darling, that's just— I don't know what to say. This is unexpected. We thought your surprise visit might be related to the photoshoot you did for us, but this… Dead? Are you sure?'

I explain what happened.

'Oh, you poor thing, come here.' Anton pulls me into a hug, and I start crying again. Hopefully, his purple suit wasn't as expensive as it looks, because I'm leaving a growing damp patch on his shoulder.

I make myself sit straight. 'I can't believe she's gone.'

I'm starting to realise how empty I feel without her

presence, like a light has left my life. I can't risk this happening again; it's just not an option. I'd never forgive myself if Anton or Saif were next, or Leverett or Bonnie.

'I want—' I sniff. 'I want someone to pay. Amphorn killed my friend. I want them to answer for it.'

I'm no longer crying into Anton's expensive suit, but he hasn't left my side. I'm grateful for his presence, for his and Saif's warmth, for the tea. Even that comfort doesn't feel the same knowing that Kate is gone.

'And do you have a way to reach this Amphorn?' Saif asks. 'What do you intend to do?'

I shrug and deflate into the sofa. 'I don't know. Surely sylphs have trials and a justice system of some sort? I'll ask for that.'

'If a sylph really has killed Kate unprovoked then yes, that sylph would be expected to answer for it,' Saif says. 'But it's not as easy as that. How will you reach them? There's also the issue of standing against a sylph in an argument. They are rather rhetorically gifted.'

'I don't know,' I say again. 'I haven't prepared a speech. I just know I can't leave it like this.'

'I must say,' Anton says, 'we are surprised you've come to see us. We would have thought you'd talk to Leverett first.'

'Ah, crap.' I pull out my phone. 'Do you mind if I message him? I wanted to talk to all of you together, but I forgot.' I wasn't exactly thinking clearly when I rushed off to drive here.

Anton exchanges a glance with Saif.

'We don't mind,' Saif says, 'but we'd like to know what exactly you're involving us in.'

241

I bite my cheek. 'Nothing, really. I just want to discuss options, if that's alright? I don't expect anyone to actually do anything. That's all on me.'

'Message him, my dear. We're happy to hear you out. Aren't we, my love?'

Saif nods. 'We'll help if we can.'

'Thank you,' I say. 'That's all I'm asking.'

I don't know what they can realistically do, but Saif at least is bound to know something. He's been to the sylphs' library—he must know how to get there. Maybe he can get me in, too, as long as that wouldn't get him into trouble. I'm not expecting him to drop me off at their front door, but maybe he can point me in the right direction.

I message Leverett and ask him to meet me here. He can fly, so it probably won't take him too long if he can get away immediately. It's Tuesday, so his shop is open today.

My fingers fly to Kate's number out of habit before I catch myself. New tears burn my eyes and nose, but I do my best to force them back down. I can't change what happened, but I can make sure her murderer doesn't get to go free. I'll accept whatever the sylphs see as justice, just as long as something happens.

That doesn't mean it doesn't hurt, though. I've had so much love and respect for her, and now that's got nowhere to go except memories that can't respond.

I quickly message Bonnie, too. 'Gone to Anton's. Might be back late <3'

I don't know what'll happen today, but I know I don't want my very human, very mortal friend anywhere near it. She can tell me off later for not telling her.

'Take a moment to gather your thoughts,' Saif says.

I nod. They leave the room, and I cry into a pillow.

I fall apart again when Leverett arrives. This isn't the first time he's seen me since Sunday, but seeing him makes me feel safe to be vulnerable. Anton and Saif are in another room, and Leverett arrived via the open balcony door in the sitting room. I've held on to him since he got here. He hasn't complained or asked me what's wrong; he knows I can't speak right now, that him being here is enough.

I try to pick myself up again, but it's hard with his arms around me and his hand stroking my back.

'Give me a moment,' I say when I finally trust my voice again. 'Anton and Saif are next door, I think. I just need to call Zeru.'

'I can wait if you like,' Leverett says. 'In case Amphorn shows up instead. They might be waiting to catch you alone.'

I shake my head. 'They've had plenty of chances for that. I'll be fine.'

Leverett kisses my head, then goes to find Anton and Saif.

Maybe I'm deluding myself, but I don't think Amphorn wants to hurt me. I think they genuinely believe that taking my magic or killing me is the only way to prevent a tragedy so great they can't quantify it. In a way, this is no different from when the Dreamcatcher invaded my mind. I believed him when he said he had no choice, that it was the safest way to ensure peace, so why shouldn't I believe Amphorn, too? They told me several times that they regret the necessity of removing me from the picture one way or another.

I've been on my own most of the time since Zeru took me home two days ago. Amphorn could easily have found me and finished the job, but they haven't. Zeru said it's being handled; maybe that involves Amphorn being locked up. It may be that they want to hunt me down but can't.

Besides, if everything works out, I'll be going to them soon enough.

I step onto the balcony and hope it's enough. 'Zeru? Do you have a moment?'

Nothing happens for several seconds. I begin to think I've either worried them too much this morning or they're just too busy to talk right now. After my angry outburst, I've given them every reason to second-guess their decision to help me.

'I'm sorry about earlier,' I say, hoping they can hear me. 'I'm grieving my friend, but that doesn't mean I can take it out on you. I know you're on my side.'

A small breeze picks up, and Zeru appears next to me. 'It is more accurate to say that I am on the truth's side, but yes. I believe you have a right to keep your magic. I accept your apology.'

I feel like a boulder lifts from my heart. 'Thank you. I, uh… You said you're looking into it? Into what happened, I mean. Is there anything I can do?'

I still want to ask if they can just take me to their library, but I don't want to sound too desperate. I'll resort to begging later if I have to.

'You can give us your word,' Zeru says. 'You might say the matter has escalated. We are not violent creatures, as you know. What Amphorn did goes against several of our beliefs. We consider killing of any kind to be an emotional response; therefore, Amphorn lost control. There is also the matter of your developing magical ability. We have much to consider. I have passed on your request to speak of the incident, and Paralda agrees that your insight would be valuable.'

My heart skips a beat. 'You mean your *ruler* is involved? You don't have, I don't know, police?'

'For matters such as this, only Paralda's decision is acceptable, and their decision will be final.'

My heart drops again. Amphorn must have known this was a possibility, but they tried to kill me anyway. They must be one thousand percent convinced that eliminating me is the only way.

'What if Amphorn is right?' I ask. 'If sylphs don't easily resort to violence and they did *this*... Do you know something? You're all keepers of knowledge, right? Do you know what I will do with this magic?'

'We know only possibilities, as we have discussed before. Will you come with me? You called me here because you are prepared for the possibility, correct?'

I sigh. I suppose that's as good as it's going to get.

'You'll really take me to your library?'

'No.'

I frown. 'I don't understand.'

'We are not going to our library, Esta,' Zeru explains. 'Paralda oversees all knowledge, but their... Hm. I'm unsure how to describe it in your words. You might call where I'm taking you their office or tower, though it's a crude term for the reality.'

I freeze. A tower? Like the card Jirina drew for me? That doesn't bode well.

'Do not be alarmed,' Zeru says. My face must have spoken volumes. 'It may sound ominous, but the reality is far simpler. I am merely taking you into our natural habitat, because this is where Paralda dwells and makes all of their decisions. They have asked that the vampire Saif joins us as well.'

'What for?' I blush. 'I mean, I don't mind, but why him?'

Perhaps Paralda trusts his opinion? Saif wasn't there when Kate fell, though. I don't understand what he could add to this case, or why Paralda has asked for him rather than Anton or Leverett. I'm not about to argue with the leader of all sylphs, though. Or, okay, yes, I guess I am, but not about their choice of witness.

'I'm sorry, Esta, I'm unsure myself. Paralda has not shared their motivations with me. Will you take me to your friend so I can bring you both to Paralda?'

I'm about to nod but stop myself. 'Let me get him. You're probably more comfortable waiting out here, right?'

It's not exactly stuffy in this house, but it is inside closed-in walls and under a roof.

Zeru does this thing where they watch me for a moment as if they're trying to read my mind or aren't aware that I've stopped talking. Then, they say:

'Very well. I appreciate your consideration.'

I promise to hurry, and then I rush to the room next door where everyone is waiting for me.

'How did it go with Zeru?' Leverett asks when I enter the

room.

'Fine,' I say, and look to Saif. 'Their leader is ready to hear my side of the story, and they've asked that you come, too.'

Saif looks as taken aback as I was by the request. 'Me? Did they say why?'

I shake my head. 'No idea.'

'Where exactly would you and my husband go?' Anton asks. 'Can't you talk here?'

I shake my head again. 'I don't really know, either, but Zeru said we're going to their tower?'

Saif nods and smiles. 'Of course. All elementals have their demesnes, as you know. The Eastern Watchtower belongs to the sylphs. It's from where Paralda rules the air and weather phenomena. I've never been, of course, but it's an honour to be invited.'

Leverett takes my hand. 'I'll come with you.'

'Zeru won't permit it,' Saif says, 'and neither will Paralda. Much like the sylphs' library, this is not a place anyone can walk into uninvited. You might struggle to call it a place at all when you first arrive.'

My heart does uncomfortable flips. Last time a sylph took me to their natural habitat, I lost Kate. I tell myself it'll be fine, that Zeru and Saif are with me this time, but Zeru was there last time, too, and as much as I love Saif, I'm not convinced he'll be any safer.

'There's no need to worry, Esta Anderson. We are merely going so that Paralda can discern the truth of what happened and make a just decision. They have likely invited us into their realm so they may easily keep the situation from escalating as it did last time. There's no one more powerful in the air than Paralda.'

I don't feel overly reassured by that, but what choice do I have?

I kiss Leverett's cheek. 'Wait for me here?'

'I won't go anywhere,' he says, pulls me in, and kisses me.

'Don't worry, Esta, my dear,' Anton says. 'We will both be waiting for you. You go do what you need to.'

Zeru glides on the slight air current when we get back to them, near-invisible merged with the breeze. They solidify when they see us.

'Are you ready to go?' they ask.

I nod.

'I'm honoured to accompany you,' Saif says.

I do feel at least slightly reassured by Saif coming with us, but I also can't shake this growing discomfort in my gut. I hope I'm just overthinking it; the mention of a tower has reminded me of Jirina's reading, so of course I'm worried. That doesn't mean that the disaster she foretold strikes today.

'Relax your bodies and your minds,' Zeru says. They place one hand on my shoulder, the other on Saif's...

And then I see only blinding white.

CHAPTER TWENTY FIVE

One moment I'm on Anton and Saif's balcony, the next I'm back in the same strange white space where I waited to talk to Amphorn My heart races faster at the sight; the memory of what happened next is too fresh. But Saif puts his hand on my other shoulder, and I will myself to calm down. It'll be fine this time. He won't die, and neither will I.

A slight breeze sighs through here, though I don't know where it could possibly come from. I decide it must be sylph magic. Seeing Zeru here makes it easy to believe—they look more like the breeze than ever, a soft wispiness to their already smooth edges and an effortless, flowy elegance to their every movement. I remember the first time I saw them in Kate's living room, where they looked so oddly out of place—like those toddler toys with the shaped bricks, and someone tried to shove a star through the triangle hole. But here, they *flow*. They look otherworldly and magical. Their form is solid but airy, warm and cool, sharp as a sword and impossibly soft like a cat's belly fluff. They are the duality of wind given a physical body. One whisper from them might comfort me more than a velvet blanket. Another might cut me to pieces.

It's a sobering thought. I mustn't forget where I am or why Zeru has brought us here.

'I will inform Paralda you are here,' they say. 'Please wait. I will—'

I shake my head before they can leave me alone again… well, alone with Saif , I guess.

'Where exactly are we?' I ask.

I'm grateful that Saif is here. Just like the last time I was in this light space, my eyes struggle with the lack of things to focus on. At least with Saif here, I can look at someone else. I realise *light* is the perfect way to describe wherever we are. This space is the incredible lightness of a sylph's calm brilliance.

Zeru is quiet long enough that I think they'll deny me an answer, but then they say:

'It may be hard to grasp for a mortal. Imagine a cloud in an endless sky. Imagine a breeze you cannot see, only feel. We are in the space where the two meet.'

They're right, that *is* hard to grasp. It also doesn't tell me anything, but that's on me for not being a sylph.

'I will return when Paralda is ready to hear you,' Zeru says before I can blink.

With that, they vanish like wisps of smoke in wind.

I turn to Saif, hoping to find solidarity for my confusion, but he looks in awe. Saif raises his hand, draws it through the air as if to test its thickness, then vaguely smiles at something I can't see.

'Did that make sense to you?' I ask.

To my dismay, he nods. 'They explained it as well as they

can. Don't be discouraged if it made no sense to you, Esta Anderson. Places such as this one aren't meant to be travelled by outsiders. You must have seen your share of impossible sights in the last two months?'

I huff in disbelief. 'Sure, but those were nothing like this. I could see and feel the void lake. I can see fairy wings. I don't even understand where I am now. Are you seriously telling me I'm in a *breeze*?'

Saif gives me a mysterious smile. 'It's close enough to the truth.'

This is frustrating. How am I supposed to argue my case when I can't even wrap my head around where I'm standing?

Something shifts, like wind scattering leaves in autumn. For a moment, I think Zeru has already returned, but they haven't. The reality is even more baffling.

It's Mischief.

I gasp, and then I freeze. My eyes burn from the relief of seeing her alive and well. How am I allowed to react? If I run over to her and hug her, it'll just show her superiors that she can't ever be my dream guide again. I hate that I can't do anything that gives away we're friends when I want to hold her and make sure she's real.

Mischief doesn't seem to care, though. She runs over on her kitty legs and throws herself into my arms.

I burst into tears. This is too much—first I lose her, then I lose Kate, and now Mischief is here? I hold on to her like my life depends on it—shit, maybe it does, given why we're here—and she doesn't try to wriggle away. Instead, she purrs louder than I've ever heard. I kiss her head, and she washes the tears off my face. It should feel weird given that she isn't really a cat but a Veiled choosing to lick my face, but it doesn't. Mischief shaped herself around my desire to have a cat, and this is what cats do. She might not even know any better. I don't know how dream guides perceive personal space.

My laugh comes out strained and broken and snotty. 'Saif, this is my dream guide. Mischief, this is Saif.'

He inclines his head with a knowing smile. 'It's an unusual but welcome pleasure to meet you.'

Mischief purrs, 'Sure,' and nuzzles her head into my neck, too overjoyed with our reunion to spare half a thought for Saif.

'How are you here?' I ask. 'Are you alright?'

I don't care if I die anymore, this is the best gift ever.

'I've been given leave to attend your hearing.' She sits back and washes her paw. 'What, did you think I ran away? Really now, Esta.'

I laugh and hug her again. This time, she does squirm out of my arms, but there's no force behind it.

'Alright, that's enough affection,' she says. 'How are you holding up?'

My lip quivers. 'Badly. Kate is gone, Mischief. A sylph killed her.'

She gives me a long look that might have translated as the mother of all eye rolls were she human. 'Yes, I suppose that happened.' She paws at my face. 'I know why I'm here, Esta. Tell me how you feel.'

I want to reach out to pet her for comfort and moral support, but I keep thinking that she isn't really a cat, isn't really a figment of my dreamscape. Mischief exists outside of that, like all Veiled. Now that my initial shock of seeing her has worn off, I can't just stroke her head.

Saif has wandered a few steps to the right to give us privacy.

'Conflicted,' I admit. 'Can I... This isn't your real shape, is it?'

Now Mischief is here and I've had my emotional outburst, I feel so much better for having seen her. I'm still furious that Kate was killed, and I still want justice—of course I do—but hugging Mischief's tiny, soft, fur-covered body has taken the fight right out of me. I'm not even sure I can move. How am I supposed to out-argue a sylph, anyway? If Zeru gave me the chance to just go home right now... Maybe I'd take it.

Mischief stretches and yawns. 'You want to see the real me?'

'Are you allowed to do that?' I ask. 'Or would that be weird?'

She washes her other paw a moment. To buy time to think, maybe.

'You, vampire,' she calls towards Saif. 'No need to sneak a peek. I don't mind if you see me.'

Saif softly chuckles to himself but doesn't hide that he's watching.

Then Mischief glows, her shining body stretches, and then a girl stands before me... or someone who looks like a girl, anyway. She looks around ten years old, I think? Her skin, her eyes, her hair are all black like obsidian, white lines like veins streaking across her skin like she's marble. She looks so different to my dream guide cat that I'm very aware I'm staring, but I don't know how to stop.

She smiles, and all doubt falls away. I've seen this expression countless times on her cat-self.

'Relax,' she says. Her voice is the same; it lets me smile a little. 'It's just me. This place isn't dream-guide territory, and it's well protected from prying outsider eyes. My people don't know what I'm doing here, only why I'm here and why it was important they let me come. I can't stay long, Esta.'

I nod. 'Thank you. I thought I'd never see you again.' My voice breaks. The idea that she may leave again in five minutes is too painful. 'You're beautiful.'

She waves me off. 'I'm not supposed to look like this, you know. We're more like marbled quicksilver. I violated the boundaries of my contract to you; this is the result.' She gives me a withering look before I can apologise and turns her nose up. 'Thing is, I rather like it. But we're not here to talk about me. Be honest: How are you feeling? I'm not assigned to you anymore, Esta, I don't know what's going on inside your head. I imagine it's more naked Leveretts now you've had each other?' I hear Saif stifle a laugh. 'Congrats on that, by the way. I really was happy for you. I just also knew I'd have to leave, which ruined the moment somewhat.'

I smirk. She may look like a child, but she definitely doesn't sound like one.

I cross my arms. 'How old are you, exactly?'

'Esta! Don't you know, it's rude to ask a Veiled her age.' She shrugs. 'A few hundred years, a little older than Leverett, I think. Just a kid.'

I giggle. 'Yeah, right.'

She laughs. 'Stop deflecting. What are you going to do?'

I deflate and stare at her a moment, hoping the answers will come to me, but I still don't feel it. I have all the conviction for Kate's case, but the hatred I felt earlier left my body the moment I saw Mischief. I can't bear that Kate died, but I understand Amphorn's worry. They know the future of the universe and whatnot so much better than I ever could. I understood the Dreamcatcher's view and worries back then, and I understand Amphorn's now.

'Ah, I know that look. You're overthinking. Stop it.'

I glare at her. 'What else can I do? If you know an argument that'll help, please tell me, 'cause I got nothing.'

Mischief reaches out to paw at my face like she used to do as her cat-self, then pulls back when she sees her beautiful black-marble fingers and awkwardly holds my hand instead.

'It must feel like you're going to court, but you're not. You're on trial, sure. So is Amphorn. No one is expecting a rehearsed defence speech from either of you—no offence, Esta, but they're certainly not expecting it from an unprepared human. Be honest, and don't hold back. You managed it with the Dreamcatcher and the Mara. This is the same thing: same argument, new people. Alright?'

I smile, but I'm tired. 'Will I ever not have this argument?'

She shrugs again and lets go of my hand. 'Who knows? Maybe if you stop running away.'

I scoff. Easier said than done.

'I don't even know who I would confront, though. All these people who've come after me are just intermediaries, right? They're all acting on someone else's command.' I trail off a little at the end, because I just remembered something. I'm not sure if it's okay to ask. Then again, if I don't do it now, when will I get another chance? 'Mischief. Is there any chance your people are the ones who—'

'Don't be ridiculous.'

I feel like she punched me with a fluffy paw. 'I thought you can't read my mind anymore.'

'I can't. You're just that obvious. I've known you a long time, remember? No dream guide or spirit guide is after you, Esta. Why would we be?'

'I don't know. I don't even know your real name.' I freeze. I didn't mean for that to sound like an accusation, only to make the point that I don't know that much about her or her people. 'Sorry. That wasn't fair.'

Mischief is still a moment. Then: 'Names have power, Esta. Maybe I will tell you mine one day.' She looks away from me and her gaze goes soft. 'If I can get out of my current problems, that is.'

'I'm really sorry I got you into this situation. If there's anything I can do to help, tell me, I'll do it.'

She smirks at me. 'There you go, being ridiculous again. I chose to help you with Chiara. I let my guard down. I chose to become your friend when I knew I shouldn't, long before you knew you didn't just make me up. It's on me. Alright?'

I nod, but I don't feel it. I used to think I'd invented her, which I now know was incorrect. Then I thought dream guides had one job, one purpose, one desire, which is to guide. She did that, but clearly that's not all there is to her, either, or she wouldn't have wanted to be my friend.

'Don't look at me like that,' she says. 'I got myself into

trouble, and I don't regret a thing. Maybe that's proof that I'm not fit to be a dream guide anymore, but I don't care. So, let's drop it, okay?'

'Okay.'

My smile is sad, though. Isn't this exactly why the Dreamcatcher was sent after me, exactly what Amphorn and their secretive employer are scared of? All Mischief did was be my friend before I knew anything, and now she's suffering because of it. Because she *met* me. It's completely out of my control, but it still happened. I don't know what'll happen to her if she can't be a dream guide anymore. Can she just retrain as something else? Or was the dream guide gig her entire reason for existing?

'Focus on your own problems for a change, Esta. Promise me you'll be honest with Paralda?'

'Yes, sure.' It'd be easier if I still knew what my honest answer is.

The air shifts again like it did when Mischief appeared, and for one brief, hopeful moment, I think it's Kate. But I couldn't have been more wrong. In strides the Mara, followed by the twisted stick-and-thread creature that is the Dreamcatcher. I forget how to breathe.

'Esta.'

I barely hear Mischief. I was terrified they'd come to demand answers. After all, Kate can't teach me anymore, so our agreement is basically void, isn't it? And I took photos of the Veiled. I expected them much sooner than this, but—

'*Esta.*' Mischief gently touches my face as if she's still in her cat form pawing at me. 'They are not here to hurt you. Paralda

257

has asked them both to speak of you.'

Saif appears next to me, not so close to take my agency away but close enough to guard me if needed. I want to hide behind him, but I'll stand my ground. Mischief says they aren't here to hurt me; I believe her.

The Dreamcatcher shifts to look at me, I think, though it's hard to tell. Twigs snap and branches crack with the movement.

'We were once sent by her, just as Amphorn was sent now,' the Dreamcatcher says in his deep, cold voice that makes my bones rattle. 'We chose to go against her and spare you. Paralda wants to know why.'

I'm still frozen, so I don't move when the Mara approaches me and takes my hands in her wrinkled ones. 'I hear you've lost your Mother, dearie. Our condolences.'

There's a lump in my throat when I nod and croak out, 'Thank you.' I don't correct her about Kate not actually having been my mother. Clearly, it's some kind of title, and frankly I'd be proud if she had been. I'm not here to argue with the Mara or the Dreamcatcher but against Amphorn. I never thought I'd see them again—I hoped I wouldn't—certainly not to speak for me.

'Can I ask what you told Paralda?'

It's more likely they took Amphorn's side, isn't it? I can't honour our agreement anymore. Nothing bad has come from the photography shoots I did and I had full consent each time, but maybe they don't care about that.

But the Dreamcatcher says, 'We don't believe you are the danger she has convinced Amphorn you are. We spoke of what we know about you.'

I swallow. That's delightfully vague.

'Thank you,' I say again. I never thought they'd come to my defence like this.

The air shifts again, and Zeru arrives on a breeze.

'Paralda would hear from you, Esta,' they say. 'All of you, please join us.'

I stand on shaking legs. Mischief takes my hand and walks with me, her smile encouraging. In this form, she barely comes up to my belly. Saif walks next to me, his presence reassuring. Zeru gives me a reassuring smile, too, but the Mara and Dreamcatcher are silent behind me save for the swish of her skirt and the sound of snapping twigs when he moves.

And when the air shifts once more and I find myself in the most sacred-looking space I've ever seen, suddenly face-to-face with Amphorn and a sylph I assume to be Paralda, I feel like I'm walking to my execution.

CHAPTER TWENTY SIX

The space is magnificent. Like before, there are no defined walls, no furniture, no structural features. The space appears wide open with seemingly no end. It is bright, it is ethereal, almost heavenly, and it is stunningly beautiful in its impossibility and simplicity. What looks like mist rises up to my ankles; it's neither cold nor warm to stand in, only soft as satin. The only kind of architecture as far as I can see is three arches so tall I don't see their end. They remind me of windows, except I see no glass. The smooth light of a permanent dawn emanates from behind them and makes me feel hopeful.

And before them, looking like a fucking *god*, stands who I assume to be Paralda. They are at least two heads taller than Zeru and Amphorn, their alabaster skin is streaked with silver, and their long silvery hair flows freely down their back. I feel like I should bow or fall to my knees or do something equally reverent, but Paralda grants me a kind smile and gestures for me to come closer.

Whatever fight I still had left in me withers. I feel like I've done nothing but defend myself these last two months, usually badly, and I just don't know what else I can say. Seeing the Mara and the Dreamcatcher again has reminded me of that and makes the last months feel like years. Seeing Mischief again has sapped the last of my energy. I don't think bringing either of them here was a tactical move; I understand why they've been asked to speak. I'm just tired.

Making eye contact with Amphorn, who stands to Paralda's left before a dawn arch, I feel downright exhausted. They don't look like they wish me any harm; they look like a chided sylph who made a mistake. It doesn't excuse what they did to Kate, but I was there on that day, and as angry as I am, even I can see it was an accident. They tried to kill me, sure, but only because they believe it's the only way to save the future or whatever. I'm not angry about their reasoning. I'm angry they killed Kate, who, it seems, just happened to be in the wrong place at the wrong time.

Then again, maybe Amphorn is quietly seething behind their calm eyes. It's really hard to tell. It's clear to me that Zeru has worked on their facial expressions, likely before we met, but Amphorn hasn't put in any such efforts. I don't know if it's because they don't normally spend this much time in their humanoid form or if it's because they consider it beneath them.

'I welcome you, Estelle Marie Anderson,' Paralda says, their voice warm and melodious.

I swallow, too shocked at hearing my full name to form a coherent response right away. Even Eloise never went that far. 'Thank you. Just, uhm, Esta is fine. Thank you.'

'As you wish.' Their gaze takes in all of us. 'I have asked you all here to settle two matters: the sylph Amphorn's transgression, and the human Esta's right to her dormant magic and the potential risk to the Veiled community. As both are linked in this instance, I have decided to hear both together. Esta, you are the common denominator in both cases. I would hear from you first.'

'Erm…' I wring my hands, unsure what to do. I don't see a witness podium to step up to. This is the first time I've ever had to publicly defend myself, and I hope it'll be the last. I'm woefully underprepared.

'Please, do not worry,' Paralda says. 'I merely mean to discern the truth before I make my final decision. Tell me first how you came upon your magic.'

I don't know what I can say. Mischief is in so much trouble already, and while I know she said her superiors aren't listening to this, the worry is still there.

'That was me,' Mischief jumps in. 'Esta was in trouble. I was searching her mind for a way to help her and stumbled across it.'

'Ah, yes,' Paralda says. 'I am familiar with the incident. Your dream guide's timely intervention saved your life, correct?'

I quickly nod. 'Yes. I didn't even know I could do that, it just burst out of me.'

Amphorn glares at me in their infuriatingly calm manner. 'And yet she managed to fend off a vampire. Since then, Zeru has taught her how to control said magic, which is not hers to wield. That power belongs to a previous incarnation that is otherwise unrelated to this human.'

'All her incarnations are part of her whole, are they not?' Paralda asks. 'Should we refuse her right to learn because she did not immediately become a master?'

'Her willingness to learn is admirable,' Amphorn says, 'but it doesn't change facts. Her learning magic endangers Balance. We cannot encourage it.'

The topic aside, it's a strange argument to watch. Most humans I know would have raised their voices or even begun to shout, but both sylphs sound so calm, like they're discussing the weather out of habit.

Paralda fully turns to Amphorn. 'Yes, it has come to my attention that you have taken orders from a new superior without my knowledge. You are, of course, free to live your life as you wish, but you went against my direct orders when you interfered with Zeru's lesson. What's more troubling is that you have allowed her to infect you with her fear, yet you would call us unreasonable. How do you defend yourself?'

'As the only sane one here!'

Even I take a step back in surprise. That's the most emotional response I've heard from a sylph. Amphorn seems to realise they've made a mistake, too; they fall silent, and for a moment, I think I see the fear everyone's talking about behind their eyes.

Paralda is silent for a moment. I doubt they're speechless often, but maybe they're considering what to say next. Zeru has stared at me while they figured out their response often enough.

Finally, Paralda says, 'Must I remind you that you have access to most knowledge in the universe, while I have access to all of it?'

I deeply adore Paralda for how calm they are. I no longer feel like I'm walking to my death; I'm actually starting to feel alright about this. It kinda sounds like Paralda is on my side.

'Then you must have seen the risk this human represents,' Amphorn says. A small but growing whirlwind picks up around them. What would Paralda do if Amphorn trashed their office?

'I have,' Paralda says. 'I have also seen greater risks in many Veiled. One human is not the greatest threat to Veiled-kind, Amphorn. Other Veiled are. Even now there are ancient fae who remember the war and want nothing more than revenge. Even now there are mermaids who long for clean waters, dryads who mourn the loss of their forests. As Esta has seen for herself, there are many vampires who would return to enslaving anyone they wish for blood. They are few examples, but they are all greater risks than this one human woman. Esta, come to me. I must assess the full extent of your magical potential. Don't worry, it won't hurt.'

I wonder how Paralda would take to being hugged. Gratitude aside, my heart is in my throat when I approach them and they place their hands on my temples.

'Relax,' they say.

I do my best to breathe evenly, but I don't know what to expect, and everyone here is watching us.

I'm about to ask if I should do something when Paralda withdraws their hands and gives me a curious look.

'Interesting.' They look at Amphorn. 'The extent of her magical talent is not a serious threat.' In other words, I really am just that untalented. It's hard to be disappointed right now. 'This does not, however, eliminate the overall risk she poses. As her mentor can no longer fulfil her role, Esta faces a decision.'

I think I might throw up. My knees buckle; I desperately wish I had something to hold on to, but Saif and Mischief are all the way over there and I don't want to appear weak by hurrying back to them. I think it matters that I don't run right now. This is where I choose if I'd rather have death or ignorance.

Paralda turns their silver eyes back on me. 'I can remove your magic. It will not be dormant once more but gone completely. This is irreversible, but it won't hurt. However, as you were willing to learn before, I would assign the sylph Zeru and the vampire Saif as your new teachers. Would this be acceptable?'

I blink, too stunned to form a response. 'So, no one is throwing me out a dawn arch?'

I blush furiously. I can't believe I said that.

Paralda smiles. 'No, Esta. As Zeru has no doubt told you, we sylphs favour knowledge. We believe you should have the opportunity to learn if you so choose.'

Gods, I think I'm going to cry. I look to Zeru and Saif for confirmation. Zeru inclines their head while Saif smiles at me.

'Y-yes,' I say. 'Yes, of course.'

The wind around Amphorn grows as they glare daggers at me. I take an instinctive step back; I've seen how easily sylphs can create a storm without moving a muscle.

It takes me a second too long to realise their glare isn't

directed at me but at Paralda.

'You would choose this over our safety?' Amphorn demands.

Paralda shuts them up with one look. 'I would, because my decision in this does not matter. If she truly is destined to walk the path you fear, she will find her way regardless of what I allow. We both know the different branches before her. The one you fear is but one of many. Having a mentor will help to set her on the path of learning and growth, not destruction.'

There's a finality in Paralda's tone I really hope Amphorn takes seriously.

'We are not the only ones with access to knowledge,' Amphorn says. 'She has seen the different paths, too, and she is certain—'

Paralda holds up a hand. 'She is not sylphid. Esta's magic is sylphid in nature, and it was you, a sylph, who attacked with the intention to cause harm. That makes both matters firmly my responsibility. It saddens me that you lured her away under the lie that I ordered you to do so. However, it saddens me even more that you let fear control you and would have killed a human because of it. This contradicts your nature.'

Amphorn is silent for a long time. They both stare at each other; I don't know if sylphs can communicate telepathically, but something must pass between them, because if they're not, we're all just silently waiting for someone to say something.

'I apologise,' Amphorn finally says. 'I acted as I believed was right.'

Paralda acknowledges their apology with a gentle nod. 'Do you agree to step down and allow Zeru and Saif to teach Esta?'

I feel so much better now. I have two weeks left before I go back to work; I think I'll take them off everything, maybe even photography. Gods, my mind needs the break.

But Amphorn crushes my hopes when they shake their head.

'No. Even we are not infallible, Paralda. We can make mistakes, too. I believe you are making one now. I must insist you let me settle the issue as she asked of me, for all our sakes.'

'I order you to step down.' Paralda still sounds calm, but there's an unmistakable command to their voice. A rumble in the distance that may or may not turn into a storm. 'Think about your actions. Reflect. We shall speak again once you've had time to yourself.' They turn to me. 'Is my decision acceptable to you? Or would you rather face Amphorn?'

I pale. 'Oh, gods, no.'

There's nothing I want more than to go home and sleep. My limbs feel as exhausted as my brain.

'Good. Then there is no further need for you to remain here. Zeru may take you and Saif back.'

I thank Paralda again and turn around. Saif is waiting for me with a reassuring smile. I cannot wait to collapse into Leverett's arms. But first, I will hug Mischief one more time before I probably never see her again.

I feel the breeze whip up before I know anything is wrong. On instinct, I turn back around to find Amphorn balancing a storm in their palm.

'I cannot allow you to leave. I'm sorry, human.'

Paralda raises their hands to interfere. 'Amphorn, step down! That's an order!'

Zeru flies towards Amphorn to stop them.

Saif turns to me and into fog mid-step.

But Amphorn is faster.

I see the concentrated ball of air rush towards me before I can comprehend it, and it's coming right for my heart. A gasp escapes me. I flick my hand at Amphorn like it'll make them go away, raise my arms to shield myself like that'll do anything, and then I close my eyes and prepare myself for pain.

It doesn't come. The room is silent. Maybe that's what death is like, though—quiet and peaceful. I open my eyes, relieved to see I'm still where I was five seconds ago. Everyone is staring at me.

Everyone except Amphorn. Where they stood, there's nothing. My wrist tingles, my palm aches and crackles as if electrified.

Saif throws his arms around me and puts himself between me and Paralda.

'It was an accident,' he says. 'She tried to protect herself. It's not her fault.'

The truth hits me the same second Paralda turns their eyes from the spot where Amphorn was to me:

I killed a Veiled.

And I have nothing to say in my defence.

I look at my hands like I expect to see them covered in blood, but of course, they're clean. That doesn't seem right.

'I saw, Saif,' Paralda says. 'Esta reacted in self-defence. Amphorn lied and betrayed me as well as themself by attacking a human who did not want to fight. Their actions are inexcusable.'

Their words grow fainter as the drowning in my ears gets louder. I keep staring at the spot where Amphorn was only a few minutes ago. How can they be dead? I didn't mean— I— I *killed* them.

How can I say I want peace now?

Saif puts his hand on my shoulder and gently turns my head to look at him. He says something; I don't hear it. He grips my shoulder; for a moment, it's forceful enough to make me look at his hand instead. But then I remember.

The air shifts. Suddenly, Paralda is right in front of me. I never wanted to hurt Amphorn. I wanted them to face justice, yes, but not like this. Paralda will strip my magic from me now, and I don't blame them. I meant well, but I still killed someone.

'Esta.' Paralda places a hand on my other shoulder, and Saif retreats a few steps. 'I recognise that you acted in self-defence. I do not blame you. Amphorn intended to kill you. Unlike your reaction, theirs was a conscious decision.'

I'd scoff if I could make my muscles move. Amphorn killed Kate by accident, too, and I still wanted them to pay for it. Who will call for my head now I've committed the same crime?

'I apologise,' Paralda continues. 'I could have stopped you as I stopped Amphorn's magic before it could reach you, but I didn't believe your magic powerful enough for this.' They are silent for a moment, probably because I've exceeded their expectations in the worst way possible. 'It is rare for a sylph to be ruled by strong emotion. We see it as a corruption. You might say Amphorn was sick. Look at me.' I'm not sure how

269

I can. I feel compelled to do as they say—perhaps there's sylph magic at work to make it easier for me—but how can I take my eyes off that spot? Paralda places their other hand on my neck, and for a second, I think they'll snap it, that they've lured me into a false sense of security to make my own death easier, but instead, they repeat, 'Look at me.'

They sound so gentle and kind and sympathetic. How can they be so nice to me when I just killed one of their people?

A small breeze starts around my head and flows down until it surrounds me. Paralda repeats their request, voice as calm as always, and I finally make myself look.

Their eyes are deep silver and impossibly light. It's like looking into eternity.

'None of the blame is yours,' they say. 'Go home. Rest. Mourn, if it helps. Zeru and Saif will continue your teaching when they deem you ready. If you wish it, Zeru will answer your questions about Amphorn's corruption, too. All this will happen when you have recovered. Right now, you need to give yourself time.'

I want to believe them, but I don't know how I can. My eyes fly back to the spot, but Zeru appears between us, and Saif returns to help me stand.

'Let's go home, Esta.'

Mischief takes my hand. 'I wish I could come with you,' she says. 'But I'm glad you're in good hands.' She looks up at Saif. 'All of you better look after her for me.'

My eyes fill with tears, but I don't remember how to speak. I also don't have the strength to argue, let alone fight him, when Saif picks me up and carries me.

Zeru places their hand on my shoulder. 'I will take you home.'

My eyes are back on that spot until the bright space disappears, and the ground vanishes from under us.

CHAPTER
TWENTY SEVEN

The breeze isn't as comforting as it used to be. This would have been lovely—me sitting in the forest near home with Lady next to me, watching the brook flow gently over rocks with the wind rustling through the trees and over my skin—but it reminds me too much of Amphorn. Of the time they killed Kate. The time I killed them.

Bonnie insisted I get some fresh air. She made up an excuse for why she can't walk Lady, but I know she thinks it'll help. Maybe it will, if I sit here long enough. I still mostly feel numb, though I do feel a little better than I did a week ago.

Paralda's kind words before Zeru took me home don't make it any easier. No one's come for me, though. No one's demanded I face justice, like I did with Amphorn. I almost wish someone hunted me down.

Leverett says the way I feel is normal. I'm not a violent person; I'm definitely no murderer. He says it's normal to drown in guilt, that some vampires go through this, too. He says he himself battled with guilt for a long time.

I hear it. I believe it. It's no easier because of it.

Bonnie suggested I make an appointment with the therapist Sunny recommended. Leverett agrees. Deep down I know it's a good idea, that I desperately need to speak to someone about everything that's happened since I stepped into the void lake, but I can't face it just yet. I can't leave it too long, either, though. Next week, I'll be back at my gallery job, this time under Marvin's supervision, and that's not likely to make me feel any better.

The werewolf Bee gave my card to emailed me. He wants a photoshoot with his wife and pups. That was three days ago; I haven't replied. What if I slip up again and kill them, too? Even if I don't, doing a photography shoot for an unknown client requires a level of energy and conviction I simply don't have right now. I don't know when I will. He's probably given up, so there's no point in me replying.

I press my palms into the soil and dig my fingers in until I feel earth under my nails. Since the wind can't comfort me anymore, maybe grounding myself will help, but all it does is annoy me. There's soil stuck under my nails now—great.

Lady whines at me. She shoves her nose at me and gazes at me with big eyes. My nose burns; I fight back tears. Damn it, how does she do that? How can my dog make me cry with one look? I always thought it's because she's so damn cute, but now she looks concerned. Worse, she looks like Paralda's words sounded: like an earnest plea for me to understand that I just defended myself and need to give myself grace. Gods, what Paralda said about Amphorn's condition almost made it sound like I did them a favour by putting them out of their unnatural misery, but how can I possibly see it like that?

273

Besides, it wasn't self-defence. Paralda had already rendered Amphorn's attack useless, I just didn't realise it. They said so themself.

A sob escapes me, accompanied by two thick tears. Lady gets on all four paws and snuggles against me with so much adoring force that I have no choice but to put my arms around her. She's so warm, her eyes so loving and compassionate, and her hug is everything the wind used to be. I hide my face in her neck, just until the tears have dried and I've composed myself, but instead, I start crying in earnest.

Damn it all. Kate would have known what to say.

It's a mercy that no one else seems to be going for a walk today or they'd have seen me have a meltdown. Or maybe my sobs are scaring people away? I'm so glad Kate showed me this place. Maybe I should have asked her how to ask the spirits of the dead for advice, too; I might have used it to speak with her. It never came up, and there was no reason to cover something like that. She taught me so much, but there's even more she'll never get to teach me. Saif and Zeru will make great teachers, but I want my friend.

Her dogs still haven't returned. I'm not really surprised, but at the same time, I don't understand where they've gone. It's like they sensed that Kate is gone and have either gone to look for her or they've gone to mourn somewhere else. I don't know what'll happen to the house. I imagine it'll be sold or rented out, but I don't want new neighbours. I want Kate.

I want to go back in time and tell the me from back then that I mustn't learn magic from Zeru. If I hadn't, Kate would still be alive, and I wouldn't be a murderer. All I wanted was to learn something I didn't think would cause any issues, but instead, two people are dead despite my good intentions and best efforts. How can I reply to the werewolf, how can I tell Zeru and Saif that I'm ready to resume my lessons, when I've messed up so much?

Lady licks my tears away, her breath warm on my face and smelling of meat. I kiss her head. Mischief did something similar while I was waiting to see Paralda, when she was still in her cat form. I can't believe she came to defend me when I did nothing to help her. She's a victim of knowing me, too. It's not fair. She deserves everything, but instead, she faces so much uncertainty just for having been close to me. I don't know for sure what'll happen to her now and I know she said she doesn't regret it, but I feel like I should do something. She came to speak for me. Can't I go to where she is and speak for her? Feels like the least I can do is return the favour.

Although, with my luck, I'd probably kill her supervisors and she'll end up taking the blame, so it's best if I stay far away from her.

I haven't spoken much to anyone this past week, but I know a little from Leverett. He didn't want to tell me, but I insisted. Apparently, the Veiled are a lot less sure about me now that I've killed one of their own. I don't know how they found out, but we suspect that the two sylphs who were working with Amphorn spread the news before Paralda could detain them, if they stepped in at all. Leverett says it's not as bad as it sounds, that plenty of Veiled are on my side and know I acted in self-defence, but I think he's lying to make me feel better. After what I did, how can any of them trust me near them? If our roles were reversed, I'd be more paranoid, too.

I said all that to Leverett, and he said I only feel that way because the incident with Amphorn is still too recent. Maybe he's right. Maybe I really haven't placed a massive target on my back.

But all I can think is that I've validated every single one of my secret would-be assassin's fears. I've no idea how she'll retaliate, but she probably won't need to. There must be plenty of Veiled who'd rather kill me than risk what I might do next, what'll happen regardless. Maybe I was on to something before Kate figured out I was actually haunted by a boggart that time. Maybe I really am cursed after all. Maybe I'm destined to ruin lives.

Lady nuzzles my neck. I kiss her head again and struggle to my feet with her leaning into me.

'Come on,' I say. 'Let's go home.'

It's so much effort to just speak those words. I want to find the energy to help Mischief like she helped me, at least, but I just... can't. Every step I take feels like lead. Besides, what could I possibly do? Wanting to do something doesn't mean I should. Mischief said her higher-ups didn't send my would-be assassin after me, but how can she be sure? She likely doesn't know about everything that happens in her organisation, either, same as I don't know everything that happens at my university. I didn't even see Eloise's redundancy coming. Isn't it possible that Mischief is wrong? It's the only lead I have that might piece all this mess together. But just the thought of researching a way to help her, to take whatever steps might be necessary to finally get some answers, is too much. It's like a massive weighted blanket has me pinned down, and I don't have the strength to get up. Not right now.

Lady trots next to me. I don't want to feel this breeze anymore. I don't want to worry about strangers seeing me cry anymore. I don't want anyone to see me at all.

Whatever Veiled comes after me next will have an easier time than the Dreamcatcher, the Mara, the boggart, than Chiara and Amphorn. I won't argue. I won't fight back again.

Gods know it'll be better for everyone if I don't resist next time.

Alright, folks, I'm gonna try to keep this short because trust me, I can talk about this *a lot*. Sylphs are an important part of this book, so at the very least I wanted to give you a better overview than Zeru probably gave Esta. They didn't have a good reason to bombard Esta with sylph lore, so I'm stepping in to bombard you! You're welcome! *thumbs up*

The first, most basic thing you need to know about sylphs is that they're air elementals/spirits who are also known as sylphids.

They are said to live inside clouds, and as such they're present in the blowing wind and in weather phenomena like heavy storms or heavy snow. They are formed of air, they live in air, and they have power over the air.

As ethereal creatures, they generally can't be seen by humans. However, their appearance depends somewhat on who you ask, which made it harder to figure out how I wanted to present them for this book. Some will tell you they can't be seen by us lowly mortals at all, others that they're delicate fae-like beings who look a lot like the stereotypical tiny fairy (think Tinkerbell). Others yet will tell you that they're something between a creature and a spirit, and that they can assume a physical form, which tends to be mostly humanoid but taller, larger, stronger—I used this for my main inspiration when I thought up Zeru and the others. That depiction goes back (quite) a bit; it wasn't until later years that they were portrayed as little fairies with graceful wings. For the sylphs in my stories, I've gone for a combination: tall, strong beings who are made

279

of air and live in air, who are graceful in their element but can't be spotted in their airy forms unless they choose to assume their more humanoid bodies.

Ancient cultures believed them to bring divinatory messages to those who were willing to listen, but they have much stronger ties to knowledge than that, too: It is said that sylphs are born understanding the universe and the connections between all things. They are guardians who protect secret knowledge (but they can cause chaos as well— they *are* fae [which in itself is a massive umbrella term]), but like all elementals, they can only move freely in their own element.

They are also very mortal. Sylphs lack a soul (or so it's said), so when they die, they cease to exist. However, a sylph who marries a human gains an immortal soul (an immortal soul being a soul that can be reborn), and their children have immortal souls, too. That's not really relevant to Esta's story, to be honest. I just thought it was a neat detail. Although, if we speculate a little, then Esta's soul must have started as a sylph who fell in love with a human and could thus enter the cycle of rebirth; Amphorn, on the other hand, is unlikely to have fallen in love with a human, so this is it for them.

Sylphs are said to love flower offerings and singing. So, next time you'd like some help with an intellectual pursuit or communicating with someone, why not leave a few flowers outside while whistling your favourite song? And, of course, do your part not to pollute the air. This probably goes without saying, but spirits who live in the air and can't move freely in other elements aren't fond of that.

Addendum 2: A Meditation

You may have noticed that, throughout this book and before, Kate will ask Esta to sit however she's comfortable, usually outside, and close her eyes. Listen to the birds. Let go. She's basically telling Esta to meditate real quick. Esta does a version of this on her own, too, without being prompted.

So, I wanted to give you an easy version of this you can do anywhere in order to centre yourself.

First thing's first:

Contrary to popular belief, the point of meditation is not to clear your mind of every thought completely. Have you tried that? It's impossible. (Or maybe that's my ADHD talking?) There's usually something swirling around up there, whether it's something that's currently bothering you, a regret you for some reason still have from when you were ten, or just an image. This is normal. If you sit down with the intention of clearing your head of everything entirely, you're setting yourself up for failure, and we're not about that here.

So, let me teach you something easy you can try.

Kate is right when she tells Esta to sit comfortably for this. You can totally try the crossing-your-legs-until-they-look-like-a-pretzel look if you want, but if you're not used to it, you'll probably get uncomfortable pretty quickly, and then the magic's gone. That's not why we're here, either. If you want to sit on your bed (yes, even inside is fine!), your favourite chair, on the floor on a soft cushion, outside in the summer rain (please don't get a cold), go do that. Honestly, anywhere is fine—the idea is that you're comfortable. You can even lie

281

down if that's when you're most relaxed, but if you fall asleep, that's not on me, child, that's on you.

Before you close your eyes, decide what kind of background sound you want. If you're new to this and get easily distracted, consider using some meditation music you can find via apps, video-sharing sites on the interwebs—places like that. This helps set the mood, and it gives you something to focus on.

While I said before that clearing your mind of all thoughts whatsoever isn't really why we're here, we do want to reach a place of calm, and that includes your many thoughts. Having meditation-specific music is a great help. If music isn't really your thing, you might prefer something like birdsong tracks, wind chimes, ocean waves... you get the idea. (Of course, you can also follow a full guided meditation if you find one that speaks to you, but you don't need this guide to do that.)

So, now you're sitting comfortably and know what background sounds you want, what do you do?

Close your eyes. Even your breathing.

Try this: Breathe in for five seconds, hold your breath for five, breathe out for six. Repeat. You can gently increase the seconds, too, but make sure you keep the same pattern of breathing out for longer than you breathed in. It'll help you relax and let go.

(Pro tip: If you need a bit of calm *any*time during the day, repeat the breathing exercise until you feel better. I can't guarantee this will help you in literally any scenario, but I find it can make a difference.)

By now you've probably got all kinds of unhelpful thoughts pouring into your head, such as *I really should be doing laundry right now*, *why did I say* that *when I was ten??*; *I really hope I got this job*, or *Why am I even doing this? I bet I look silly.*

That's fine. Yes, honestly. Acknowledge that the thoughts are there, and then gently nudge them away. If that sounds too hard, try not to focus on your thoughts at all.

But, Sarina, HOW?

Well, you could, for example, focus on your breathing. Feel the air fill your lungs. Feel it leave. Actively focus on how it feels inside yourself. Feel it with every fibre of your precious, wonderful being.

If you put on music, you can focus on that, too. Fixate on it until nothing else exists. Feel the gentle rhythm. Listen to the birdsong or wind chime or whatever it is you put on.

(Oh, and another pro tip: If you find the daylight or swaying shadows of the branches too distracting even with your eyes closed, you can blindfold yourself. I've done this; it's an excellent way to block whatever distracting light source there might be around you. Alternatively, you can focus on the light beyond your eyelids. Whatever helps the most and relaxes you the most.)

That's it. You're doing it. Meditation can be as simple as that.

Sit like that for as long as you like. When you're just starting, you might get bored quickly, or you might find that you open your eyes for the first time in thirty minutes only to see that it's barely been five. Slowly go for longer periods of time, if you like.

You don't need to meditate for an hour or more. You also don't need to sit completely still. If your knee starts to itch, you can try to ignore it and hope it goes away, but you might find it easier to just quickly scratch it and get back to it; otherwise, it might distract you the whole time you're there, and then how relaxing do you think that'll be?

A quick word on visualisation: If you like, you can absolutely visualise something you find grounding as you meditate, like a tree for example, or a sphere of glowing, golden light. However, there are many people who can't visualise anything (this is called aphantasia). Since many meditations make some form of visualisation a key part of their routine, it's really rather excluding. **Don't worry if you can't create an image out of nothing in your mind. It's really not necessary to meditate.**

An easy way I meditate you're welcome to borrow is with my first tea of the morning. I can't always do this for various reasons, but I find nothing sets the tone for the day ahead better than going outside with my first tea of the day, finding a spot to sit (either on that low wall halfway up our garden or under that huge tree at the back), and just *being*. Touch the soil. Feel its temperature, its texture on your palm and fingers. Touch a tree branch or trunk and feel the softness of the moss, the surface of the bark. Listen to the birds. Hear the buzz of a nearby bee. Find a flower and smell it. Take in the scent of nature. Feel the breeze on your skin, the sunshine warming your face. Watch that butterfly, this ant, those clouds.

Focus entirely on those things.

In short: Become fully aware of the nature around you and appreciate it. All this was here before you, and it will be here long after you. Appreciate its existence and your own alongside it for all its worth.

But what if you don't have a garden? The good news is that you don't need one. As you can see from my example, you don't need to close your eyes. If you're out in public, you quite possibly wouldn't want to (and probably shouldn't, either—please be safe while you're out and about).

There are many more complicated ways to meditate, but this should provide you with a good beginner's overview. You can now shape this however you want and need until it's entirely individual to you (and, most important of all, it works for you).

And finally, don't let anyone tell you that there's only one way to meditate correctly. If you really want to do this, try a few things. Experiment: music or nature sound; sitting outside on concrete or inside on a soft cushion; eyes open or shut; focus on your breathing or music or the breeze on your arms. The correct way to meditate is the way that helps you find peace and calm in the chaos of your every day.

Thank you so much for reading *A Dream of Storms and Mourning*. This series means a lot to me, and your support does, too. I hope you've had as much fun with Esta as I have! I'm really looking forward to writing the next 7 (provided nothing changes – this may be Book 3, but it's still relatively early days when I've got a total of 10 books planned). Hopefully, you're looking forward to reading them.

If you have two minutes, I'd be grateful for a review. This helps readers find their next favourite book, so your review or even just a rating makes a big difference even if it doesn't seem like it. It doesn't need to be long, either! One sentence (or again, just a rating) is plenty.
Thank you.

Like Freebies?

Join my mailing list for regular updates and freebies, most of which aren't available anywhere else! (For an up-to-date list of what freebies are available *right now*, check the link below.) You'll also hear about upcoming releases, early cover reveals, teasers, and all other announcements.

BUT WAIT, THERE'S MORE.

If you're wondering what the hell Amphorn meant when they reminded Zeru of their failure, what happened with Aither, and what exactly Zeru is regretting, you'll find answers in *Air of Magic*, also available exclusively to newsletter subscribers.

Join at:

sarinalanger.com/newsletter

If you'd like to hang out with me in an informal setting and

get early peeks at new covers and maps, join my Facebook Reader Group, 'Sarina's Sparrows':
facebook.com/groups/sarinassparrows

Let's Connect

sarinalanger.com

facebook.com/groups/sarinassparrows

goodreads.com/sarinalangerwriter

bookbub.com/profile/sarina-langer

For an up-to-date list and links to the social media sites I'm on, go to: beacons.ai/sarinalanger or scan this QR code:

Acknowledgments

Folks, this book has been on a journey! The first two books were absolute delights to write, and while I got there with this one eventually, it wasn't quite as straightforward. I actually scrapped my initial first draft and started over with a new plot. Because of that, publishing this book took a little longer than I originally planned. Thank you for waiting. Thank you for being patient. We got there in the end… after the rather awkward and sudden realisation one evening that I'd been writing the wrong book and should start over, really.

Thank you so much to Rachel Oestreich, my incredible editor who said, *and I quote*, 'NGI, I have been looking forward to it so much—a bit of whimsical urban fantasy (I know it gets REAL but your writing style for this series is so gentle and lovely to read).' You don't know how much I love you for this, and yes, I've shown this to everyone I love. Thank you for letting me bug you with questions and concerns whenever I have them, and thank you for generally being a wonderful supportive treasure.

Thank you to Miss Dia, my lovely cover designer who came in from this book and has since done a marvellous job of creating new covers for Books 1 and 2, and now this one as well. Your dedication to and love for this series warms my heart so much, as do your mind-blowing emojis I wouldn't know how to recreate if I tried.

Thank you so much to Becky Wright for doing all the formatting I don't have the patience to do myself. Your work is beautiful, as always.

Thank you to Zoe, my amazing PA as of recently. Thanks to you I have a presence on TikTok. Thank you for everything you do and being so lovely and fun to work with.

Thank you to Jules Appleton, Beverley Lee, Tania Rina Perry, and Dana Fraedrich for reading early drafts of this book in various stages. Thank you for helping me make it even better and for spotting those tiny error that slip through all too easily.

Thank you to my reader group on Facebook for being at the forefront of all news. Thank you for getting excited with me <3

Thank you to my new street teams on Facebook and Discord. It means everything to me that you love my books enough to want to help me spread the word. Getting the news out is amongst the hardest things an author has to do. You make it easier (and more enjoyable). Thank you.

And finally, thank you SO MUCH to everyone who reviews my books and shares my news and shows me and my characters so much love. Every positive review, every excited social media post, fills my heart with joy.

About the Author

Sarina Langer is a dark fantasy author of both epic and urban paranormal novels from the delightfully cloudy South of England.

She is as obsessed with books and stationery now as she was as a child, when she drowned her box of colour pencils in water so they wouldn't die and scribbled her first stories on corridor walls. ('A first sign of things to come', according to her mother. 'Normal toddler behaviour', according to Sarina.)

In her free time, she has a weakness for books, pretty words, and spends what's probably too much time playing video games.

She believes that the best books are those where every ray of light casts a shadow.

Milton Keynes UK
Ingram Content Group UK Ltd.
UKHW031155251124
451529UK00001B/33

9 798230 731474